GREY MASK

Mollie Lee
Pryor

Books by Patricia Wentworth

GREY MASK

PATRICIA WENTWORTH

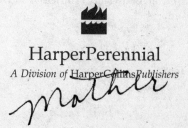

HarperPerennial
A Division of HarperCollins Publishers

Wentworth, Patricia.
   Grey mask: a Miss Silver mystery/Patricia Wentworth.—1st
HarperPerennial ed.
      p.   cm.
   ISBN 0-06-092364-4 (pbk.)
   I. Title.
PR6045.E66G7   1993
823'. 91—dc20   92–53392

93   94   95   96   97   WB / CW   10   9   8   7   6   5   4   3   2   1

CHAPTER 1

Mr. Packer dangled the heavy bunch of keys for a moment before laying it on the table.

"Four years is a long time to be away," he said.

His voice was so drily polite that Charles Moray could not fail to be aware that in the eyes of his solicitor four years' absence, and a consequent neglect of all the business arising out of his father's death and his own succession, was a dereliction. An only son who succeeded to a large estate had no business to walk the uttermost parts of the earth. He should step into his place as a citizen, stand for Parliament in the constituency represented by three generations of his family, and—settle down.

Charles picked up the bunch of keys, looked at them with an odd fleeting frown, and put them in his pocket.

"You won't be going to the house tonight, I suppose," said Mr. Packer.

"No. I'm staying at The Luxe. I just thought I'd look in and get the keys."

"I asked because I believe—in fact I know—that the caretaker Lattery, is out. He is always out on Thursday evening. I am aware of the fact, because it is his practice to call at this office for his wages; he comes very punctually at five o'clock. And I thought that if you had any intention of calling at the house, his absence might surprise you."

"No, I shan't go round there tonight," said Charles. He

glanced at his watch. "Haven't time—Millar's dining with me. I expect you remember him."

Mr. Packer remembered Mr. Millar; not, apparently, with enthusiasm.

Charles got up.

"Well. I'll be round in the morning. I can sign anything you want me to then. I hope I haven't kept you. I'd no idea it was so late."

He walked back to The Luxe in the dusk of the October evening—dampish, coldish—a gloomy, depressing sort of climate to welcome a man who has had four years of tropical sunshine.

Charles sniffed the cold wet air and found it good. It was surprisingly good to be at home again. The rage and pain which had driven him out of England four years ago were gone, burnt to the ash of forgetfulness by the very fierceness of their own flame. He could think of Margaret Langton now without either pain or anger. She was married of course; a girl doesn't turn a man down like that on the very eve of their wedding unless there's another man. No, Margaret must be married. Very likely they would meet. He told himself that it would be quite an interesting meeting for them both.

At The Luxe a telegram from Archie Millar—"Awfully sorry. My Aunt Elizabeth has wired for me. She does it once a month or so. Hard luck she hit on tonight. Cheerio. Archie."

Charles ate his dinner alone. During the soup he regretted Archie Millar, but with the fish the regret passed. He did not want Archie or Archie's company; he did not want to go to a theatre or do a show; he wanted vehemently and insistently to go to the house which was now his own house, and to go to it whilst it stood empty of everything except its memories. He didn't want to hear Lattery's account of his stewardship, or to listen to Mrs. Lattery deploring the way that the damp got into things. "No matter what you do, sir, or how much you air—and I'm sure I'm such a one for airing as never was." Her high-pitched, querulous voice rang sharply in his ears. No, he didn't want to talk to Mrs. Lattery. But he wanted to see the house.

His impatience grew as he walked westward facing a soft wind that was full of rain. The house drew him. And why not? His great-grandfather had built it; his grandfather and his father had been born there; he himself had been born there—four generations of them—four generations of memories. And the house stood empty, waiting for him to come to it.

A hundred years ago Thorney Lane was a real lane, whose hedgerows were thick with thorn that blossomed white as milk in May and set its dark red haws for birds to peck at in October. It was a paved walk now, running from one busy thoroughfare to another, with wooden posts set across it at either end to show that it was for the use of foot passengers only. When Mr. Archibald Moray built his big house the thoroughfares were country roads.

Half-way up Thorney Lane a narrow alley separated the houses which looked on to Thornhill Square from the houses of the more modern George Street. The old lane had wandered pleasantly between high brick walls. No. 1 Thornhill Square was the corner house.

Charles Moray, walking up Thorney Lane, turned to the right and proceeded for about a dozen yards along the alley-way. He stopped in front of the door in the brick wall and took out the bunch of keys which Mr. Packer had given him. This key, at least, he thought he could find in the dark. How many times had he and Margaret walked the narrow alley in the twilight, in the dusk, in the dark?

He wondered if the Pelhams were still at 12 George Street, and if Freddy Pelham had learned any new stories in the last four years—Freddy and his interminable pointless tales about

3

nothing! Even when he had been at the height of his love for Margaret it had been hard work to put up with Margaret's stepfather. Well, he wouldn't have to laugh at Freddy's stories now.

He ran his fingers over the keys until they touched the one he wanted; it had a nick in it half-way down the shaft. He let the other keys fall away from it and put out his left hand to feel for the keyhole. His fingers touched the cold, wet wood and slid down on to colder iron. Under the pressure of his hand the door moved. He pushed, and it swung. There was no need for him to use his key on a door that had stood not only unlocked but unlatched. Lattery had grown slack indeed if he made a practice of going out by the back way and leaving the door ajar.

It was very dark in the garden. The high brick wall cut off the last glimmer of the lamp which was supposed to light Thorney Lane and the alley that ran into it.

Charles walked down the flagged path with as much assurance as if he had had daylight to show him what only his mind was showing him now. Here the thorn tree, a seedling eighty years ago, dropped from some survivor of the old hedge. Next, lavender bushes, sweet in the dark as he brushed them by. The garden was of a good size, and had been larger before his grandfather built out a ballroom upon what had once been a formal terrace.

Charles passed the long dark windows with slender fluted columns between them. It was inevitable that he should think of the June night which had seen every window brilliant, open to the soft summer dusk. The dancers had only to step out from between the pillars and descend two marble steps to find themselves amongst flowers.

He frowned and walked on; then threw up his head and stopped. What was that June evening to him now, that he should shirk the remembrance of it? If the past had any ghosts, it was better to look them in the face and bid them begone for ever. The June night rose vividly. The last hours of his engagement to Margaret rose; he saw himself and her; her father, proud and pleased; Margaret in white and silver, radiant and for once beautiful. He could have sworn that the radiance and the beauty flowed from some lamp of joy within; and, with their wedding day only a week ahead, he had not doubted what flame burned high in that lamp of joy. Yet next day she had sent him back his ring.

Charles stared at the dark windows. What a fool he had been! His incredulity was the measure of his folly. He could not believe Margaret's own words in her own writing—not till the telephone had failed him; not till he had forced an entrance into the Pelhams' house, only to hear that Margaret had left town; not till he read in every newspaper the cold announcement that "the marriage arranged between Mr. Charles Moray and Miss Margaret Langton will not take place."

Did he accept the facts? It is not a pleasant thing to be jilted. Charles Moray flung out of England in as bitter a rage as the galling humiliation warranted. He had never had to think of money in his life: if he wanted to travel he could travel. His father made no demur. India first, and Tibet; then China—the hidden, difficult, dangerous China which only a few Europeans know. Then in Peking he fell in with Justin Parr, and Parr persuaded him into an enthusiasm for the unexplored tracts of South America.

He was still hesitating, when his father died suddenly; and there being nothing to come home for, he set off with Parr on a voyage of adventure with a secret unacknowledged lure, the hope of forgetting Margaret.

Charles looked steadily at these ghosts of his and saw them vanish into the dark, thin air. He was immensely pleased with himself for having faced them, and it was with a glow of self-approbation that he came to the end of the flagged path and groped for the handle of the garden door.

The glow changed to one of anger. This door was open too. He began to have serious thoughts of celebrating his return by sacking Lattery. He stepped into a passage. It ran a few feet and ended in a swing door which gave upon the hall. There was a light here; not one of the hanging lamps which could flood the whole place, but a small, discreet shaded affair set away in a corner.

There is something very melancholy about a big empty house. Charles looked at the light and wondered if this house was really empty. It ought to have felt empty. But it didn't. And he ought, perhaps, to have felt melancholy. Instead, he was experiencing a certain elated feeling which was partly expectancy, and partly the instinct that scents adventure. He went up the stairs and turned into the right-hand corridor. This floor was in darkness. A faint glow came up from the well of the stairs and made the gloom visible. He had his hand on the switch which controlled the light, when he paused and after a moment let his hand fall again.

At the end of the corridor two doors faced each other. The right-hand door was invisible in the darkness, but across the threshold of the left-hand door lay a faint pencilling of light.

Charles looked at this pencilling, and told himself that Mrs. Lattery was in the room. All the same he walked softly, and when he reached the door he stood still, listening. And as he stood, he heard one man speak and another answer him.

Moving quite noiselessly, he stepped backwards until he could touch the opposite door; then, putting his hand behind him, he turned the handle, passed into the dark room, and closed the door again.

The room into which he had come was the one which

had been his mother's bedroom. The room opposite was her sitting-room, and between the two, across the end of the corridor, there ran a windowless cupboard—a delightful place for a child to play in. He could remember his mother's dresses hanging there, silken, lavender scented, whispering when you touched them. She died when he was ten; and then there were no more dresses hanging there.

Charles opened the door very softly. The seven feet of black emptiness gave out a cold, musty smell—Mrs. Lattery had not done very much of her boasted airing here. He went forward into the blackness until his fingers touched the panelling on the far side of it. Long ago there had been a door here too; but it had been shut up to make more space for Mrs. Moray's dresses. The keyhole had been filled and the handle removed.

Charles had regretted the keyhole. It had figured in his games, and he could still remember the thrill with which he had discovered a peep-hole which replaced it handsomely. Four feet from the floor on the extreme edge of the panelling a knot-hole had been filled with glue and sawdust stained to match the wood of the door. With infinite patience the little boy of nine had loosened the filling until it could be withdrawn at will like a cork. It was the memory of this peep-hole which brought him into the cupboard now. An unlatched gate, and an open door, and men's voices—these things seemed to require an explanation.

He knelt down, felt for the knot-hole, and gently, cautiously, pulled out the plug that filled it.

CHAPTER 2

Charles Moray looked through the hole in the panelling and saw what surprised him very much. The room beyond was half in shadow and half in light. There was a lamp with a tilted shade on the rosewood table which held his mother's photograph albums. It stood perched on the fattest album with its green silk shade tipped back so as to throw all the light towards the door.

Charles drew back instinctively lest he should be seen; but the ray fell away to the left of his panelling and was focused on the door across whose threshold he had seen the pencilled line of light.

There were two men sitting at the table. One of them had his back to Charles, who could see no more than a black overcoat and a felt hat. The other man was in the shadow facing him. Charles, peering and intrigued, beheld a white shirt-front framed, as it were, in a sort of loose black cloak. Above the shirt-front a blur, formless and featureless. Certainly the man had a head; but, as certainly, he seemed to have no face. However deep the shadow, you ought to be able to see the line where the hair meets the forehead, and the outline of the jaw.

Charles drew a longish breath. The man didn't seem to have any hair or any jaw; he was just a shirt-front and a cloak and a greyish blur that had no form or feature. It was rather beastly.

Then as he felt the short hairs on his neck begin to prickle, the man with his back to him said,

"Suppose there's a certificate?"

The shoulders under the black cloak were shrugged; a deep, soft voice gave an answer;

"If there's a certificate, so much the worse for the girl."

"What do you mean?" The first man hurried over the question.

"Why, she must go of course. I should think a street accident would be the safest way." The words were spoken with a gentle, indifferent inflexion. The man in the shadow lifted a paper, looked down at it with that blur of a face, and inquired, "You are sure there was no will?"

"Oh, quite sure. The lawyer took care of that."

"There might have been a second one—millionaires have a curious passion for making wills."

"Twenty-seven was quite sure: Here's his report. Will you look at it?"

A paper passed. The lamp was turned a little, the shade adjusted. Charles saw the light touch part of a hand, and saw that the hand wore a grey rubber glove. His heart gave a jump.

"By gum! That's what he's got on his face too! Beastly! All over his face and head—grey rubber—a grey rubber mask!"

The lamp was his mother's reading-lamp. The room, unused since her death, remained for Charles Moray a place of warmth and shaded light, a place where he mustn't make a noise, a fire-lit evening place where he sat cross-legged on the floor beside a sofa and a soft, tired voice told him stories. What were these unbelievable people doing in this place? It made him feel rather sick to see the light slant from the reading-lamp across that grey, smooth hand on to the pages of Twenty-seven's report; it made him very angry too. Of all the infernal cheek—

9

The pages turned with an even flick; Grey Mask was a quick reader. He dropped the report in a heap and said, in that deep purring voice,

"Is Twenty-seven here?"

The other man nodded.

"Are you ready for him?"

"Yes."

Charles jerked back from his peep-hole. Someone had moved so near him that the recoil was instinctive. Coming cautiously forward again, he became aware that there was a third man in the room, away on his left, keeping guard over the door. When he stood close to the door he was out of sight; but when he opened it he came sufficiently forward to be visible as a blue serge suit and the sort of khaki muffler which everybody's aunts turned out by the gross during the war. The muffler came up so high that the fellow was really only a suit of clothes and a scarf.

Through the open door there came a man who looked like a commercial traveller. He wore a large overcoat and a bowler hat. Charles never got a glimpse of his face. He walked up to the table with an air of assurance and looked about him for a chair.

There was no chair within reach, and under Grey Mask's silent, unmoving stare some of the assurance seemed to evaporate. The stare was a very curious one, for the holes in the smooth grey face were not eye-shaped but square—small square holes like dark dice on a grey ground. They gave Charles himself an indescribable feeling of being watched.

"Twenty-seven—" said Grey Mask.

"Come to report."

Grey Mask tapped the sheets of the written report sharply.

"Your report is too long. It leaves out essentials. There's too much about you—not enough about the facts. For instance, you say the lawyer took care of the will. Did he destroy it?"

Twenty-seven hesitated. Charles suspected him of a desire to hedge.

"Did he?"

"Well—yes, he did."

"How?"

"Burnt it."

"Witnesses?"

"One's dead. The other—"

"Well?"

"I don't know. It's a woman."

"Her name?"

"Mary Brown—spinster."

"Know who she was?"

"No."

"Find out and report again. That's essential. Then there's another point. There was no certificate?"

"No."

"Sure?"

"I couldn't find one. The lawyer doesn't know of one. I don't believe there is one—I don't believe there was a marriage."

"Too much 'you,'" said Grey Mask. "Find out about that witness. You can go now."

The man went, looking over his shoulder as if he were expecting to be called back.

Charles did not see his face at all. He was cursing himself for a fool. He ought to have got downstairs before Twenty-seven. He had his plan all made, and he ought to have been attending to it instead of listening to the gentleman confessing his criminal activities. Twenty-seven would now get away, whereas if Charles had cut along the corridor and locked the

11

door at the end of it, he might very well have had a bag of four waiting for the police.

At a very early stage of this interview his thoughts had dwelt hopefully on the fact, so much deplored by Mr. Packer, that his telephone subscription had been kept going during those four years of absence.

Twenty-seven had faded—must fade if the other three were to be bagged. It was a pity; but perhaps the police would gather him in later.

"I'll get along," said Charles; and as he said it, he heard the invisible man on his left move again. He moved and he said, in a whispering Cockney voice,

"Twenty-six is 'ere, guvnor."

Grey Mask nodded. He had pushed Twenty-seven's report across the table, and the other man was straightening the sheets and laying them tidily together.

"Shall I let 'er in?" The " 'er" brought Charles's eye back to the knot-hole again. He had withdrawn it an inch or two preparatory to getting noiselessly on to his feet; but the Cockney's "Shall I let 'er in" intrigued him.

There was the sound of the opening door. The blue serge suit and the khaki muffler bulged into view again, and, passing them, there came a straight black back and a close black cap with a long fold of black gauzy stuff that crossed the cap like a veil and hung down in two floating ends.

Charles received such a shock that the room went blank for a moment. He saw, and did not see; heard words, and made no sense of what he heard. He was within an ace of lurching sideways, and actually thrust out a hand to save his balance. The hand encountered the panelling against which his mother's dresses used to hang. He kept it there pressed out against the cold wood, whilst with all his might he stared at the straight black back of Number 26 and told himself

12

with a vehement iteration that this was not, and could not be, Margaret Langton.

The iteration died; the rushing sound that filled his ears dwindled. His hand pressed the wall. The blankness passed. He saw the room, with its familiar furnishings—the blue curtains, dark and shadowy; the faded carpet with the wreaths of blue flowers on a fawn-coloured ground; the table with the photograph albums and the lamp with its tilted shade. The ray of light crossing the room showed him the edge of the closing door. It passed out of sight and shut without a sound.

Margaret was standing with her back to him. Margaret was standing at the table with her back to him. The light would miss her face because she was standing above it. He needed neither the sight of that face nor any light upon it to be sure that it was Margaret who was standing there. Her hands were in the light. They were ungloved. She was putting down a packet of papers; they looked like letters.

Charles saw the hands that were more familiar to him than any of the familiar things in the room which he had known ever since he had known anything at all. He looked at Margaret's hands. He had always thought them the most beautiful hands that he had ever seen—not small or slender, but strong white hands, beautifully formed, cool and alive to the touch. The hands were quite bare. He had made sure that Margaret was married, but there was no wedding ring on the finger that had worn his square emerald.

As he saw these things he became aware that Margaret was speaking, her voice so very low that the sound barely reached him and the words did not reach him at all. She stood holding the edge of the table and speaking in that low voice; and then with a quick movement she turned and came back along the ray of light to the door, which swung open to

13

pass her through. The light was at her back. The scarf with the floating ends veiled her face. She moved with her old free step and the little swing of the shoulders that he knew by heart. She held up her head. The ends of the scarf moved behind her. She passed through the door and was gone. The door shut.

Charles drew a very long breath. He had not seen her face.

CHAPTER 3

Charles continued to look into the room. The place where Margaret had stood was just at the edge of where the thick double wreath of fat blue flowers began to twine itself about a central medallion. There was a little worn place just to the right of where she had stood. He stared at the worn place. Margaret had been here and was gone again—*Margaret*. Well, that put the lid on telephoning to the police. Yes, by gum it did!

A quick spasm of laughter shook him. He had said that it would be interesting to meet Margaret again—*interesting*.

"Oh, my hat!" said Charles to himself.

Interesting enough—yes, and a bit to spare if he and Margaret were to meet in a crowded police court. A very pretty romantic scene. "Do you recognize this woman?" "Oh yes, I almost married her once." Headlines from the evening paper rose luridly: "Parted Lovers meet in Police Court." "Jilted Explorer and Lost Bride." "Should Women become Criminals?" No, the police were off.

He came back from the headlines at the sound of a name:

"Margot." It was the man sitting at the table with his back to him who had spoken.

Charles withdrew his hand from the wall and listened intently. He had thought for a moment that the fellow was going to say Margaret. Then he heard the man say,

"Thirty-two is kicking."

Grey Mask moved one of the smooth gloved hands; the gesture indicated that Thirty-two and any possible protest he might make were equally negligible.

"He is kicking all the same."

Grey Mask spoke; the purr was a sneer.

"Can a jellyfish kick? What's it all about?"

The man with his back to Charles shrugged his shoulders.

"Says ten per cent isn't worth the risk."

"Where's the risk? He gets the money quite legally."

"Says he ought to get more than ten per cent—says he doesn't want to marry the girl—says he'll be hanged if he marries her."

Grey Mask leaned a little forward.

"Well, he won't be *hanged* if he doesn't do what he's told, but he'll go down for a seven years' stretch. Tell him so." He scribbled on a piece of paper and pushed it over. "Give him this. If he doesn't prefer liberty, ten per cent, and a pretty wife to seven years' hard, he can have the seven years. He won't like it."

The other man took up the paper.

"He says he doesn't know why he should marry the girl. I told him I'd put that to you. Why should he?"

"Provides for her—looks well—keeps her quiet—keeps her friends quiet."

The other man spoke quickly:

"Then you think there might be a certificate?"

15

"I'm not taking risks. Tell Thirty-two he's to use the letter as we arranged."

"Then you do think—"

There was no answer. The other man spoke again:

"There's nothing at Somerset House. Isn't that good enough?"

"Not quite. Everyone doesn't get married at their parish church or the nearest registry office—everyone doesn't even get married in England."

"Was he married?"

Grey Mask straightened the shade of the reading-lamp; the lane of light that had led to the door disappeared.

"If Forty there had ears, he could answer that question."

"Forty—"

"Perhaps. Forty says he used to walk up and down the deck. He says he talked. Perhaps he said something; perhaps he talked of things he wouldn't have talked about if he hadn't known that Forty would be none the wiser. In the end the sea got him and none of us are any the wiser. Pity Forty there never learned lip-reading."

He lifted his hand and signalled with it. Forty, then, was the janitor. And he was stone-deaf—useful in a way of course, but awkward too. Charles wondered how he knew when there was anyone on the other side of the door. Of course if he had his hand on the panel and anyone knocked, he would feel the vibration. Yes, it could be done that way—a code of signals too.

He had just reached this point, when the light went out. The door had begun to open, and then Grey Mask put his hand to the switch of the lamp, and the room went dark, with just one blur of greenish dusk which faded and was gone in the gloom.

Charles got up. He was rather stiff. He got back into his

16

mother's room without making any noise, and before he put his hand on the door, he stood for an instant listening, and could hear no sound. He would have liked to rush them from behind, catch them perhaps at the head of the stairs and send them sprawling, a loud war-whoop and their own bad consciences to aid. It might have been a very pleasant affair. He liked to think of Forty's square bulk coming down with a good resounding thud upon the wild writhings of the other two.

Hang Margaret! If she hadn't come butting into heaven knew what of a dirty criminal conspiracy, he might have been really enjoying himself. Instead, he must mark time, must tiptoe through his own house after a pack of scallywags.

Charles tiptoed. He reached the head of the stairs and looked down into the hall. Someone moved in the twilight; a light went on. Lattery, the caretaker, crossed the lighted space whistling *Way Down Upon the Swanee River*. He whistled flat.

Charles charged down the stairs and arrived like an exploding bomb.

"Where the devil have you been, and what the devil have you been doing?"

Lattery stared, and his knees shook under him; his big stupid face took on a greenish hue.

Charles ran to the garden door. It was still open. He ran up the garden, and heard the door in the wall fall to with a slam. By the time he got it open and burst into the alley, someone was disappearing round the corner into Thorney Lane. He sprinted to the corner and round it. The someone was a whistling errand boy with a crop of red hair that showed pure ginger under the street lamp.

At the bottom of Thorney Lane there was a woman. He ran after her. When he reached the roaring thoroughfare, there were half a dozen women on every couple of yards of pavement. The two big cinemas at either end of the street had just come out.

He went back to the house in a black bad temper.

CHAPTER 4

He interviewed Lattery, and could not determine whether he had to do with an unfaithful steward or a great stupid oaf who was scared to death by the sudden apparition of a gentleman whom he believed to be some thousands of miles away.

"Where had you been?"

"Seeing it was Thursday," said Lattery in his slow perplexed voice.

"Where had you been?"

"Seeing it was Thursday, Mr. Charles—I beg your pardon, *sir*—seeing it was Thursday and the day I take my pay from the lawyer same as he arranged—and I put it to him fair and square, and so he'll tell you. I put it to him, sir, wouldn't it be convenient for to fix on Thursday for me to take the evening off like? And the lawyer he says to me—and one of his clerks was in the room and could tell you the same—he says to me as how there wasn't any objection."

"Thursday's your evening off?"

"Yes, Mr. Charles—I beg your pardon—*sir*."

"You always go out on Thursday?"

"Yes, sir."

Lattery's face had regained its florid colour, but his round eyes dwelt anxiously on Charles.

"Do you always leave the garden door open?" Charles shot the question at him suddenly.

"The garden door, sir?"

"The door from the little passage into the garden. Do you generally leave it open?"

"No, sir."

"Why did you leave it open tonight?"

"Was it open, sir?"

"Don't you know it was? Didn't you come in that way?"

"I come in through the front door," said Lattery, staring.

They were in the study, which opened out of the hall. Charles crossed to the door, flung it open wide, and looked across.

"If you came in through the front door, who bolted it and put up the chain?"

"Please, sir, I did."

Charles felt a little ridiculous. He banged the door and came back to his seat.

"When I reached this house an hour ago," he said, "the door on the alley-way was open. I came in by it. The garden door was open, and I came into the house by that. I went upstairs, and there was a light in my mother's sitting-room."

"Someone must have left it on, sir."

"The people who left it on were still in the room," said Charles drily. "They were men—three of them. And they got away down the stair just before me. Are you going to tell me you didn't see anything?"

"I take my oath I didn't see anything."

"Or hear anything?"

Lattery hesitated.

"I sort of thought I heard a door bang—yes, I certainly thought I heard a door, for it come into my mind that the missus was early."

CHAPTER 5

Miss Standing sighed, sniffed, dabbed her eyes with rather a tired-looking handkerchief, and plunged an experienced finger and thumb into the depths of a large box of Fuller's chocolates. Having selected a luscious and melting chocolate cream, she sighed again and continued the letter which she had just begun. She wrote on a pad propped against her knee, and she addressed the bosom friend whom she left behind only two days before at Madame Mardon's very select and expensive Swiss Academy. The words, "My darling angel Stephanie," were scrawled across the pale blue page.

Miss Standing sucked at her chocolates and wrote on:

It's all too perfectly horrid and beastly for words. All the way across M'amselle could only tell me that poor papa had died suddenly. She said there was only that in the telegram, and that I was to come home. And when I got here last night, there wasn't any Mrs. Beauchamp like there always is in the holidays, and the servants looked odd. And M'amselle went off this morning, and I don't really know what's happened, except that Papa was at sea in his yacht somewhere in the Mediterranean. So there isn't any funeral or anything, and of course I haven't got any black—only just the things I came away with. And it's all frightfully miserable. If you don't write to me, I shall die. It's frightful not to have anyone to talk to. The lawyer—Papa's lawyer—is coming to talk to me this morning. He telephoned to say he was coming. I suppose I shall be simply frightfully rich. But it's so depressing. It makes me wish I'd got some relations, even frightfully dull ones like Sophy Weir's. *Do* you remember her aunt's hat? I haven't any relations at all except my cousin Egbert, and I'd rather have no relations than him—so would anyone. He's the most appalling mug you ever saw.

Miss Standing frowned at the word *appalling*, which she had written with one p and two l's. It didn't look quite right. She took another chocolate, struck out one of the l's, put in another p, and continued:

I shan't come back to school of course. After all, I am eighteen, and they can't make me. I do wonder if I shall have a guardian. In books the girl always marries her guardian, which I think is too frightfully dull for words. You'll have to come and stay with me, and we'll have a frightfully good time.

She stopped and heaved a sigh, because of course Stephanie wouldn't be able to come till Christmas, and Christmas, to use Miss Standing's own simple vocabulary, was a frightfully long way off—nearly three months.

She stared gloomily into the rich and solemn room. It was a very large room, running from front to back of the big London house, and it had the ordered richness of a shrine rather than any air of everyday comfort. There were priceless Persian rugs upon the floor, dim with the exquisite colouring of a bygone age. The curtains were of historic brocade, woven at Lyons before Lyons ran blood in the days of the Terror. The panelling on the walls had come from a house in the

21

Netherlands, a house in which the great Duke of Alba had lived. On this panelling hung the Standing Collection; each picture a fortune and a collector's prize—Gainsborough; Sir Joshua; Van Dyck; Lely; Franz Hals; Turner. No moderns.

Miss Standing frowned at the pictures; she thought them hideous and gloomy and depressing. She hated the whole room. But when she began to think of what she would do to it to make it look different, she got the sort of feeling that there would be something almost sacrilegious about doing anything to it at all. A pink carpet now, and a white wallpaper to cover up all that dark wood. It was silly to feel as if she had laughed in church; but that was the sort of feeling she got.

She consoled herself with a very succulent chocolate. It had a nougat centre. The very sofa on which she was sitting was like a sort of stage funeral pyre, all purple and gold and silver.

"I wonder what I shall look like in black. Some people look so frightful in it. But that silly man who came to the fete with the De Chauvignys said I ought to wear it—he said it would flatter me very much. And of course people always do say that fair women look nicer in black than in anything else. It's a frightfully dull thing to look nice in."

Miss Standing opened a little leather vanity case which lay beside the box of chocolates. She took out a powder puff and a tiny mirror and began to powder her nose. The powder had a very strong scent of carnations. A glance in the mirror never failed to have a cheering effect. It is very difficult to go on being unhappy when you can see that you have a skin of milk and roses, golden brown hair with a natural wave, and eyes that are much larger and bluer than those of any other girl you know.

Margot Standing's eyes really were rather remarkable. They were of a very pale blue, and if they had not been surrounded by ridiculously long black lashes they might have spoilt her looks; as it was the contrast of dark lashes and pale bright eyes gave her prettiness a touch of exotic beauty. She was of middle height, with a pretty, rather plump figure, and a trick of falling from one graceful pose into another. She wore a pleated skirt of blue serge and a white woollen jumper, both very plain; but the white wool was the softest Angora, and the serge skirt had come from a famous house in Paris.

A door at the far end of the room was opened. William, the stupidest of the footmen, murmured something inarticulate, and Mr. James Hale came slowly across the Persian carpet. Margot had never seen him before. He was her father's lawyer and that sounded dull enough; but she thought he looked even duller than that—so very stiff, so very tall, so narrow in the shoulder, and so hairless about the brow. She said "Ouf!" to herself as she got up rather languidly to meet him.

Mr. Hale had a limp, cold hand. He said "How do you do, Miss Standing?" and cleared his throat. Then Margot sat down, and he sat down, and there was a silence, during which Mr. Hale laid the dispatch-case he had been carrying upon a chair at his side and proceeded to open it.

He looked up to find a box of chocolates under his nose.

"Do have one. The long ones are hard, but the round ones are a dream."

"No thank you," said Mr. Hale.

Margot took one of the round ones herself. She had eaten so many chocolates already that it was necessary to crunch it quickly in order to get the flavour. She crunched it, and Mr. Hale waited disapprovingly until she had finished. He wished to offer her his condolences upon her father's death, and it appeared to him in the highest degree unseemly that he should do so whilst she was eating chocolates.

As she immediately replaced the chocolate by another, he abandoned the condolences altogether and plunged into business.

"I have come, Miss Standing, to ask you if you have any knowledge of the whereabouts of Mr. Standing's will."

Margot shook her head.

"Why, how on earth should I?"

"I don't know. Your father might have spoken to you on the subject."

"But I haven't seen him for three years."

"So long as that?"

Miss Standing nodded.

"He was very seldom here for the holidays, anyhow, and the last three years he was always in America, or Germany, or Italy or some of those places."

"Not Switzerland? You were at school in Switzerland, I believe."

"Never Switzerland," declared Miss Standing taking another chocolate.

"Did he ever write to you about his will?"

Margot's eyes opened to their fullest extent.

"Good gracious no! Why, he practically never wrote to me at all."

"That," said Mr. Hale, "is unfortunate. You see, Miss Standing, we are in a difficulty. Your father's affairs have been in our hands for the last fifteen years. But it was my father who had full knowledge of them. I know that he and the late Mr. Standing were upon terms of considerable intimacy; and if my father was still with us, the whole matter would probably be cleared up in a few minutes."

"Isn't your father with you?"

Mr. Hale cleared his throat and fingered a black tie.

"My father died a month ago."

"Oh," said Miss Standing. Then she paused, leaned forward with a sudden graceful change of attitude, and said, "Nobody's told me anything about Papa. M'amselle said she didn't know—only what was in the telegram, you know. You sent it, didn't you? And so I don't really know anything at all."

"Mr. Standing died very suddenly," said Mr. Hale. "He was in his yacht off Majorca."

Margot repeated the name.

"Where is Majorca?"

Mr. Hale informed her. He also put her in possession of what he termed "the sad particulars" of her father's death. It appeared that the yacht had been caught in a heavy gale, and that Mr. Standing, who refused to leave the deck, had been washed overboard.

Mr. Hale at this point offered his belated condolences, after which he cleared his throat and added:

"Unfortunately we are quite unable to trace any will, or to obtain any evidence that would lead us to suppose that he had ever made one."

"Does it matter?" asked Margot indifferently.

Mr. Hale frowned. "It matters a good deal to you, Miss Standing."

"Does it?"

"I am afraid that it does."

"But I'm his daughter anyway. Why should it matter about a will? There's only me, isn't there?" Her tone was still indifferent. Mr. Hale was an old fuss-pot. He wasn't a man at all; he was just a suit of black clothes and a disapproving frown. She said with sudden irrelevance: "Please, I want some money. I haven't got any. I bought the chocolates with my last bean. I made M'amselle stop the taxi whilst I rushed in and got them. Everything was so frightfully dismal I felt I should expire if I didn't have chocs—it takes me that way, you know."

Mr. Hale took no notice of this. Instead, he asked, with a gravity that was almost severe.

"Do you remember your mother at all?"

"No—of course not. I was only two."

"When she died?"

"I suppose so."

"Miss Standing, can you tell me your mother's maiden name?"

She shook her head.

"Come! Surely you must know it!"

"I don't." She hesitated and then added, "I think I was called after her."

"Yes? What are your names?"

"I've only got one. I think I was christened Margaret, and I think perhaps it was my mother's name. I've always been called Margot."

"Miss Standing, did your father never speak about your mother?"

"No, he didn't. I keep telling you he practically never spoke to me at all. He was always frightfully busy. He never *talked* to me."

"Then what makes you think you were called after your mother?"

A slight blush made Miss Standing prettier than before.

"There was a picture that he kept locked. You know— the sort with doors and a keyhole, and a miniature inside. I always wanted to know what was in it."

"Well?"

Miss Standing shut her lips tightly.

"I don't know that I ought to tell you," she said with an air of virtue.

"I think you *must* tell me," said Mr. Hale.

Something in his voice frightened her. She drew back, looked at him out of startled eyes, and began to tell him in a hurrying, uncertain voice.

"I wasn't supposed to go into the study. But one evening I went because I thought he was out. And he wasn't. And when I heard him coming I had only just time to get behind the curtains. It was frightful, because I thought he was never going to go away, and I thought I should be there all night."

"Yes? Go on."

"He wrote letters, and he walked up and down. And then he gave a sort of groan, and I was so frightened I looked out. And he was opening the picture. He opened it with a little key off his watch-chain. And when he'd opened it he went on looking at it for simply ages. And once he gave another groan, and he said 'Margaret' twice in a sort of whisper."

"Quite so," said Mr. Hale.

The colour rushed into Margaret's cheeks.

"Why do you say that, just as if I was telling you about the weather, instead of a frightfully secret, romantic sort of thing like I *was* telling you about?"

"My dear Miss Standing!"

"It was frightfully thrilling."

"Did you see the picture?"

"N-no. Well. I just got a peep at it—when he turned round you know."

"Yes?"

"It was a miniature, and it had little diamonds all round it. They sparkled like anything, and I could just see that she was fair like me. And that's all. I just saw her for a moment. She was awfully pretty."

Mr. Hale cleared his throat.

27

"There is, of course, no evidence to show that the miniature was a portrait of your mother."

"Why, of course it was!"

"It may have been. May I ask if the picture is in the house?"

"He always took it away with him. Perhaps it's on the yacht."

"I'm afraid it went overboard with him. The steward spoke of a portrait such as you describe; he said Mr. Standing carried it about with him. Now, Miss Standing, you are quite sure that you have no knowledge of your mother's maiden name?"

"I told you I hadn't."

"Or where your father met her?"

Margot shook her head.

"You don't know where they were married?"

"No. I don't know anything at all—I told you I didn't."

"Do you know where you were born?"

"N-no. At least—No, I don't know."

"What were you going to say? You were going to say something."

"Only—no, I don't know anything—only I don't think I was born in England."

"Ah! Can you tell me why?"

"He said—it was long ago when I was a little girl—he said, talking about himself, that he was born in Africa. And I said 'Where was I born?' And he said 'A long way from here.' So I thought perhaps I wasn't born in England."

Mr. Hale made the clicking noise with his tongue which is generally written "Tut-tut!" It expressed contempt for this reminiscence. As evidence it simply didn't exist. He cleared his throat more portentously than before.

"Miss Standing, if no will is found, and no certificate of your mother's marriage or of your own birth is forthcoming, your position becomes extremely serious."

28

Margot paused with a chocolate on its way to her mouth.

"Why does it become serious? I'm Papa's daughter."

"There is no proof even of that," said Mr. Hale.

Margot burst out laughing.

"Oh!" she said. "How frightfully funny that sounds! Why everyone knows I'm his daughter! How frightfully funny you are! Who do you think I am, if I'm not Margot Standing? Why, it's too silly!"

Mr. Hale frowned.

"Miss Standing, this is a very serious matter, and I beg that you will treat it seriously. I do not believe that Mr. Standing made a will. I know that he had not made one six weeks ago, for he paid my father a visit on the twentieth of August, and after he had gone my father told me that he had been urging upon Mr. Standing the necessity of making his will. My father then used these words: 'It is a very strange thing,' he said, 'that a man in Mr. Standing's circumstances should have deferred such a simple and necessary action as the making of a will. And in his daughter's peculiar circumstances he certainly owes it to her to make sure of her provision.' Now, Miss Standing, those are the exact words my father used, and I take them to mean that he was cognizant of some irregularity in your position."

Margot opened her eyes very wide indeed.

"What on earth do you mean?"

"In the absence of any information about your mother, and in the light of what my father said—"

"Good gracious! What *do* you mean?"

"I mean," said Mr. Hale, "that it is possible that there was no marriage."

"But good gracious, there's *me*!" said Miss Standing.

"It is possible that you are illegitimate."

Miss Standing gazed at him in silence. After a moment she repeated the word illegitimate in a tentative way; it seemed to touch a chord. She brightened visibly and said in a tone full of interest,

"Like William the Conqueror—and all those sons of Charles II?"

"Quite so," said Mr. Hale.

"How *frightfully* thrilling!" exclaimed Miss Standing.

CHAPTER 6

When Mr. Hale had finished explaining the exact legal position of an illegitimate daughter whose father had died intestate, Miss Standing's eyes were round with indignation.

"I never heard anything so frightfully unjust in all my life," she said firmly.

"I'm afraid that doesn't alter the law."

"What's the good of women having the vote then? I thought all those frightful unjust laws were going to be altered at once when women get the vote. Miss Clay always said so."

Mr. Hale had never heard of Miss Clay, who was in fact an undermistress at Mme. Mardon's. He himself had always been opposed to women's suffrage.

"Do you mean to say"—Miss Standing sat bolt upright with her plump hands clasped on her blue serge knee—"do you actually mean to say that I don't get anything?"

"You are not legally entitled to anything."

"How absolutely disgraceful! Do you mean to say that Papa had millions and millions, and I don't get any of it at all? Who gets it if I don't? I suppose somebody does get it. Or does Government just *steal* it all?"

"Your cousin, Mr. Egbert Standing, is the heir-at-law. He will—er—doubtless consider the propriety of making you an allowance."

Miss Standing sprang to her feet.

"Egbert! You're joking—you *must* be joking!"

Mr. Hale looked the offence which he felt.

"*Really*, Miss Standing!"

Margot stamped her foot.

"I don't believe a single word of it. Papa didn't even like Egbert. He said he was a parasite. I remember quite well, because I didn't know what the word meant, and I asked him, and he made me look it up in the dictionary. And he said he didn't know what he'd done to deserve having Egbert for a nephew. He said it was a great pity someone hadn't drowned his brother Robert when he was a baby, because then he couldn't have had Egbert. That's what Papa said, and do you suppose he'd want his money, and all his things, and his pictures to go to someone he felt like that about? Papa simply adored those horrible gloomy pictures, and he'd hate Egbert to have them. Egbert adores them too—I can't think why—and that used to make Papa angrier than anything else. Aren't people funny?"

When Mr. Hale had taken his leave, Margot continued her letter to Stephanie.

Oh, Stephanie, he's been! Mr. Hale, the lawyer, I mean. He's the most frightful old stiff, with the sort of boring voice that makes you go to sleep in church when a parson has it. Only I didn't go to sleep, because he was saying the most frightfully devastating sort of things. There are a whole heap of the most frightful family secrets, and he says he thinks I'm illegitimate like the people in history. And I didn't know anyone ever was except in history books. But he says he thinks I am, because he doesn't think my father was ever married to my mother. And I don't understand about it, but he says there isn't any certificate of their being married, and there isn't any certificate of my being born. And doesn't that just show how stupid the whole thing is? Because if I hadn't been born, I shouldn't be here. So I can't see what on earth anyone wants a certificate for. And he says I shan't have any money . . .

Mr. Hale returned to his office, where he presently interviewed Mr. Egbert Standing. He had not met him before, and he looked at him now with some disfavour. Mr. Hale did not like fat young men; he did not like young men who lolled; he disapproved of bow ties with loose ends, and of scented cigarettes. He regarded the curl in Egbert's hair with well-founded suspicion. For a short moment he shared a sentiment with Miss Margot Standing—he did not like Egbert. The young clerk who took notes in the corner did not like him either.

Everything else apart, Mr. Egbert Standing was a most difficult person to do business with. He lolled and yawned, and ran his fingers through the artificial waves of his mouse-coloured hair. He had a round featureless face with light eyes, light lashes, and no eyebrows. Mr. Hale disliked him very much indeed. It seemed impossible to get him to take any interest either in Miss Standing's predicament or his own position as heir-at-law.

Mr. Hale repeated Mr. Hale senior's remarks very much as he had repeated them to Margot.

"My father left me in no doubt that there was some irregularity in Miss Standing's position. He pressed Mr. Standing to make a will, but Mr. Standing put the matter aside. I am quite sure that my father knew more than he told me. I believe that he was in Mr. Standing's confidence. May I ask whether your uncle ever spoke to you on the matter?"

Egbert lolled and yawned.

"I believe he did."

"You believe he did!"

"I have some slight recollection—I—er—I'm not a business man. I—er—don't take much interest in business."

"Can you tell me what your uncle said?"

Egbert ran his hands through his hair.

"I—er—really I have a very poor memory."

"Mr. Standing, this is a very important matter. Do you assert that your uncle spoke to you in such a sense as to lead you to suppose that your cousin was illegitimate?"

"Something of that sort." Egbert's voice was languid in the extreme.

"What did he say?"

"I—er—really can't remember. I don't take much interest in family matters."

"You must have some recollection."

"My uncle was, I believe, excited—I seem to remember that. He was, in fact, annoyed—with me—yes, I think it was with me. And I have some recollection of his saying—" Egbert paused and regarded his right thumb-nail critically.

"Yes? What did he say?"

"I really don't remember exactly. It was something about his will."

"Yes? That is important."

"I don't remember really what he said. But he seemed annoyed. And it was something about making his will, because he'd be hanged if he'd let the property come to

33

me. But he didn't make a will after all, did he?"

"We haven't been able to find one. Was that all he said, Mr. Standing?"

"Oh no there was a lot more—about my cousin, you know."

"What did he say about your cousin?"

Egbert yawned.

"I didn't take any interest in her, I'm afraid."

Mr. Hale strove for patience.

"What did your uncle say about his daughter's position?"

"I don't remember," said Egbert vaguely. "Something about its being irregular—something like he said before, when he wrote to me."

Mr. Hale sat bolt upright.

"Your uncle *wrote* to you about his daughter's position?"

Egbert shook his head.

"He wrote to me about the club I was putting up for—said he'd blackball me."

Mr. Hale tapped on the table.

"You said he wrote to you about his daughter."

"No, he wrote to me about blackballing me for the club. He just mentioned his daughter."

"In a letter of that sort? *Mr. Standing*!"

"Come to think of it, it wasn't that letter at all. I told you my memory was awfully bad."

"Oh, it was another letter? And what did he say?"

"I really can't remember," said Egbert in an exhausted voice.

"Have you got that letter—did you keep it?"

Egbert brightened a little.

"I might have it, but I don't know—I'm so awfully careless about letters. I just leave them about, you know, and sometimes my man throws them away, and sometimes he doesn't. I could ask him."

"He'd be hardly likely to remember, but perhaps you will have a search made."

"He reads all the letters," said Egbert thoughtfully. "He *might* remember."

Years of self-control do not go for nothing. Mr. Hale merely pressed his lips together for a moment before saying:

"Will you kindly ask him to make a thorough search? This letter may be a very important piece of evidence. Indeed, if it contains Mr. Standing's own admission that his daughter's birth was irregular, the whole question would be settled." He paused, and added, "In your favour."

"I suppose it would," said Egbert vaguely.

Mr. Hale shuffled some papers.

"It is, perhaps, a little premature to raise the point, but if you succeed as heir-at-law you will, I presume, be prepared to consider the question of some allowance to your cousin. I mention this now, because if we had your assurance on this point, we should be prepared to make her a small advance. She appears to be entirely without money."

"Does she?"

"Entirely. She in fact asked me for some money to go on with only this afternoon."

"Did she?"

"I am telling you that she did, and I should be glad to have your views on the subject of an allowance."

Egbert yawned.

"I don't go in for having views. Art is what interests me—my little collections—a bit of china—a miniature—a print—*Art*."

"Mr. Standing, I must really ask you whether you are prepared to guarantee a small allowance to your cousin."

"Why should I?"

Mr. Hale explained.

35

"If you succeed to the late Mr. Standing's fortune, you will be a very wealthy man."

Egbert shook his head again.

"Not after everybody's had their pickings," he said.

Mr. Hale understood him to refer to the death duties.

"There will be a good deal left," he said drily. "An allowance to your cousin—"

For the third time Egbert shook his head.

"Nothing doing. If there's a will, or if it turns out that my uncle really married her mother, would she make me an allowance? *Not much.*"

"The positions are hardly analogous."

"There's nothing doing," said Egbert—"not in the way of an allowance. Someone—" he ran his hand through his hair—"someone suggested we might get married. What do you think of that?"

"It is rather a question of what Miss Standing would think of it."

"Why? It would put her all right, wouldn't it? I thought it was rather a bright suggestion myself—puts us both right, don't you see? If there's a will or a certificate it makes it all right for me. And if there isn't a will or a certificate, it makes it all right for her. I thought it was quite a bright suggestion."

"It would certainly be a provision for Miss Standing."

"Or for me," said Egbert.

CHAPTER 7

That evening Mr. Archie Millar fulfilled his deferred dinner engagement. He and Charles had a small table in a corner of the huge dining-room of The Luxe. Archie was in very good form—full of virtue, full of bonhomie, full of real affection for Charles.

"I am The Virtuous Nephew out of *Tracts for Tiny Tots*. This is the seventeenth time this year that I have been summoned to my Aunt Elizabeth's death-bed. She's no end bucked because I always come. She isn't goin' to die for the next hundred years or so, but it keeps the old dear no end amused to go on sendin' for me, and alterin' her will, and givin' good advice all round. She always tells me about all my little faults and failin's, and I say 'Righto' and she's no end bucked. Her doctor says it's a splendid tonic. But I wish she didn't always send for me when I'm dinin' with a pal."

Charles was debating the question of just how much he was going to tell Archie. Margaret—hang Margaret! She did nothing but get in the way. He frowned and broke in on Archie's flow of conversation with an abrupt question:

"Tell me about the Pelhams. Are they still at 16 George Street?"

Archie laid down his fish-fork.

"Haven't you heard?"

"Not a word since I left."

"Mrs. Pelham died six months ago."

Charles felt shocked. Margaret adored her mother. If he had

sometimes thought she adored her too much, he admitted the temptation. Esther Pelham, beautiful, emotional, with a charm as potent as it was difficult to define, never lacked adorers. Charles himself had bent the knee. Unfair, therefore, to complain if Margaret did so too. He was shocked, and showed it.

"Poor old Freddy was awfully cut up. Bit of a bore Freddy Pelham, but everyone's awfully sorry for him now—no end of a facer for him after takin' her abroad and all—rotten for him comin' home alone, poor chap."

"Did she die abroad?"

Archie nodded.

"Freddy took her off for a long voyage. No one thought she was really ill. Beastly for poor little Freddy comin' home alone."

Charles told himself just what he thought of an idiotic reluctance to speak Margaret's name. He spoke it now:

"Wasn't Margaret with them?"

"No—it was an awful shock for her."

Charles prodded himself again.

"She's married, I suppose?"

"Margaret! Who told you that yarn?"

"No one. I just thought she'd be married."

"Well, she isn't—or she wasn't last time I saw her, and that was about ten days ago. She isn't livin' with Freddy, you know."

"Why isn't she?"

"Nobody knows. Girls are so dashed independent nowadays. She went off on her own when Freddy took her mother abroad—and she's stayed on her own ever since—works for her livin', and doesn't look as if it agreed with her. I think it's a pity myself." He looked at Charles apologetically. "I always *liked* Margaret, you know."

Charles laughed.

"So did I. What's she doing?"

"Job in a shop—low screw, long hours. Rotten show I should call it. Fancy workin' when you don't have to. Girls don't know when they're well off."

"Where's she living?"

"She told me," said Archie, "but I'm hanged if I remember. Sort of minute flat affair. She had a little money from her own father, didn't she?"

"Yes—nothing to speak of."

"You're such a beastly plutocrat!"

"She couldn't live on it."

"She is livin' on it, plus a pound a week."

Charles exclaimed:

"A pound a week!"

"That's her screw."

"Impossible!"

"I told you you were a beastly plutocrat. Pound a week's her market value. She told me so herself."

"It's sweating! What's her job?"

"Tryin' on hats for ugly old women who can't face 'emselves in the glass. Margaret puts on the hat, the old woman thinks she looks a bit of a daisy in it, pays five or ten guineas, and goes away as pleased as Punch. Give you my word that's how it's done. Amazin'—isn't it?"

Charles frowned.

"What's the shop?"

"Place called Sauterelle in Sloane Street—frightfully smart and exclusive."

Charles detached himself with a jerk from a vision of Margaret trying on hats for other people.

"The Hula-Bula Indians say that a vain woman is like an empty egg-shell," he observed.

39

"Women are all vain," said Archie. "I only once met one that wasn't, and I give you my word she was a grim proposition. You should see my Aunt Elizabeth's night-caps. By the way she's just made a will leavin' every farthin' to a home for decayed parrots. She says the lot of parrots who outlive their devoted mistresses is enough to make a walrus weep. She says she feels a call to provide for their indigent old age. I shall have to marry an heiress—I see it loomin'. I think I'd better make the runnin' with the Standing girl before there are too many starters."

"Who's the Standing girl?"

Archie very nearly dropped his knife and fork.

"My dear old bean, don't you read the evenin' papers? Old man Standing was a multi-millionaire who got washed overboard in one of the late weather spasms in the Mediterranean. Beastly place the Mediterranean—nasty cold wind, nasty choppy sea—draughty sort of place. Well, he got washed overboard; and they can't find any will, and he's got an only daughter, who scoops the lot. I'm just hesitatin' on the brink as it were, because they haven't published her photograph, and that probably means she's a bit of a nightmare—I mean, think of the photographs they do publish. And my Aunt Elizabeth might alter her will again any old day if her parrot bit her, or came out with some of the swear words she thinks she's broken him of. She told me with tears in her eyes what a reformed bird he was. But you can't ever tell with parrots."

Charles had not been attending. He had decided that he would tell Archie just what had happened the other night; only he would leave Margaret out of it. He interrupted an ingenious plan for priming the parrot with something really hair-raising in the way of an expletive.

"The other night, Archie, when you didn't come, I walked down to have a look at the old house."

"Did you? Did you go in?"

"Anyone might have walked in," said Charles drily. "The door into the alley-way was open, and the garden door was open too. I walked in, and I walked upstairs, and I found a cheery sort of criminal conspiracy carrying on like a house on fire in my mother's sitting-room."

"I say, is this a joke?"

"No, it isn't. I saw a light under the door, and I heard voices. You remember the cupboard where we used to play, across the room of the passage between the bedroom and sitting-room?"

"Yes, of course."

"I got in there and looked through the hole we used to keep corked up, and there was a gentleman in a grey rubber mask and gloves giving orders to a very pretty lot of scoundrels."

"Charles, you *are* jokin'."

"I'm not—it happened."

"What were they doin'—"

"Well, I rather gathered they'd destroyed a will, and it wouldn't very much surprise me to hear that they'd made away with the man who'd made it. They seemed to be think-ing about murdering his daughter if another will turned up, or some certificate—I didn't quite understand about that."

"Charles, you don't mean to say you're serious?"

"Absolutely."

"You weren't drunk, and you weren't dreamin'?"

"I was not."

Archie heaved a sigh.

"Why on earth wasn't I there? What did you do?—bound from your place of concealment hissin' 'All is discovered,' or what?"

"I went on listening," said Charles. He proceeded to give Archie a very accurate account of the things he had listened

41

to and the things he had seen. He left Margaret Langton out of the story, and in consequence found himself making rather a poor figure at the finish.

"You *didn't* bound from your place of concealment!" Archie's tone was incredulous.

"No, I didn't."

"You let them get away and just trickled round to the police station?"

"Well—no," said Charles, "I didn't go to the police station."

"Why didn't you?"

"Because I didn't want to." He paused. "As a matter of fact I used to know one of the crowd pretty well, and I thought I'd keep the police out of it if I could."

Archie considered this.

"I say, that's bad! I mean destroyin' wills and plannin' to murder people isn't the sort of game you expect to find your pals mixed up in—is it? Did you know the fellow well?"

"Fairly well," said Charles.

"Well, d'you know him well enough to put it to him that it isn't exactly the sort of show to be mixed up in?"

"That's what I was thinking of doing."

"I see. Then there's the girl. They won't be getting up to any murderin' games for the moment, I take it."

"No," said Charles, "that was only if this certificate turned up."

"And you don't know what it is? And for all you know it may be turnin' up any day of the week. Pity you don't know her name—isn't it?"

"Her Christian name is Margot. I heard that."

Archie upset his coffee.

"Charles, you've been pullin' my leg."

"I haven't."

42

"Honest Injun?"

"Honest Injun."

"Not about the name? You swear you're not pullin' my leg about that?"

"No, I'm not. Why should you think I am?"

Archie leaned across the table and dropped his voice.

"You swear the girl was called Margot? You're sure?"

"Positive. Why?"

"Because that's the name of the girl I was talkin' about—the Standing girl—old Standing's daughter."

"Margot?"

"Margot Standing," said Archie in a solemn whisper.

CHAPTER 8

Mr. Hale was considerably annoyed next morning by the arrival of Mr. Egbert Standing and a large leather suitcase full of unsorted papers. One of Mr. Hale's clerks brought in the suitcase and placed it on the floor, whereupon Egbert with a wave of the hand commanded him to open it.

"It isn't locked—I never lock things—you just slide back those what-d'you-call-its."

The clerk slid back the what-d'you-call-its and lifted the top. A mask of crumpled paper met the eye.

"There!" said Egbert. "My man tells me that's the lot."

Mr. Hale looked at the suitcase, and Mr. Hale's clerk looked at Mr. Hale. A large envelope marked Income Tax lay across a pale blue note. Mr. Hale sniffed. A surprisingly vigorous scent of patchouli arose from the suitcase. He suspected the pale blue note—income tax officials do not use patchouli.

"Go on—sort them," said Egbert in a tone of languid encouragement.

"I should have thought you would prefer to sort them yourself."

Egbert shook his head.

"I couldn't be bothered."

"Your private correspondence—" began Mr. Hale. He eyed the pale blue note.

Egbert yawned.

"I can't be bothered. Let him get on with it."

After receiving a nod from Mr. Hale, the clerk proceeded to get on with it. The contents of the suitcase appeared to consist chiefly of unpaid bills. There was a sprinkling of other scented notes—pink, mauve, and brown. There were two sock-suspenders, an artificial flower in a condition of extreme old age, a green satin slipper with a gold heel, and several photographs of damsels in brief skirts and a great many pearls.

"Put the letters on one side, Cassels," said Mr. Hale. "We're looking for a letter in the late Mr. Standing's hand. I don't know if you remember it."

"I think I do, sir. Isn't this his writing?"

Mr. Hale took it, looked at Egbert, and inquired,

"Do you wish me to read this? It seems to be part of a letter from your uncle."

"Read away—out loud if you like—I'm sure I don't mind."

Mr. Hale turned the sheet in his hand, frowning.

"There is nothing about Miss Standing here. I think I will not—er—read it aloud."

"Is it the one about blackballing me for that club I told you about?"

"No," said Mr. Hale.

Egbert looked slightly puzzled.

"What is it then?"

"Mr. Standing appears to have been refusing a request for a loan."

"Oh, *that* one. He's got a nasty way of putting it—hasn't he?"

Mr. Cassels unfolded a piece of paper which had been crumpled into a ball. Still on his knees, he turned and laid it on the edge of the writing-table.

"Am I to read this, Mr. Standing?"

"You can read them all—it doesn't worry me. I can't be bothered myself."

The letter was very badly creased indeed. Mr. Hale uttered an exclamation as his eye lighted upon the address and the date. The paper was stamped with the name of a hotel in Majorca, and the date was only a fortnight old. He read the address aloud and repeated the date; then glancing down the sheet, he spoke to the young clerk still rummaging among bills.

"That will do, Cassels. This is the letter we were looking for."

Mr. Hale turned sharply upon Egbert.

"This letter was written the day before your uncle was drowned. It is, as far as we know, the last letter he ever wrote. It is impossible to over-rate its importance. How could you fail to realize this?"

"I don't take any interest in business," said Egbert. "I told you I didn't. I told you my line was Art."

Mr. Hale rapped the table.

"You cannot possibly fail to realize the importance of this letter."

Egbert yawned.

45

"I don't know that I read it very carefully. My uncle's letters don't interest me, you know."

"Mr. Standing, I will ask you to listen attentively whilst I read you this letter."

Egbert sprawled in the big armchair with half-shut eyes. It is possible that he listened attentively; but he had all the appearance of being half asleep.

Mr. Hale's voice was sharp as he read from the crumpled page:

My dear Egbert,

I will neither lend you any money, nor will I give you any money. Your letter serves to remind me, not for the first time, that I had better make my will and have done with the chances to which Margot's irregular birth exposes the fortune which I have laboured to build up. Even if she were legitimate, I would not expose her to the risks involved in the possession of so much money. I shall make a will as soon as I return to England, and I advise you not to expect too much from me. What you want is a good hard bout of honest work.

E. Standing

"It's a rude letter—isn't it?" said Egbert sleepily. "I remember I nearly tore it up."

"You would have been tearing up about three million pounds if you had," said Mr. Hale in his most impressive voice.

CHAPTER 9

Charles Moray walked twenty yards up Sloane Street, and then walked twenty yards down again. He continued to do this. Across the street was a lighted window with one hat on a stand and a piece of gold brocade lying carelessly at the foot of a bright green bowl full of golden fir-cones. Charles was aware that these things were there, because he had stood in front of the window and peered in; all that he could actually see from across the road was a blue of light in the fog. He hoped he would be able to see Margaret when she came out.

He went up close to a street lamp and looked at his watch. It was past six o'clock and the fog was getting thicker every minute. He crossed the street and again began to walk up and down.

It was a quarter past six before Margaret came out. He was only a couple of yards away, and even so, he nearly missed her. There was a shadow that slipped past him in the fog and was gone.

Charles ran after the shadow. He could not have said how he knew that it was Margaret who had passed him; he did not stop to think about that at all. He ran after her, came in sight of the shadow, and kept pace with it, a little behind.

He was in a strange mood. There came first the quick certainty that this was Margaret. And then, like a flood, this sense of her and of her nearness swept over him. She walked before him; but if she had been in his arms, as she once had been, he could not have felt her more near. If he looked, he

47

would see her very thoughts. He told himself that all he had ever seen was a mirage—the real Margaret had never shared a single thought with him.

He had been quite sure that it was going to be immensely interesting to meet her again; it had not entered his head that he would be angry. Yet he had not walked half a dozen yards behind her before he was as angry as he had ever been in his life. He was angry in a new way—angry with Margaret for earning her living, angrier because she had mixed herself up in who knew what ridiculous and criminal conspiracy, and angriest of all because she had made him angry. Mixed with his anger—curiosity. What was at the bottom of it? What did it all mean? The explorer in him was most keenly on the alert. He meant to get to the bottom of the business.

Perhaps his step quickened a little; he was nearer her than he had meant to be when they passed under a street lamp. The light hung above it like a faint white cloud.

He said, "How d'you do, Margaret?" and said it lightly and pleasantly. To Margaret Langton the voice came out of the fog and out of the past. There was a step that kept pace with her own. And then Charles Moray said her name—*Charles*. She turned, a ghost in a nimbus. The quick movement was Margaret, the rest a blur.

"*Charles!*"

Her voice was unbelievably familiar; it might have been some voice of his own speaking to him. It shook him, and a hotter anger than before leapt in him.

"*Charles!* How dare you frighten me like that!"

"Did I frighten you?" He spoke smoothly and easily.

Margaret caught her breath.

"I thought someone was following me. It's horrible to be followed in a fog."

"I was waiting for you, and I nearly missed you. That ass Archie had forgotten your address, so I had to try and catch you here."

They walked on; the lamp receded. Margaret said,

"Why did you want to—catch me?"

He shrugged his shoulders.

"I've been away. Perhaps you haven't noticed. One comes back, one sees one's friends—"

"*Friends*—are we friends? I shouldn't have thought you would ever want to see me again."

This was the old Margaret, fiercely untactful. Charles leapt at the opening. He wanted to hit hard, to hurt her as much as possible. He kept his indifferent tone very successfully.

"Why on earth shouldn't I want to see you? After all, we were friends for about ten years before we ever thought of getting engaged. Wasn't it ten years? We were friends for ten years, and then we were engaged for six months, and then—we stopped being engaged. Well, the engagement being only an episode, it can be just wiped out. You see?"

No woman likes to be told that she was only an episode. Charles was pleasantly aware of this; aware too that he had succeeded in piercing some armour of defence.

She said with a hot resentment in her voice,

"How can we be friends? How can you possibly want to be friends with me?"

Charles laughed.

"My dear girl, why not? Do let us be modern. These things don't last, you know. Do you expect me to be tragic after four years? I was naturally a bit peeved at the time. But one doesn't go on being peeved." He paused, then struck again and struck hard. "I've been looking forward immensely to seeing you—but of course I thought you would be married."

"*Married! I!*"

"Well," said Charles, "I didn't suppose you turned me down just for the fun of the thing. Naturally there was someone else."

Margaret turned on him, her head up.

"Did you say that just to hurt? Or did you believe it?"

Charles laughed again.

"A bit of both. I believed it all right."

She made a sound—not a sigh or a sob, but a quick angry breath.

"Look here," said Charles, "I'll put nearly all my cards on the table if you like. I suppose that we should wash out the *episode* and revert to the *status quo ante*. If you won't do this, I shall naturally conclude that you mind meeting me, that you find it embarrassing or painful."

Margaret was certainly very angry.

"My dear Charles, doesn't it occur to you that I might simply be bored?"

"No, it doesn't. We could fight like fiends, and we could hate each other like poison; but we could never be bored. When can I come and see you?"

"You can't come and see me."

"Too embarrassing? Too painful?"

There was no answer. He thought he heard her catch her breath again. He continued in a pleasant social manner:

"I was proposing, you know, to revert to the days before the *episode*. You were ten, weren't you, when your people came to George Street? I seem to remember that you didn't mince your words in those days. Why bother to mince them now? Why not revert—say anything you like?"

Margaret said nothing; she walked without turning her head. Charles walked beside her. He was sorry there was a fog; he would have liked to see her face. He gave her a moment; then he spoke again.

"No words bad enough?"

There were no words at all.

"When can I come and see you?"

Silence—the fog—a black slippery crossing—Basil Street. They crossed, and passed through another patch of hazy light.

"You used not to sulk," said Charles meditatively.

She flung round on him then like an angry schoolgirl.

"How *dare* you?"

Charles was immensely pleased.

"*Touche!*" he said to himself; and then aloud, "I'm sorry— I haven't any manners. I've been deprived of the refining influence of woman for four years, you see. When can I come and see you?"

They had reached the Knightsbridge pavement, and he stopped instinctively on its dark brink. It was very dark, the lights of the crawling cars only just discernible, the noise of the traffic a bewildering dull sound that seemed to come from everywhere at once.

Charles stopped, but Margaret Langton never hesitated; she walked straight on, and even as he looked round for her she was lost in the shuffling, whispering, hooting gloom. Charles plunged after her. Someone swore, a hoarse voice shouted. "Where are you gettin' to?" The hooter of a car went off right in his ear, and his shoulder collided violently with somebody's driving-mirror. The next half-minute continued to be like that, only more so.

He fetched up on the island in the middle of the road with feelings of relief. The island was crowded. Under the powerful light it was possible to see one's next-door neighbour. Charles annoyed all the rest of the people on the island by being neighbour to each of them in turn. He trod on several toes, was prodded in the ribs by a very powerful umbrella, and a number of people asked him what he thought he was doing. As it was impossible to explain that he was looking for Margaret, he had to say he was sorry a good many times.

Margaret was not on the island. He came to a standstill behind a broad blue serge back. A heavily built man stood just in front of him. He wore a rough blue coat of the peak-jacket style and had about his neck a large khaki muffler—the sort of thing that one's aunts knitted stacks of during the war. The thought passed through Charles's mind and then pricked him so sharply that he very nearly cried out. He had made the same comparison before, within the last few days; and he had made it about the same muffler. He had stared at that blue serge back and that khaki comforter before. He had stared through the knot-hole of his mother's cupboard and seen that lumpy shoulder and that bullet head come into view as Number Forty, the deaf janitor, opened the door to Grey Mask's visitors.

He pushed against the man, hoping to see his face; and as he did so, he said mechanically,

"I beg your pardon."

In a moment his interest was dashed. The man turned half round and said,

"Granted."

Charles saw a square fresh-coloured face, clean-shaven, and then the man turned again and stepped off the island into the road. Charles stepped off too.

Forty was stone deaf. This man was not stone deaf. He must have heard Charles say "I beg your pardon," because he immediately turned round and said "Granted." He might have turned because Charles pushed him; but you don't say "Granted" when someone barges into you from behind. No, he must have heard. Then he wasn't Forty, because Forty was deaf. Grey Mask said that Forty was deaf.

Charles considered what he knew of Forty. He was Grey Mask's janitor—in other words a villain who was trusted by other villains. And Grey Mask said he was deaf. To Charles he was merely a bullet head, a blue serge coat, a pair of broad shoulders, and a khaki muffler.

Charles inclined strongly to the evidence of his own eyes. He followed the muffler. He followed it to the corner and along twenty yards or so of pavement. Then he followed it into a Hammersmith bus.

CHAPTER 10

The bus went creaking and clanking on its way. It was quite full, and it smelt very strongly of fog, petrol and wet umbrellas. Charles sat opposite the man with the muffler and looked at him curiously. He had a square, fresh face and very blue eyes; he had the look of a man who has followed the sea. Forty had been with Mr. Standing on his yacht. But Forty was deaf, and this man wasn't deaf.

Just on the impulse Charles leaned across and addressed him.

"Bad fog—isn't it? I'm glad I'm not at sea."

The man looked at Charles after a pleasant puzzled fashion and shook his head.

"Sorry, sir, but I'm deaf."

Charles raised his voice:

"I only said it was a bad fog."

He shook his head again and smiled deprecatingly.

"It's no good, sir. Hill 60 going up was the last thing I heard."

The other people in the bus looked round with interest. A fat woman in a brown velvet dress and stout laced boots said, "What a shime!"

Charles sat back and closed his eyes. Grey Mask had said Forty was deaf—and that this was Forty, Charles had now no more doubt than that he himself was Charles Moray; yet Forty, apologized to by a casual stranger in a fog—no, let's get it clearer, Forty taken unawares—had answered a casual stranger's apology. But Forty in a crowded, lighted bus not only maintained that he was stone deaf but produced a picturesque reminiscence to account for it. What did it mean?

Charles thought that he would find out what it meant; and when presently the man in the muffler got out of the bus, Charles got out too.

"The one point about this perfectly beastly weather," he explained to Archie over dinner, "is that you can follow a fellow without his spotting you. I followed him very successfully and tracked him to his lair. He appears to be lodging at No. 5 Gladys Villas, Chiswick. The house belongs to an old lady and her daughter who've been there for about forty years—I found that out at the grocer's. But there I'm stuck. The old lady's name is Brown, and she's the widow of a sea captain. I could have found out lots more of that sort of thing. But how am I going to find out the things I want to know about Forty?"

"Get a trained sleuth to do it," said Archie firmly. "That's what they're for. I can put you on to one if you like."

"A good man?"

"A sleuthess," said Archie impressively. "A perfect wonder—has old Sherlock boiled."

Charles frowned.

"A *woman*?"

54

"Well, a sleuthess. She's not exactly what you'd call a little bit of fluff, you know."

"What's her name?"

"Maud Silver."

"Mrs. or Miss?"

"My dear old bean!"

"Well—which is she?"

"Single as a Michaelmas daisy," said Archie.

"But who is she? And why drag in a sleuthess when there are lots of perfectly good sleuths?"

"Well," said Archie, "I put my money on Maud. I only saw her once, and she didn't make my heart beat any faster. I went to see her because my cousin Emmeline Foster was in the dickens of a hole. She'd done one of the silly sort of things women manage to do—can't imagine how they think of them myself. I can't give you the lurid details; but what it amounted to was that she'd gone and lost the family jewels, and she was shakin' in her shoes for fear her mother-in-law would find out. Well, little Maudie got them back. No fuss, no scandal, no painful family scene—a *very* neat piece of work. That's only one story. I know half a dozen more, because Emmeline just rushed round with her mouth open tellin' all her friends what a wonder Maudie was, and all the friends who had private scrapes of their own went and bleated to Maudie about 'em, and when Maudie had got 'em all straightened up again, they came back and told Emmeline, and Emmeline told me."

Charles took down Miss Maud Silver's address. If she specialized in getting silly women out of messes, she would just about suit his book. He put the address away in his pocket-book, and as he looked up he caught sight of Freddy Pelham dining at a table with Massiter, the artist, and a large, dull, respectable couple whom Charles did not know.

Massiter had the air of a man who is bored to the verge of coma. Freddy looked so forlorn that Charles felt a genuine pang of pity.

Later, when he and Archie were going out, he found himself almost touching Freddy in the doorway, and in a moment Freddy was shaking him by the hand.

"My dear fellow! You're back—yes, you're back! Dear me, you're back again!"

"As you see," said Charles.

Freddy dropped the hand he had been shaking; his little grey eyes looked deprecatingly at the young man whom his stepdaughter had jilted; his rather high and plaintive voice became more plaintive still.

"My dear fellow—you're back! Pleased to see you—very pleased to see you!"

"I'm pleased to be back," said Charles cheerfully.

At another time it might have amused him to observe Freddy's embarrassment. He plunged straight into the cause of it.

"By the way, can you give me Margaret's address?"

Freddy blinked.

"Margaret's *address*—er—*Margaret's* address?"

"Yes."

Freddy blinked again.

"You've heard that she's deserted me," he said. "I don't know why girls can't stay at home. But it seems to take them all the same way. Now there's Nora Canning—now let me see, was it Nora? Or is Nora the married one, and am I thinking of Nancy? Or is it Nancy who is the married one? And who the deuce did she marry? It wasn't Monty Soames, and it wasn't Rex Fossiter. Now who *was* it she married? I know I was at the wedding, because I remember they gave us deuced bad champagne—and Esther couldn't go, but Margaret and

56

I went—" He broke off, and looked down like a shy child. "You've heard about Esther?"

Charles felt horribly sorry for him.

"Yes, I—heard. I can't say how sorry I am. She—there was something about her."

Freddy wrung his hand.

"I know, my boy, I *know*. No one like her—was there? Can't think what she ever saw in me. Well, well, I'm glad to see you back, Charles. She always liked you very much. I'd be sorry to think there was any sort of feeling now you've come back."

"Oh, there isn't."

"Bygones be bygones, eh? That's right! Stupid to keep things up—that's what I've always said—what's the sense of keeping things up? I've always said that. I remember now saying that twenty years ago to Fennicker—no, if it was Fennicker it couldn't have been twenty years ago, because that Fennicker was in China until 1914, unless I'm thinking of the other one—their mothers married cousins you know— deuced pretty women both of them—lovely shoulders. Women don't have shoulders now, eh? Nothing but bones— that's what I say—*scraggy*, my boy—and it don't make them look any younger—"

"What about Margaret's address?" said Charles quickly. If he had to wait whilst Freddy disentangled the Fennickers for a few generations or so, he would do so; but there seemed to be just a chance of escape; Archie was punching him in the ribs. "What about Margaret's address?"

"I thought she might have stayed with me," said Freddy. "But I don't want you to think we quarrelled—I shouldn't like anyone to think that."

"Can you give me her address?"

It took Charles another ten minutes to get it, and Archie had reached groaning point before they finally got away.

They walked the short distance to the show Archie had insisted upon. The fog was still heavy. Charles found himself thinking curiously and angrily about Margaret. Where was she? What was she thinking? What was she doing? He had a furious desire to know, to break away from Archie and to walk to the address which Freddy Pelham had given him.

At intervals during the evening that desire to know what Margaret was doing swept over him again. If he could have looked into Margaret's room, he would have seen nothing, because the room was dark. It was very dark and very cold, because there was no light and no fire.

Margaret Langton lay face downwards in front of the cold hearth; her forehead rested upon her crossed arms. The fire had gone out a long time ago. It was hours since she had moved at all, but the hot, slow tears went on soaking into the black stuff of her sleeve. Her right arm was crossed over her left arm; her forehead rested upon it. The stuff of her sleeve was quite wet through.

CHAPTER 11

Charles sat in Miss Maud Silver's waiting-room. He was not one of those who wait patiently. Having arrived at ten o'clock, he was exasperated to find that he was not the first upon the scene; a murmur of female voices stimulated his annoyance. "Probably talking millinery," was his embittered comment.

Then all of a sudden through the thin partition came a sharp little cry of *"I can't!"* The cry had a quality which did not suggest millinery. There was a silence; and then the murmur of voices went on again.

It was almost half past ten before the inner door opened and a woman came out. She kept her head turned away and passed quickly out on to the landing.

Charles entered Miss Silver's office with a good deal of curiosity, and found himself in a small, light room, very bare—furnished, to the first glance at any rate, by a chair, a writing-table and Miss Silver herself. The writing-table was immense, of the large old-fashioned flat kind with drawers all round it; the top was piled high with exercise-books of different colours very neatly stacked.

Miss Silver sat in front of a pad of pink blotting-paper. She was a little person with no features, no complexion, and a great deal of tidy mouse-coloured hair done in a large bun at the back of her head. She inclined her head slightly, but did not offer to shake hands.

Charles introduced himself, mentioned Archie's name, mentioned Emmeline Foster's name, and received no indication that Miss Silver had any recollection of either of them.

"What can I do for you, Mr. Moray?" The voice was rather a hesitating one; a quiet voice without tone.

Charles began to feel sorry he had come.

"Well—I wanted some information."

Miss Silver picked up a brown copy-book, wrote Charles's name at the head of a page, asked for and added his address, and then inquired what sort of information he wanted.

Charles did not mean to tell her very much—not at first anyhow. He said,

"I want information about a man who is lodging at 5 Gladys Villas, Chiswick. He's a middle-aged man with a fresh colour. I don't know his name. I want to know anything you can find out about him; and I most particularly want to know whether he is really deaf."

Miss Silver wrote in the copy-book. Then she asked,

"Anything more?"

"Yes," said Charles frowning. "I want to know something about Mr. Standing's family affairs. You know the man I mean—he's been in all the papers."

"His affairs," said Miss Silver, "are largely public property. I can tell you a good deal about them now. He was washed overboard whilst he was yachting off Majorca, and he didn't leave any will. His immense fortune will therefore be inherited by his only child. Her name is Margot. She is just eighteen, and until a week ago was at school in Switzerland. Was that what you wanted to know?"

Charles shook his head.

"Everyone knows that. I want news from day to day of what is happening. I want to know who is in the house with the girl—what she does—who her friends are. I want to be told at once if she goes away, or if there is any sudden development in her affairs. I'm afraid it's all rather indefinite; but I expect you can see the sort of thing I want."

Miss Silver had been using the right-hand page of the brown copy-book; she now wrote something quickly on the left. Then she said;

"I see what you want. But you haven't told me why you want it."

"No."

Miss Silver smiled suddenly. The smile had the most extraordinary effect upon her face; it was just as if an expressionless mask had been lifted and a friendly, pleasant face had looked out from behind it.

"It's no good, Mr. Moray."

Charles said, "I beg your pardon?"

The smile was still there.

"I can't take your case unless you're going to trust me. I can't work for a client who only tells me snippets and odds and ends. 'Trust me all in all, or not at all' is my motto. Tennyson is out of fashion, but I admire him very much, and that is my motto."

Charles looked at her with the suspicion of a twinkle. What a Victorian little person! He became aware of a half-knitted stocking on her lap, still needles bristling. It seemed to him very appropriate. He twinkled, and replied to her quotation with another:

"The Taran-Tula Indians say that you may catch a snake by the tail, but you should never trust a woman."

Miss Silver looked sorry for the Taran-Tula Indians.

"Poor ignorant heathens!" she said; and then, "Of course, if one has been very badly treated, it makes one cautious. But I can't take your case unless you are frank with me. Frankness on your part—discretion on mine."

She picked up the stocking and began to knit, holding the needles in the German way. After one round she looked at Charles and smiled again.

"Well, Mr. Moray?"

Charles told her everything that he had told Archie Millar, and came away wondering whether he had made a fool of himself.

CHAPTER 12

At a quarter to seven that same evening Charles Moray rang the bell of Miss Langton's tiny flat. Margaret opened the door and stood facing him across the threshold.

"Charles!" Her voice betrayed no pleasure.

She had left the sitting-room door open behind her. At the first glance the effect was one of colour—dark red curtains; bright coloured cushions; Margaret a silhouette, in her black dress with the light behind her. She kept her hand on the door and did not move to let him in.

"Well?" said Charles. "Now that you're quite sure it's me, couldn't we come in?"

Margaret dropped her hand, turned and walked past the table to the hearth. A handful of sticks just lighted crackled there. She bent and put a lump of coal on them.

Charles came in behind her and shut the door. He was in a fever of impatience to look at her, to see her face. And then she rose suddenly from the fire and swung round; the light shone on her. She was pale—clear, and pale, and fine; the only colour was in her eyes—brown sombre colour with a dark fire behind the brown. She had changed; sorrow had gone over her and changed her. But under the change there was still Margaret, a Margaret who was so familiar that his heart jumped.

She spoke quickly:

"I'm afraid I can't ask you to stop. I've only just got in, and I have to get my supper."

"The soul of hospitality!" said Charles. "As a matter of fact I came to propose that we should dine somewhere and dance or do a show—whichever you like best."

She had changed—he supposed that he himself had changed; but Margaret ought not to have changed so much as this. The strong lines of cheek and jaw showed too plainly. Her eyes were too large; they looked darker. That was because she was so pale, and because of her black dress. Something welled up through his anger.

"Freddy told me you were here. Margaret, I want to say I'm so sorry about—her. Archie told me. I hadn't heard."

Margaret moved quickly.

"Yes—I can't talk about it. Where did you see Freddy?"

"He was dining with some people at The Luxe. I haven't gone down to Thornhill Square yet. The Luxe is—more sociable. I thought we might dine there tonight."

"No," said Margaret.

"Now look here! Just be a reasonable creature for once in a way. The change will do you good. I propose that we strew a little decent dust over the hatchet just for tonight. We needn't really bury it, you know—quite without prejudice, as the lawyers say. After all, one must dine."

Margaret looked at him out of those big dark eyes. He thought they mocked him.

"My dear Charles, I don't dine—I sup. When I'm very affluent I have an egg or a sardine. When I'm not—"

"Revolting!" said Charles. "Come and dine—real dinner."

"No," said Margaret. Her tone was a little fainter. Last night's bitter weeping had left her weary and cold. Now her mood began to change; there came over her an impatience of all this dreary round into which her life had fallen. Charles standing there brought back the old days; his voice, his teasing, smiling eyes, his air of cheerful vigour, all brought with them a longing for the old life, the old natural enjoyment in a hundred things which had slipped away from her.

"Come along," said Charles. He let his voice soften and his eyes look into hers.

She stopped resisting the turn of her mood. Why shouldn't she go back for an hour like a ghost, eat, drink and be merry, dance through an evening, and leave tomorrow to take care of itself?

"Well?" said Charles. "You've just time to dress."

He looked over her shoulder at the clock on the mantel-piece, a pretty trifle of bright green china with wreaths of gold and painted flowers. He and Margaret had bought it together in an old shop in Chelsea; he had given it to her on her nineteenth birthday, a month before they became engaged. The hands pointed to a quarter to seven.

He said, "Well? You're coming?" and saw the colour come into her face.

She laughed unexpectedly and picked up the clock. He watched with surprise and amusement. What was she going to do?

What she did was to open the clock and turn the hands. They went round with a little whirr; she was turning them back-wards—once—twice—three—four—five times; and as they turned, she became the glowing, young, live Margaret of that nineteenth birthday.

"What are you doing?" asked Charles smiling.

"I'm putting back the clock five years," said Margaret. There was a shade of defiance in her tone. Five years took them back to the days before what Charles had called the "episode"; it took them back to the time they were just neighbours and friends, seeing one another every day, full of common interest, engagements, diversions, quarrels.

Charles lifted his eyebrows.

"Five years?"

She nodded.

"Yes, five. Is it a bargain?"

"Go and dress," he said.

Charles made himself very agreeable over dinner. Incidentally he began to learn something of Margaret's life during the past four years. To his surprise he found that she had been working during the whole of the time, though she had gone on living in George Street until her mother's death.

"Freddy was very anxious I shouldn't think you had quarrelled with him." He laughed. "How would one set about quarrelling with Freddy? Has anyone ever done it?"

"I shouldn't think so."

"You didn't?"

"My dear Charles!"

"No—but did you?"

"Would it be your business if I had?"

Charles considered.

"You're not playing the game. This is five years ago and I am thinking of asking you to marry me. Yes, I think it's my business, because you see, if a girl has quarrelled with her step-father and left home, one might want to know why before one took the fatal plunge."

Margaret put down her left hand and clenched it on the sharp edges of the chair on which she sat. Just for a moment all the lights in the long room seemed to swing, and the room itself was full of a grey mist. She looked steadily into the mist until it lifted and showed her Charles leaning towards her across the table with his charming malicious smile.

"Are *you* playing the game? You can't have it both ways, you know. If it's now, it's not your business; and if it's five years ago—" her voice broke in a sudden laugh—"why,

65

if it's five years ago, I haven't left home at all."

"Your trick!" said Charles. But he had seen her colour go, and just for one horrid moment he had thought that she might be going to faint.

After dinner they danced in the famous Gold Room. Margaret was a beautiful dancer, and for a time they did not talk at all. Perhaps they were both remembering the last time they had danced together, a week before the wedding day which had never come.

Charles broke the silence. Memories are too dangerous sometimes.

"All the old tunes are as dead as door-nails. I don't know the name of anything. Do you?"

"The last one," said Margaret, "is called *I don't mind being all alone when I'm all alone with you.*"

"And this one?"

They were close to the orchestra, and a young man with a piercing tenor uplifted his voice and sang through his nose: "Oh, baby! Don't we get along?"

"Ripping!" said Charles. "I like the way these fellows burst into song."

"I'm happy! You're happy!" sang the young man in the band.

"In fact," said Charles, "the libretto has been specially written for us. I must thank the management. You wouldn't like to come with me, I suppose?"

Margaret laughed.

"No, I wouldn't. And you needn't think you can get a rise out of me by saying things like that, because you can't."

"Sure?"

"Quite sure."

"Then let's talk about swimming the channel, or flying to Tierra del Fuego, or something nice and safe like that."

Margaret laughed again; and when she laughed, the dark fire sparkled in her eyes.

"My charwoman—I have her once a week when I feel rich enough—doesn't think flying at all nice—not for a lady 'as calls herself a lady'. She said to me this morning that days and nights alone with a 'pirate' was what she didn't call respectable. She's a priceless treasure, and if I could afford to have her every day, it would cheer me up quite a lot."

"Do you need cheering? And if you do, must it be a charwoman?"

Another dance had begun. They glided into it. Margaret did not perhaps think that Charles's last remark called for an answer. The young man in the band broke forth once more: "Can't we be sweethearts now?"

"This song and dance business is *very* amusing," said Charles. "Not a dull moment anywhere. What's that step the fellow over there's doing? It looks tricky. Do you know it? You do? Then we'll practise it together."

He saw her home, and it was on the dark doorstep that he said,

"The clock's turned back again, and I want to ask you a question?"

"It's too late—I must go in."

"Yes, it's too late; but I want to ask you all the same. You wouldn't give me the chance four years ago, you know. Why did you do it, Margaret?"

He heard her take her breath; felt, rather than saw, that she stepped back.

"I can't tell you."

"Why can't you?"

"I can't. It's all over and done with, and dead and buried." Her rather deep voice sank deeper. "It's all *over*."

"I wonder," said Charles.

Margaret pushed her latch-key into the lock with a fierce thrust.

"It's *over*," she said.

The door shut between them heavily.

CHAPTER 13

Margot Standing wrote again to her friend Stephanie at the *pension*.

Oh, Stephanie, I do wish you were here! I haven't got anyone to talk to, and it's so frightfully dull. You can't call Mr. Hale a person to talk to, because he does all the talking himself, and everything he says is simply deadly. He says I shan't have any money at all unless there's a will, or those certificates turn up. And he says he's sure there isn't a will because of what poor Papa said to his father. And yesterday he said he was sure there weren't any certificates, because there was a letter from Papa to say so. And he said not to worry, because perhaps Egbert and I could come to some arrangement, and that that would be much the best thing. But I've made up my mind to go out and earn my living. I think it's rather romantic to earn one's living and to be a penniless orphan instead of a great heiress. I think it's frightfully romantic to be a penniless orphan, and in books they always have a frightfully exciting time. But great heiresses get married for their money, so I think it's much better not to be one. Don't tell anyone, but I answered an advertisement, and I got an answer, and I'm going to someone who wants a nice-looking girl for a secretary. I was afraid I might be too young, but he wrote and said he liked them young and wanted to know what colour my hair was and a lot of things like that. So I sent him the little snap-shot Mademoiselle took last term, and he said he was sure I should suit him, and I'm going there tomorrow. I haven't told anyone. And—this is the most secret part of all, and what you're most particularly not to tell anyone. And *please* tear this up, because you know you do leave letters about, and it's most frightfully secret. I'm not calling myself Margot Standing, because I don't want anyone to know where I am—Egbert, I mean, or Mr. Hale, or anyone. So I'm calling myself Esther Brandon. Don't you think it's a frightfully good name and very romantic? I didn't make it up—I *found* it. I was really looking to see if I could find those certificates or anything about my mother. There is a big box full of old things in one of the attics. I wanted to use the things for dressing-up on holidays, and when I asked Papa, he said "No" in a most *frightful* voice, and Mrs. Beauchamp said I oughtn't to have asked, and she expected the things belonged to my mother. So I thought I'd look and see if I could find anything. But there were only dresses—awfully funny and long, with frills and huge sleeves and lots and lots of little bones. I *can't* think how they breathed. And right at the bottom there was an old green desk. It had M. E. B. on the lid in gold letters, and I thought it was going to be frightfully exciting. But it wasn't, because it was empty. The only thing that was in it was a twisted screw of paper that had got wedged in under a little drawer at the side. I got it out, and it had Esther Brandon written on it like you sign your name. It looked like a little bit torn off the end of a letter. I thought it was a frightfully romantic name, and I expect it must have been my mother's name because of E. B. on the lid of the desk. When I wanted a name to go and earn my living with, I thought I'd be Esther Brandon. But you're not to tell anyone at all. And mind you tear this letter up at once, and *tear it up small*—not like the people in books who leave bits about, and the villain puts them together and finds out all the things they don't want him to know.

When Miss Standing had finished her letter, she threw a wistful glance at the empty chocolate box and wandered into the drawing-room. She was not prepared to find her cousin Egbert there, and if she had been a shade less bored, she might have retreated unobserved. As it was, even Egbert was someone to talk to, and she was perhaps a little curious as to what he was doing standing on one of the drawing-room chairs and gazing fixedly at the picture furthest from the door.

He turned round when he heard her, but remained standing on the chair.

"It's no more a Turner than I am!"

"What isn't?"

"That picture isn't." He laughed rather rudely. "My uncle's geese were all swans. He didn't know enough to pay the prices he did. Of course he wouldn't ask me, but I could have told him from the very beginning that that wasn't a Turner."

"It's awfully ugly anyway," said Margot.

Egbert gave a snort and jumped down from the chair.

"Ugly? Who cares whether it's ugly or not? If it was a Turner, it would be worth thousands of pounds. But it isn't a Turner, and it isn't worth a thousand pence."

"Good gracious, Egbert, what does it matter? You'll have simply piles of money anyhow."

"It's not a question of money. Besides—"

"You *will* have pots—won't you? I shouldn't think you'd know what to do with it."

Egbert looked annoyed.

"Nobody ever has too much money," he said. "Besides there won't be so much as you seem to think, by the time the death duties are paid and one thing and another."

"Good gracious!" said Miss Standing again. "You're frightfully sure you're going to get it. Suppose I've just found a will, or one of those certificates Mr. Hale keeps bothering about—what would you do then?"

Something just flickered across Egbert's face—fear, and something uglier than fear. Margot, without understanding why, felt her breath come quicker; she wanted to run out of the room and bang the door. Instead she repeated her question:

"What would you do?"

"Have you found anything?" said Egbert in a different voice; and again Margot would have liked to run away.

"I might have found something. There was an old box that belonged to my mother."

He came a step nearer.

"Was there? What was in it? What did you find?" Margot went back a step.

"I found some old dresses. They must have been *very* uncomfortable to wear."

"What else did you find?"

"I found a desk. Wouldn't you like to know what was in it?"

"Papers?" said Egbert.

Margot laughed. She couldn't think why she felt frightened.

71

"You're talking nonsense!" said Egbert pettishly. "I don't believe there were any papers."

"Perhaps there weren't."

"You'd have shown them to Mr. Hale fast enough."

"Perhaps I should, and perhaps I shouldn't."

"Nonsense! Look here, I want to talk to you."

"You are talking to me."

"I want to talk to you about something special. You're only chaffing about that desk, you know. There's no chance of a will turning up now, and your father's own letter makes it quite clear that it's no use your buoying yourself up thinking you've got any claim on his money. But, as I said to Mr. Hale, there's no reason for you to worry, because I'm quite willing to go shares."

Margot opened her eyes very wide indeed.

"Shares!"

"Well, that's just a way of putting it. It wouldn't really be shares of course, but it would come to just the same thing as far as you were concerned. I mean if a girl's got plenty of pretty frocks and some pocket-money, and a good home, and a car—I don't say it wouldn't run to a car—well, she doesn't want anything more—does she?"

"She might."

"She wouldn't. Why should she?"

"I don't know. I don't know what you mean."

"I mean if we were married," said Egbert.

Margot gave a little shriek:

"If *who* was married?"

"We. I said if we were married."

Margot stared at him.

"Good gracious, Egbert! What a *frightful* idea!"

"It wouldn't be frightful at all—it would be a very good provision for you."

Margot giggled.

"It would be frightful!" She giggled again. "Are you proposing to me?"

"Yes, I am." There was very little of the ardent lover about his tone.

"I've never been proposed to before. I didn't know it would be like this."

"You ought to take it seriously. It would be a very good thing for you."

Margot retreated towards the door. Something was making her feel frightened all the time.

"No, it wouldn't. I should hate it—I should hate it most frightfully. I'd rather marry anyone—I'd rather marry Mr. Hale or old Monsieur Declos who taught us drawing and took snuff—I would really!"

"I suppose you're joking. You won't have a penny if you don't marry me—not a single penny."

Something came with a rush into Margot's eyes—hot, wet, smarting.

"I don't want a penny, and I'd rather marry an *organ-grinder*!" she said.

This time she did run out of the room and bang the door.

CHAPTER 14

Margot ran out of the drawing-room and down the stairs. Half-way she stopped running and began to walk quite slowly. Why on earth should she run away from Egbert? It wasn't his house yet, though he had begun to behave as if it were.

She stopped, looked down, and saw her letter to Stephanie sticking out of the pocket of her white jumper. She thought she would go out and post it; but it wanted a stamp. There were always stamps in the study—

She stamped her letter and went to the post with it. It wasn't very nice out; the fog was coming up again, and it was wet under foot although there had been no rain.

Margot let herself into the house with the feeling that it was pleasanter after all to be indoors. If she had only had some chocolates. But they were all gone, and though Mr. Hale had given her ten shillings "just to go on with," she would want that for the great adventure of going out as a secretary. She would just have to amuse herself with the rather exciting story which she had left off to go and write to Stephanie. The bother was, she had left the book in the corner of the drawing-room sofa, and she had had enough of Egbert for one afternoon.

She stopped at the drawing-room door and listened. Perhaps he had gone away; there really wasn't anything for him to stay for. She felt sure that he had gone away; but all the same she turned the handle very softly and let the door swing open an inch or two before she looked in.

Egbert was standing on a chair again, but this time it was in front of another picture. He had his back to Margot and to the sofa on which she had left her book. She opened the door a little wider. She could see the book lying there face downwards, half on the back of the sofa and half on a sprawling purple cushion; and she could see Egbert looking hard at the picture of a very fat, bulging woman with about a hundred yards of drapery slipping off her in every direction.

Margot made up her mind to risk it. The sofa was in an angle between the wall and the window; if she was quick

74

and didn't make a noise, she could get her book without Egbert knowing anything about it. She slipped into the room, reached the sofa, and had her hand on the book, when Egbert suddenly jumped down.

For once in her life Margot moved quickly. Before Egbert had time to turn round she had ducked behind the sofa, and when he went to the bell and stood there with his finger on it, she crawled along inch by inch until she was sitting on the floor between the sofa and the wall. No one would find her now unless he leaned right over the back and looked down. The whole thing was just the outcome of a schoolgirl instinct to hide.

Margot sat in her corner giggling inwardly and wondering if Egbert would stay there long—it would be a bore if she had to miss her tea. She wondered why he had rung the bell. It was that stupid William's business to answer it. Margot thought he was quite the stupidest footman they had ever had.

Someone came through the door and shut it. Margot couldn't see anything, but she heard Egbert say, "Come here—I want to talk to you"; and then, "Where is she?"

"She went out to post a letter."

It ought to have been William who answered the bell. But this was not William's voice. It didn't sound like a footman's voice at all; it was rather bored and curt.

Egbert said, "Well, I've asked her, and she won't have me. I told you she wouldn't—I told you it wasn't any good."

It couldn't be William who had answered the bell. Egbert wouldn't tell William that he had proposed to her and that she had said "No." Margot giggled again as she thought of what she had really said.

The man who couldn't be William made an impatient sound.

"Of course you made a mess of it—you'd be bound to do that."

Who on earth could it be? None of the servants would speak to Egbert like that. But he had rung the bell, and it was William's business to answer the bell.

"I didn't make a mess of it. I pointed out what a good thing it would be for her."

"You made a mess of it. A girl of eighteen wants to be made love to—I suppose you never thought of that."

"She never gave me a chance. I don't like her, and she doesn't like me, and there's an end of it."

"Is there? You know best what your orders are, and you know whether he'll be pleased at your failure to carry them out."

"He can't expect me to marry the girl if she won't have me." Egbert's tone was pettish in the extreme.

"He expects you to marry her or *remove* her. He's not taking any risks—there's too much at stake."

Margot felt as if she were listening to a play. It was a frightening play; it made her feel creepy all down the back of her neck. Who was *he*? Why did he want Egbert to marry her? Was it Mr. Hale? What did they mean by saying that Egbert would have to marry her or *remove* her? It had a horrid sort of sound.

Egbert said, "He can't make me marry her."

And then the man who couldn't be William said, "Oh well, that was just a concession to your family feelings. He would really prefer her out of the way for good and all."

Margot's hands began to feel very cold. It was getting more frightening every minute.

"He can't make me do that either," said Egbert Standing.

The other man laughed. The laugh didn't make Margot feel any better.

76

"I think you'll do what you're told when you get your orders. I'm to report tonight, and I think we shall both do exactly what we're told to do. And I think—I rather think—Miss Margot is for it."

"Ssh!" said Egbert quickly.

The other man laughed again.

"What a rabbit you are! It's a pity, because she's quite a pretty girl. It seems a pity to waste her, but I agree with him that she's better out of the way. I'll make up the fire now I'm here. Local colour! And I won't stop in case Daniels takes it into his pompous head to wonder what I'm doing."

Margot heard a log fall on the fire, and then the scrunching rattle of coal. After a minute the door was opened and shut again. The man who couldn't possibly have been William had gone away.

She had to wait another ten minutes before Egbert Standing went away too.

CHAPTER 15

It was next day that Charles Moray walked into Miss Silver's office by appointment. The exercise-book with his name lay open before her. The pages had been written on in a small neat hand.

Miss Silver sat upright and knitted. She appeared to have finished the grey stocking he had seen last time and to have embarked on a second one, for only about three inches of dark grey ribbing depended from the steel needles. She nodded to Charles in an absent way and let him take a seat and say "Good-morning" before she opened her lips. Then she said,

77

"It is a great pity you did not come to me before."

"Why, Miss Silver?"

Miss Silver heaved a gentle, depressed little sigh.

"It is a pity. You would like to hear my report? I will begin with Jaffray."

"Jaffray?"

"The man you wished me to report upon, lodging with Mrs. Brown at 5 Gladys Villas, Chiswick."

"Yes. What have you been able to find out?"

"You shall hear." She glanced at the exercise-book, but continued to knit. "He was until recently in the employment of Mr. Standing the millionaire, on whose family affairs you also wished for a report."

"In his employment?"

"Yes, as valet and general factotum when he was on board his yacht."

"Do you mean that Jaffray remained on the yacht?"

"Yes, that is what I mean. Mr. Standing liked to have someone there who knew his ways. He used to wire: 'Coming on board such and such a time,' and Jaffray would have everything ready for him. He could afford to pay for his fancies. I found Mrs. Brown a very pleasant, talkative person. She seemed to have a very high opinion of Jaffray, who has lodged with her on and off for the last nine years."

"Was he with Mr. Standing on his last cruise?"

"Oh yes—he has only just got back." Miss Silver took out a needle, looked at it for a moment, and then began another row. "Mrs. Brown seemed to think it a little strange that Jaffray was not more upset at the loss of so good an employer. She said she wondered he didn't trouble at not having any work. And I think she was worrying about whether he would be able to go on paying his rent regularly. I have always found worried people very willing to talk. The more worried they are, the more they will tell you."

Charles leaned forward.

"Is Jaffray really deaf? Did Mrs. Brown tell you that?"

Miss Silver pressed her lips together for a moment.

"Mrs. Brown talked a good deal about what she called Mr. Jaffray's affliction. She said he lost his hearing in the war at the time Hill 60 was blown up. She very much deplored the disadvantage to Mr. Jaffray in his search for a new situation, and she repeated more than once that she could not understand why he did not take it more to heart."

"*Is* he deaf?" said Charles.

"Mrs. Brown spoke as if he were."

"But *is* he?"

The needles flashed and clicked. Miss Silver said, "I don't think so, Mr. Moray."

Charles gave a violent start.

"You don't think he's deaf at all!"

"No, I don't think he's deaf. But I'm not sure. I will report to you again. I think I can find out. Now as to the other matter on which you wished me to report. I am really extremely sorry that you did not come to me before."

"What has happened?" Charles spoke apprehensively.

"Miss Standing has disappeared," said Miss Silver in mournful tones.

A hideous sense of responsibility weighed Charles to the ground. He had known that the girl was threatened, and because of Margaret he had held his tongue. He turned a hard face on Miss Silver.

"How can she have disappeared?"

"I will tell you what I know. She left her house in Grange Square yesterday afternoon. She had a trunk with her, and she took a taxi to Waterloo Station. There she took another taxi and drove to No. 125 Gregson Street. She had engaged herself to go there as secretary to a man who calls himself Percy Smith. It was extremely ill-advised of her to take this step. Mr. Smith is not a man of good character. He has been mixed up in one or two very nasty scandals."

"Go on," said Charles, "what has happened?"

Miss Silver dropped her knitting in her lap.

"I can only tell you what happened up to a certain point. Miss Standing had dropped her own name—she called herself Esther Brandon."

"*What!*" said Charles. "No—go on!"

"She called herself Esther Brandon. And she arrived at 125 Gregson Street at seven o'clock yesterday evening. She was only in the house for about half an hour. She left in a great hurry and without any luggage, and no one has any idea of where she went. So far I have not been able to trace her; but I certainly hope to do so."

Charles stared at the floor. Esther Brandon—what on earth had Margot Standing to do with Esther Brandon? Chance—coincidence—no, not by a long chalk. If Mr. Standing's daughter had taken Esther Brandon's name, it was because the name meant something to her. Now what did it mean?

"If you would tell me everything, it would be easier, Mr. Moray," said Miss Silver.

He stopped looking at the floor and looked at her.

"Don't I tell you everything?"

She shook her head.

"You are like the people who let a house and keep one room locked up. You needn't be afraid that I shall open the door when you are not there. But it would be easier for me to serve you if you would give me the key."

"It's not my key, Miss Silver," said Charles.

Miss Silver took up her knitting again.

"I see," she said.

CHAPTER 16

Margot Standing ran out into the street. Her heart was thumping so hard that it shook her; her legs shook under her as she ran. Her world had been so violently shaken that it seemed to be falling about her. She was really only conscious of two things—that she was frightened, oh, dreadfully frightened; and that it was dreadfully difficult to get her breath. She didn't feel as if she could go on running; but she *must* go on running, because if she didn't, the man might come out of the house and catch her. The thought terrified her so much that she went on running even after it seemed as if she could not breathe at all.

It was quite dark and foggy, and she did not know in the least where she was going; she only ran, and went on running until her outstretched hands came up hard against a wall. The shock upset her balance. Her left shoulder hit the wall. She swung half round and then fell in a heap. She had not breath enough to cry out. She lay at the foot of the wall with a sense of having come to the end of anything she could do. There was nothing but fog, and darkness, and cold wet stones.

After a few minutes her breath began to come back. Presently she moved and sat up. She wasn't hurt, but her bare hands were scraped. She had run out of the house in Gregson Street without any gloves on; her gloves were on the table where the cocktails were. When she thought about the gloves, she could smell the strong sickly smell, and she could see Mr. Percy Smith standing there and holding out a little glass full of yellow stuff with a cherry and a grape bobbing about in it.

Sitting there on rough, wet cobblestones, Margot began to cry. She cried with all her might for ten minutes, and then began to feel better. She had got away. If he hadn't gone out of the room—Margot dabbed her eyes with her very wet handkerchief and saw herself sitting there quite stupid and dumb with the cocktail in her hand, and Mr. Percy Smith going out of the room and saying he wouldn't be a minute.

She scrambled up on to her knees because she didn't want to see that picture any more. It made her feel exactly like she had felt when Mrs. Beauchamp took her to the top of the Eiffel Tower and told her to look over. Margot had looked for a moment; and then she wouldn't have looked again for anything in the world. To stand on the edge of a frightful drop and to think how easily one might fall over it—

Margot got right up on to her feet and began to walk blindly forward over the cobblestones. The lights of a car flashed in front of her. Sounds of traffic came through the fog. Her foot struck against the kerb at the edge of a pavement. She turned to the right and walked along slowly without the least idea of where she was going.

She had been walking for half an hour before her mind really began to work again. Someone knocked against her, and a shrill Cockney voice said, "Look out! Where are you going?"

Margot moved on, startled. The question repeated itself: "Where are you going? Where—are—you—going?" It was this question that woke her up: "Where are you going?"—"I haven't anywhere to go." "Where are you going?"—"I don't know." "Where are you going?"—"Oh, I haven't got anywhere to go to."

She had cried so violently that no more tears came into her eyes, but she felt as if she were crying deep inside her.

It was a frightful thing not to have anywhere to go to. She couldn't possibly go back to Grange Square, where Egbert and somebody else—somebody who had answered the bell that William ought to have answered—were waiting to get their orders about *removing* her. Even after being so dreadfully frightened by Mr. Percy Smith she could still shake and turn cold when she remembered that vague, suggestive word.

What was she going to do? What did you do when you were a girl and you hadn't got anywhere to go to, and you didn't know anyone who would help you, and you only had a shilling in the world. If Papa had only let her have friends like other girls. But he had never let her know anyone except at school. And Mrs. Beauchamp was on her way to Australia. It had been her business to see that Margot didn't pick up acquaintances in the holidays. Margot would have given a great many things that she did not possess to have had just one acquaintance now.

Mr. Hale—but if it were Mr. Hale who was giving those orders—perhaps it was—perhaps it was Mr. Hale who was going to tell Egbert and William—no, it *couldn't* be William—to *remove* her.

She couldn't go home. Oh, it wasn't home any more; it was only a house where people were planning horrible things. It was Egbert's house; it wasn't hers. She hadn't got anywhere to go to—she hadn't got a home—she hadn't got anything.

These things kept coming into her mind like a lot of aimless people struggling into a room and drifting out again; they didn't do anything, they just came in, and drifted about, and went away.

Margot went on walking, and the aimless thoughts kept on coming and going. The thick moisture that filled the air with fog began to condense and come down in rain. Soon she was very wet. The rain became heavier; it soaked through her blue serge coat and began to drop from the brim of her hat. The coat had a collar of grey fur. The rain collected on it and trickled down the back of her neck.

Only that afternoon Margot had written to Stephanie that there was something frightfully romantic about being a penniless orphan. It didn't feel a bit romantic now; it felt cold, and frightening, and desperately miserable.

CHAPTER 17

Charles Moray was still living at The Luxe, but he had fallen into the way of paying unheralded visits at odd times to the house in Thornhill Square. He did not always let the Latterys know that he had been and gone. He did not always enter the house; sometimes he merely walked along the square, up Thorney Lane, and into the garden by way of the alley that ran behind it. In all his visits he neither saw nor heard anything unusual.

On this particular evening he walked round the garden, heard ten o'clock strike from the church of St. Justin, and went out through the door in the wall, locking it after him. As he stood with his back to the alley-way and withdrew the key, someone passed behind him in the darkness.

Charles turned and began to walk towards Thorney Lane. The lamp at the end of the alley showed him that it was a woman who had passed behind him whilst he was locking the door. She turned to the left and walked quickly down Thorney Lane past the opening into Thornhill Square to the big thoroughfare that lay beyond. Charles followed her.

The woman was Margaret Langton. If she had been up to her old home, the alley-way and Thorney Lane would be a short cut for her. He thought he would wait a little before catching her up.

The night was cold, but there was no fog. Heavy rain had cleared the air, and the falling temperature seemed to promise frost before morning.

As Margaret turned into the lighted thoroughfare, he saw that she was carrying a parcel. He came up with her with an easy, "Hullo, Margaret! Where are you off to?"

"I've been up to see Freddy. I'm going home."

"So you really haven't quarrelled with him?"

"No," said Margaret in a tired voice, "I haven't quarrelled with Freddy. Why should I?"

Charles took her parcel and tucked it under his arm. It felt like a box, quite light, but awkward to hold.

"Loot?" he inquired.

"Only an old desk of my mother's. It's empty. Freddy said I could have it. He's going abroad, you know."

"Freddy is!"

"Yes—he can't bear England without her. He wants to travel."

"I'm awfully sorry for him," said Charles.

He was awfully sorry for Margaret too, but he knew better than to say so. She kept her passionate feeling in a shrine which no one else must enter. He held his peace.

They walked on in silence until Margaret stopped and held out her hand.

"I go up here. Give me my parcel, please."

"I thought I was seeing you home."

"I don't know why you thought so."

"I still think so," said Charles cheerfully.

Margaret shook her head.

"No. Please give me my box."

Perhaps she expected him to contest the point. Instead, he said quite meekly,

"Very well, if you like carrying things that run into you, carry them."

"Thanks," said Margaret.

Her way lay along one of the darker streets. She felt an odd, rough disappointment as she walked along it alone. She had certainly expected that Charles would thrust his company upon her. She had told him to go; but she had not expected him to go. He was not at all a biddable person. If he let her go home alone, it was because he did not want to come with her. Margaret held her head a little higher. The old desk was a most uncomfortable thing to carry; sometimes the edge of it ran into her side, and sometimes into her arm.

In the darkest patch of the road she bumped into someone. Her "Oh, I'm so sorry!" received no answer except a sort of half sob.

"Did I hurt you?"

The distressing little sound was repeated. Margaret began to wonder what was the matter. She could just see someone standing against the brick wall that bordered the tiny front gardens of the houses on this side of the road. The dark figure seemed to be leaning against the wall in a helpless half-crouching attitude.

"What is it? Are you ill?"

The figure moved. A girl's voice said shakily, "I—don't—know."

"What's the matter?"

It was abominably stupid to ask the question—the girl would certainly beg from her.

"I haven't anywhere to go."

Margaret moved, and at once two despairing hands caught at her.

"Don't go away! Don't leave me!"

Margaret told herself she had been a fool, but she was in for it now. She took the girl by the arm, and felt that her sleeve was soaked.

"Good gracious! You're wet through!"

"It rained." The voice was one of utter misery.

"Come along as far as the lamp-post—we can't talk in the dark."

The lamplight showed Margaret a girl with drenched fair hair hanging in wispy curls. The girl was very pretty indeed; even with a tear-stained face and limp hair she was very pretty. Her dark blue coat was beautifully cut, and drenched though it was, Margaret could both feel and see that the stuff had been expensive. It had a grey fox collar, draggled and discouraged-looking, but a fine skin for all that.

The girl looked at her out of blue, tear-washed eyes set round with astonishingly black lashes.

"Have you lost your way?" said Margaret gravely.

"Yes—I have—but—"

"Where do you live?"

The girl gulped down a sob.

"I can't go back—I *can't*."

She couldn't be more than seventeen or eighteen. Margaret's eyes travelled down to her feet. Expensive shoes—real Milanese stockings. "The little idiot has had a row with her people and run away." She spoke firmly:

"Where do you live? You must go home at once."

"I can't. I haven't got a home."

"Where have you come from?"

"I can't go back. They'll do something dreadful to me if I go back."

"Do you mean they'll be angry with you?"

The girl shook her head.

"There isn't anyone to be angry. I haven't got anyone—*really* I haven't. They'll do something dreadful to me. I heard them making a plan—I did really. I hid behind the sofa and I heard them. They said it would be safer to *remove me*." She shuddered violently. "Oh, what do you think they meant?"

Margaret was puzzled. This might be delusion; but the girl didn't look unhinged. She looked frightened, and she was certainly soaked to the skin.

"Haven't you any friends you could go to for tonight?"

"Papa wouldn't let me have any friends, except at school."

"Where was your school?"

"In Switzerland."

"What on earth am I to do with you?" said Margaret. "What's your name?"

"Esther Brandon," said the girl.

The desk that Margaret was carrying fell on the pavement with a crash. The name was like a blow. She looked at the girl's brimming eyes and quivering mouth, and saw them as if they were a long way off, a very long way off. She had to put her hand on the standard of the lamp and lean hard on it for a moment before she could find voice enough to speak.

"What did you say?"

"Esther Brandon," said the girl.

Margaret felt quite numb and stupid. She bent down and picked up the desk. It had been Esther Brandon's desk when she was a girl, no older than this girl. And Esther Brandon had become Esther Langton, and afterwards Esther Pelham. Margaret straightened herself, holding the desk as if it weighed heavily. Then she spoke suddenly and sharply:

"Where did you get that name?"

The girl didn't answer. She had looked frightened when Margaret caught at the lamp-post. Now all of a sudden a vague look came over her face; her eyes clouded. She put out her hands and said "Oh!" Then she took a wavering step forward and went down all in a heap on the pavement.

Mr. Charles Moray loomed up out of the darkness.

"Charles—thank goodness!"

"What's up?" said Charles. "Who is she?"

"I don't know. Be an angel and get me a taxi."

"What are you going to do with her?"

"Take her back with me."

Charles whistled.

"My dear girl, you can't go about London collecting strange young females."

Margaret was on her knees. The girl moved a little and drew a choking breath.

Charles bent nearer.

"Take her to a hospital, Margaret."

"I can't."

She turned her face up to him, and it was as white as paper.

"My dear girl—"

"Charles—I can't." Her voice fell to a whisper. "She says her name—Charles, she says her name is Esther Brandon."

Charles whistled again.

CHAPTER 18

Margot sat curled up in one easy chair. She had a novel in her lap. The room was pleasantly warm, because before Margaret went out she had lighted the fire. There were no chocolates, and no one to talk to until Margaret got back at half-past one. If it hadn't been Saturday, Margaret would not have been back till nearly seven. Margot thought it was a very good thing that it was Saturday.

She was wearing a jumper and skirt of Margaret's, and a pair of Margaret's shoes and stockings. She was also wearing Margaret's underclothes. Her own wet things were all in a heap inside the bedroom. It simply did not occur to her to pick them up and hang them in front of the fire to dry. After a night of profound slumber in Margaret's bed she looked very little the worse for her fright and her wetting.

She wished she had some chocolates, and she wished Margaret would come back. The book was rather a dull one. Besides she didn't want to read; she wanted to talk. It was frightful not to have anyone to talk to after the sort of things that had happened yesterday.

Margaret came home at half-past one. She proceeded to get lunch. She had brought the lunch with her—a tin of bully beef, a loaf of bread, and a cream cheese.

"I'm hungry," said Margot.

Margaret considered the beef and the cheese. They were meant to last over the weekend. Well, with any luck the

90

girl would be off her hands today—she must be. She looked at Margot placidly eating beef and decided to wait until she had finished.

Margot announced a passion for cream cheese. She ate a good deal of it, and did not notice that Margaret ate bread and scrape; she was too busy talking about Stephanie and the skating parties they had had last winter—"I didn't come home for the Christmas holidays"; and how Mrs. Beauchamp had taken her to Paris for Easter—"I got my coat there. Do you like it? Of course you haven't seen it properly yet, because it's all wet; but it's rather nice, really, and Mrs. Beauchamp said it suited me."

"Who is Mrs. Beauchamp?" said Margaret. She looked at the loaf, and decided that she had better not have a second piece of bread.

"Papa got her to look after me in the holidays. Can I have some more cheese?"

"And where is Mrs. Beauchamp?"

"Well, I expect she's got to Australia by now. She was going out to see her son. Fancy! She'd never seen her grandchild—and it had the dinkiest curly hair! Don't you call that frightfully hard?"

When Margaret had put away what was left of the loaf, the beef and the cheese, she planted herself squarely in front of Margot who had returned to the easy chair.

"Look here, we've got to talk. Is your name really Esther Brandon?"

Margot gazed at her ingenuously.

"No, it isn't."

"Then why did you say it was?"

"I thought it was a romantic name, and I thought if I was a penniless orphan and going out to earn my own living, I might just as well have a *romantic* name."

"Where did you get it from?" Margaret's deep voice was almost harsh. She sat forward in her chair and kept her eyes on Margot's face.

Margot giggled.

"I found it on a bit of paper—a bit of a letter, you know. It was in an old desk. I expect it was my mother's."

Margaret drew a breath of relief. It was just a chance—a bit of some letter her mother had written long ago, perhaps to this girl's mother, perhaps to some other relative. It didn't really matter. She spoke again in an easier tone.

"You were going to earn your living? How?"

Margot told her.

"I was going to be a secretary. I answered an advertisement. And he said to send my photograph, so I sent a little snapshot M'amselle took. I've never *really* had my photograph taken you know—Papa wouldn't let me because of its getting into the papers. And the man said I'd do splendidly, and I was going there today."

Margaret heaved a sigh of relief.

"Then you've got work to go to."

"No, I haven't—not now."

"Why haven't you?"

"Oh!" said Margot. "He was a *beast*. Shall I tell you about it?"

"I think you'd better."

"Where shall I begin? Shall I begin with Egbert?"

"Who is Egbert?"

"Well, he's my cousin, and he said he wanted to marry me. And then I hid behind the sofa, and I heard him planning awful things about *removing* me."

This was what she had said last night. Margaret tried to disentangle it.

"What made you hide behind the sofa?"

Margot giggled.

"Egbert said it would be a frightfully good thing for me if I married him, and I said I'd rather marry an organ-grinder, and I banged out of the room and went and posted my letter to Stephanie. And when I came back I wanted my book which I'd left in the drawing-room, and I just opened the door to see if Egbert was there. And he was. He was standing on a chair looking at one of those frightful pictures of Papa's which are supposed to be worth such a lot of money—you know, Lely, and Rubens, and Turner, and all that lot—only Egbert says some of them aren't—not really. He says Papa got taken in over them."

Turner—Lely—Rubens.

Margaret said, "Go on."

"Well, Egbert was standing on a chair, so I didn't think he'd see me; but he got down, and I had to hide. And then he rang the bell."

"Well?"

"It was William's bell. He's new since last time I was home. He's the stupidest footman we've ever had."

"Well? What about it?"

Margot leaned forward. She looked frightened.

"Egbert rang the bell, and someone came—but it couldn't have been William, because Egbert told him all about proposing to me, and he said he expected I should have to be *removed*." She shivered and caught at Margaret's dress. "Margaret, what do you think he *meant*?"

"I don't know. You're not making this up?"

Margot giggled.

"I can't make things up—I'm not a bit good at it. But I'm quite good at remembering. Even M'amselle said I was good at that. I can tell you every word they said if you like."

Encouraged by a nod, Margot proceeded to repeat the conversation which she had overheard.

"What do you think they *meant*?"

"I don't know. Go on."

"Well, I just packed my box and sent the other footman for a taxi. I thought I wouldn't send William, and I thought I wouldn't stay till today in case of anybody trying to *remove* me. It had a frightfully horrid sort of sound—it did really— so I thought I wouldn't stay. And I thought Mr. Percy Smith might just as well let me come a day earlier, so I took a taxi— only I didn't go straight to his house because I didn't want anyone to know."

"What did you do?"

Margot looked innocently pleased with herself.

"I told the man to go to Waterloo, and when he'd gone away, I took another taxi—to Mr. Percy Smith's. And that took every bit of the money I had except a shilling. I've got the shilling still."

"And what happened at Mr. Percy Smith's?" said Margaret gravely.

Margot blushed scarlet.

"He was a beast."

"You'd better tell me what happened."

"He had a horrid face—a *frightfully* horrid face. And he said he was awfully pleased to see me. And he took me into a room, and he said now I must have a cocktail. And I said I'd rather not. And then he said a lot of other things, and I didn't like them. Need I tell you the things he said?"

"No," said Margaret.

"I don't want to. I think he was a frightfully horrid sort of man."

"How did you get away?" said Margaret violently.

Margot stared and giggled.

"He went out of the room—he said he wouldn't be a minute. And as soon as he'd gone, I got so frightened that I opened the window. And there was an area, so I didn't think I could get out that way, and I was just thinking what could I do, when the postman came up to the door. And when I saw him, I ran out of the room, and I got to the front door, and I opened it, and the postman was gone. And I heard someone call out behind me, and I was frightfully afraid and I ran. Do you think it was silly of me?"

"I should think it was probably the only sensible thing you'd ever done in your life," said Margaret.

Margot giggled again.

"You said that just like M'amselle, only she used to say, 'You are von little fool, Margot.' "

The name dropped out negligently, Margaret hardly needed it; the papers had been too full lately of Mr. Standing's affair. That he had a collection of valuable pictures, and a nephew with the unusual name of Egbert was public property. Margot Standing's name and the fact that she had just returned from Switzerland were public property too.

The bell of the flat rang sharply.

CHAPTER 19

Margaret went to the door.

The flat consisted of two small rooms with a strip of passage between them. Two-thirds of the passage had been walled off to make a kitchen about the size of a boot-cupboard. The front door and the doors of the two rooms opened into the remaining third; there was just room for them and no more.

Margaret shut the sitting-room door and opened the front door. Charles Moray stood there.

"Well?" he said.

"She's in there." Margaret indicated the sitting-room with a nod.

"Have you found out whether she's a long-lost relation?"

"She isn't."

"Look here, I want to talk to you."

"We'll go over to Agatha Carthew's flat—she's away for the weekend and I've got the key."

They proceeded across the landing to Miss Carthew's flat. It appeared to be devoted to the rigours of the simple life. There was linoleum on the floor and distemper on the walls; there were two Windsor chairs and a gate-leg table; and that was all.

Charles shut the door with a bang.

"I suppose she had your bed last night, and you slept on the floor," he began accusingly.

This was unexpected, and Margaret laughed.

"Certainly not the floor."

"That beastly hard contraption I sampled when I was waiting for you the other night then—and no bedclothes."

"A rug," said Margaret firmly.

Charles made an enraged sound.

"Who is this girl? You say she isn't a relation. Are you sure she isn't?"

"Quite sure."

"But her name—your mother's name?"

"That frightened me," said Margaret frankly. "But there's quite a simple explanation. She is—well, she's a goose, and she found what must have been a bit of a letter from my mother with her signature. She told me she thought it was a fright-

96

fully romantic name to go out and earn her living with."

Charles burst out laughing.

"What a mind! Hasn't she got a name of her own?"

There was a moment's silence. Margaret's troubled voice broke in upon it.

"I think I'd better tell you what she's been telling me. It's all so odd, and I don't know what to think. I mean she may be making it up, or she may be—" She hesitated and then said, "Odd. I don't know what to think really."

"Better tell me the whole thing. And why not sit down instead of wandering like something in a zoo?"

He himself was sitting on the corner of Miss Carthew's table. Margaret came to a standstill beside him. She leaned on the back of one of the chairs.

"I won't sit—I don't feel like it. Look here, this is what she told me."

She unfolded Margot's tale in Margot's own ingenuous words and without comment, but she kept her eyes on Charles. Charles, for his part, listened impassively. She made nothing of his expression.

"Of course, she's a first-class little fool, but I don't think she's capable of inventing all this. What do you think? And does it occur to you that she may be somebody who will be looked for?"

"What do you mean by that, Margaret?" said Charles.

"Just that."

There was a pause. Charles looked at her, dived into a pocket, and produced a copy of the *Evening Gossip*. He unfolded it with a certain slow deliberation and held it out. Margaret saw the large headlines and caught the paper from his hand:

MISSING HEIRESS
INTERVIEW WITH

She turned to get the light on the paper, and Charles got off the table and read over her shoulder:

"Has Miss Standing disappeared? When our representative asked Mr. Egbert Standing this question, he replied to it in the negative. 'My cousin,' he said, 'has suffered terribly from the shock of her father's death, and from the uncertainty of her own position. It is by no means certain that she will inherit Mr. Standing's fortune. My uncle left no will, and up to the present no legal proof of his marriage has come to light. In these circumstances my cousin decided to leave London. We are not in any anxiety on her account. We desire no publicity.' "

There was a good deal more of this sort of thing. There was an interview with the butler, who said that Miss Standing left the house at half-past six on the previous evening; she took a taxi to Waterloo and she had with her a large brown trunk, the same she always took to school.

"Well," said Charles, "what about it?"

"Oh, she's Margot Standing. I guessed that as soon as she began to talk about her cousin Egbert and her father's collection of pictures. I'm sure she's Margot Standing—it's her story I'm not sure about. What do you make of it? It's pretty unbelievable—isn't it? I don't mean the Percy Smith part—that's just the sort of trap a little fool of a schoolgirl would walk into. I don't mean that; I mean all that part about her cousin and the other man planning to remove her. What do you make of that?"

Charles was making a good deal of it. He was remembering his mother's sitting-room, and the man who had said, "Margot," and then, "The girl may have to be removed. A street accident would be the safest way." And he was remembering that Margaret—*Margaret*—had talked with this man, that Margaret had been there. He wondered bitterly whether Margot Standing had not jumped out of the frying-pan into the fire.

"Charles! Do say something! Do you think there's anything in it?"

"Do you?"

"Yes, I do." The words burst out. "There's something. She's a little fool; but she's not mad, and she's not lying. What does it mean?"

Charles was standing very close to her. He had been looking over her shoulder at the paper. Then as they talked, she moved to face him. Now he touched her on the arm, a quick, insistent touch.

"Don't you know what it means?"

"No—how can I?"

"You don't know what it means?"

His tone startled her.

"Charles—what—why should you say this?"

"Don't you know?"

She drew back, paler. Something in her eyes—distress, anger—he wasn't sure.

"Charles, what are you saying? What do you mean?"

Charles put a hand on her shoulder.

"Will you tell me that you'd never heard of Margot Standing before?"

"Of course I've heard of her. The papers—"

"That isn't what I mean. Will you tell me that you'd never heard of her from another source?"

"I don't know what you mean." Her eyes were angry.

"Don't you? Then will you tell me what you were doing on the night of the third of October?"

99

"The third?" said Margaret. "The third?" Her voice changed suddenly as she repeated the word; she was puzzled, and then she was frightened—sharply, unexpectedly frightened.

Charles felt all the muscles of her shoulder stiffen under his hand. He kept it there, holding her.

"Will you tell me what you were doing in my house that night?"

Margaret looked at him. Her eyes were dark and fierce.

"Well, Margaret?" he said; and then, quickly, "Don't lie! I saw you."

A wave of colour rushed into her face. She wrenched her shoulder free and flung away from him.

"How dare you say a thing like that? When did I ever lie to you?"

"When you said you loved me," said Charles, and saw the colour ebb away and leave her fainting white.

She kept her eyes on his. They said, "I'll never forgive you." Then she turned from him and went to the window. With her back to him, she said in a low, hard voice,

"You saw me?"

"I saw you. And I heard—*things.*"

"What did you hear?"

"I heard—no, I won't tell you what I heard. It's no good carrying coals to Newcastle."

She turned at that.

"What do you mean?"

"That you know it already. I heard enough to make me believe Margot Standing's story."

"Tell me what you heard."

"Tell me what you were doing there."

"I can't."

"Tell me whom you were meeting."

"I can't."

"Margaret, for heaven's sake! What sort of mess is this you've got into? Can't you tell me about it? Can't you trust me?"

"I—can't."

His manner changed. He said lightly,

"Then I'm afraid I can't tell you what I heard."

There was a silence. Margaret stood looking at him. Her expression changed rapidly. He thought she was going to speak; but instead she pressed her hand over her eyes. The gesture shut him out, and shut her in. He wondered what company she had in the darkness which she was making for herself.

She dropped her hands at last. Her face was composed, too much controlled to tell him anything. When she spoke, her voice was quiet and a little tired. She said,

"Charles, what are we to do with her?"

The "we" was unexpected; it startled him.

"She doesn't want to go back—she's afraid to go back."

"I think she has reason to be afraid," said Charles.

"You do think so?"

"Don't you?"

Margaret grew very much paler.

"Charles—" she said. Then she stopped.

Charles looked at her. His look did not help her. It was hard and steady.

"Charles—" she said again.

"What are you trying to say?"

"Charles, you asked me—what I know—I don't—know—anything—"

"You mean you don't know anything that you can tell me?"

"No, I don't mean that. There's something—I can't tell you. But it's not about Margot. I don't know anything about

101

Margot." She paused; and all at once fire and colour came back. "Do you think I'd hurt her?"

Charles did not think anything of the sort. No evidence, not even his own, could make him think Margaret capable of hurting any girl. Every instinct, every memory rose up in her defence. He said soberly,

"No, I don't think you'd hurt her. There might—be others."

That struck her. She winced away from it.

"She can't go back," said Charles. "Can she stay here—*safely*?"

"Why do you say that?"

"You know. Is she safe here? Is she safe with you?"

Margaret lifted her head. The proud, familiar gesture plucked at his heart.

"Yes, she's safe."

"Will you swear to that?"

"Will you ask me to?"

Something passed between them—a wordless, passionate question; a passionate, wordless answer. Charles felt a rush of emotion that startled him. He said quickly, "No"; and the moment passed.

Margaret smiled. She seemed to relax, to be more the old Margaret than he had seen her yet.

"Do you want me to keep her?"

"Could you—for a day or two?"

"I suppose I could."

Neither of them seemed to think it strange that Charles should be in charge. If Margot Standing had been a stray kitten, the affair might have passed very much as it was passing now. He led the way out of Miss Carthew's flat and into Margaret's. She threw open the sitting-room door and went in.

Miss Standing looked up very much as the kitten might have done; there was the same grace of pose, the same effect of soft roundness, the same wide-eyed innocence.

"This is Charles Moray who helped me to bring you home last night," said Margaret.

Charles looked at Margot, and Margot gazed at Charles. He saw the prettiest girl he had ever seen in his life. He said,

"How do you do, Miss Standing?"

CHAPTER 20

Margot accepted the name without protest. She blinked those very black lashes, uncurled herself, and stood up. She continued to look at Charles.

The colour in the old green jumper and skirt of Margaret's turned her pale blue eyes to turquoise green. Sometimes the black lashes darkened them for an instant. Her skin was amazingly fair and fine. The roses in her cheeks were the prettiest pink roses in the world.

She dimpled at Charles and inquired,

"How did you know my name?"

"I guessed."

"I don't see how you could guess."

"Margaret guessed too."

"Did she? Margaret, how did you guess?"

"If you want to keep your name a secret," said Charles, "you mustn't talk about your cousin Egbert."

"Or your father's collection of Lelys and Turners." Margaret's tone was a little hard.

Margot turned to Charles.

"You won't make me go back?"

"Tell me why you don't want to go back?"

Margot told him. The story was the same story that she had told to Margaret, and that Margaret had repeated to him. While she was speaking, he tried to piece together what she had heard Egbert say, and what he himself had overheard. The pieces fitted. But there were gaps which he meant to fill.

"You won't send me back—will you? It's such a big house, and what they said about *removing* me gave me a most frightful sort of creepy feeling. It really did."

It gave Charles a creepy feeling too.

"No, we won't send you back. But I think you ought to let your lawyer know where you are."

Margot turned quite pale.

"Mr. Hale!"

"Is that his name?"

"Mr. James Hale. His father was a friend of poor Papa's. He said Papa said all sorts of things to his father."

"Well, I think you ought to tell him where you are."

"Oh, I don't *want* to."

"Why on earth not?"

She leaned forward whispering,

"I *thought*—perhaps he was the person who was going to give the orders about *removing* me." She shivered a little. "It would be frightful if I told him and he *was*."

Charles agreed—he remembered a certain reference to "the lawyer." Where everything was so uncertain, it was better to take no step than a false one.

"All right. You stay here, and we don't tell anyone for a day or two. I'll try and find out about your Mr. Hale. What relations have you got?"

Margot giggled.

"Everybody asks me that. I haven't got any relations except Egbert."

"What? None at all?"

"Isn't it funny not to have any? Papa only had one brother, and he only had Egbert. Papa hated Egbert. And if my relations were going to be like *him*, I'm frightfully glad they never got born."

"What about your mother?"

Margot looked important.

"I don't *even* know her name—not for certain, you know. I *think* it was Esther Brandon."

Margaret swooped into the conversation.

"Don't say that!"

Margot stared at her.

"I do think so. That's why I took it. I think I'd better be called Esther Brandon—don't you? Because if I go on being Margot Standing, those people might find me."

Margaret turned away. She said,

"Don't talk nonsense! You can't call yourself Esther Brandon."

Then she went over to the bookcase, picked up a book at random, and began to flick the pages over.

"Why can't I? Why is it nonsense?" Margot spoke to Charles, not to Margaret.

"Well, there's quite a good reason."

"But I can't be Margot Standing."

"No, you can't—can you? Let's think of something else. You can be Miss Smith."

She gave a little shriek.

"No, I can't! Not Smith! Not after that horrible Percy Smith!"

"Brown then, or Wilson—unless you know any bad Browns or wicked Wilsons."

Margot giggled.

105

"I'll be Wilson—I'd rather be Wilson than Brown."

"Brown," said Charles reprovingly, "is a good old Scottish name."

"I'll be Wilson. Shall I be Margot Wilson?"

Charles considered the question, and shook his head.

"No, I don't think so. Margot is too uncommon. We'll make up something else out of Margaret. I suppose you *are* Margaret?"

The other Margaret stood with her back to them, flicking over the pages of her book. She had no idea what the book was. Charles and Margot, sitting close together, talking in low confidential tones, playing a foolish game of names. It was her flat, and she had known Charles Moray for fourteen years; but it was she who had the sense of strangeness and intrusion—she, and not Margot. Margot appeared to be perfectly at home. She heard her giggle and protest, "I won't be Daisy!"

Charles offered her "Rita," and got a little shriek of "Oh—*no!*" in reply.

"Why not? It's a very nice name."

"It's not—it's frightful."

"Have Madge then."

"That's worse."

"Madge is a perfectly good name."

"I won't have it."

"What about Margie?"

"Frightful! It's exactly like margarine."

"Well, there aren't any others."

"There's Meg," said Margot. "I wouldn't mind being Meg."

Margaret felt as if someone had run a sharp knife into her very suddenly. Charles had called her Meg just once or twice—just once or twice. She did not hear what he said. She turned another page and read: "Oh, Greta's banks are fresh and fair." She laughed and called over her shoulder,

"You can be Greta."

Margot got up and ran to her.

"Did you find it in your book? Let me see! I rather like it. Where is it? Oh—why is it banks? Is it a river? It says, 'Greta's banks are fresh and fair.'"

"Very appropriate," said Charles.

The bell rang. Margaret pushed Sir Walter Scott back into the bookshelf and went to the door. Mr. Archie Millar stood there with a deprecating smile.

"I say, may I come in? Is there a spot of tea going?"

He was surprised at the warmth of his welcome, surprised and a good deal stimulated. Margaret and he had been very good pals for years. He began at this moment to feel a faint dawn of sentiment.

Margaret went back into the sitting-room with a little colour in her cheeks. Archie, behind her, caught sight of Charles, hailed him, and then, beholding Miss Margot Standing, stood agaze. It was Charles who rose to the occasion.

"This is Archie Millar. You'll get used to him. Archie, make your best bow to Miss Greta Wilson. She's staying with Margaret."

The prettiest roses in the world became two shades deeper. Miss Greta Wilson giggled, looked between her black lashes, and found Archie a pleasant young man. In half a minute they were deep in conversation. In three minutes he had discovered that she had only just left school, that she didn't know anyone in London, and that she loved revues, adored chocolates, and considered *Moonlight and You* the divinest waltz *ever*.

Margaret had begun to get tea. She passed to and fro from the minute kitchen. Charles did not offer to help her. He stood by the window looking down absently upon the darkening street. The lime-tree over the way had begun to lose its leaves; those that still remained were as golden as ripe corn. What on earth were they to do with the girl, far too pretty not to be remembered, far too naïve and inexperienced to be set adrift on dangerous waters full of strange cross-currents and secret depths? A golden leaf fell wavering to the ground. Archie's voice broke in:

"Charles! Here, wake up! What about our all goin' on the bust tonight? A festive beano—what?"

Charles shook his head, and was adjured not to look like an undertaker's assistant.

"She says she hasn't seen a thing—you did say you hadn't didn't you?"

Miss Greta Wilson nodded.

"Appallin'—isn't it? I don't see how we can let it go on for another day. What about dinner for four and the best show we can get into at this sort of last moment?"

Charles shook his head again. The prospect of producing Greta in public was a daunting one—"She's too pretty by half, and Lord knows whom we should meet."

"Then what about you and me?" said Archie. "I must have somethin' to cheer me up after the horrid blow I've just had—straight out of the blue, and no time to put an umbrella up." He addressed Miss Greta Wilson, who inquired if it were raining.

Archie looked at her reproachfully.

"I've had a blow that's dashed my proudest hopes into what-you-may-call-'ems."

"What has happened, Archie?" said Margaret. "Tea is ready."

"Unconscious of their doom, the little blighters played."

"What little blighters? Yes, Charles, two more chairs."

"My fondest hopes," said Archie—"shattered by a bolt." He produced a crumpled copy of the evening paper and waved it. "I shall want heaps and heaps of tea. The blow has driven me to drink."

"What on earth's happened? Charles, will you cut the bread? The knife's most awfully blunt."

"There's womanly sympathy for you!" said Archie. "I've got a broken heart, and she talks about blunt knife! I've lost my heiress. Pain and anguish wring my brow. And no one offers to be a ministerin' angel—unless Greta will. Will you be a ministerin' angel, Greta?"

The late Miss Margot Standing dimpled, coloured, and said,

"It's frightfully romantic. I'd love to."

"Here's your tea, Archie. I didn't know you'd got an heiress. Charles, that's yours—there are four lumps of sugar in it."

"Nobody knew but me. Concealment's been preyin' like a tiddleyum upon my damask cheek—Shakespeare! And I've been sittin' like Patience on a thing-ummy-jig smilin' at grief—more Shakespeare—same speech—*ibid*, as they say in the books."

"Who was she?"

"She *wasn't* an heiress," said Archie mournfully. "What's the good of my fixin' my young affections on a girl with several millions tacked on, when the evenin' paper suddenly bursts out with the horrid bomb that she isn't goin' to have the millions after all? Alas, they are another's; they never can be mine—not Shakespeare this time. The cash is Egbert's."

Greta dropped her teacup with a splash. The tea dripped on the green jumper. She repeated, "Egbert!" giggled, and repeated it again.

"Egbert Standing," said Archie. "Revoltin' name! The daily press that never lies says that Egbert scoops the lot—he gets the whole caboodle, and Margot doesn't even get a smell of it. I've taken to drink."

He passed up his cup.

Miss Greta Wilson made no attempt to wipe the tea off her jumper. She fixed her blue eyes on Archie with the unwinking stare of a kitten and asked,

"Did you know her?"

Archie shook his head.

"Perhaps she's frightfully ugly," pursued Greta.

"She's probably hideous," said Archie. "If she weren't, there'd have been about a million photos of her in all the papers."

Greta's colour rose.

"Would you marry a girl who was perfectly hideous, just because she had heaps of money?"

"Ah!" said Archie. "If it were to keep my Aunt Elizabeth's parrot out of the workhouse, I might. Some day I'll tell you all about it—'A Hero's Sublime Sacrifice. A Parrot's Trust Rewarded. Devoted Nephew Saves Indigent Feathered Friend. Matchless Masterpiece In Seventeen Episodes Featurin' Archibald Millar.' Hullo, that's an idea! Let's all go to the pictures. I feel as if it might soothe me to sit in the dark and hold Margaret's hand." He said "Margaret," but he looked at Greta.

Greta blushed.

CHAPTER 21

They went to the cinema. Charles did not see very much of the film. What on earth were they to do with the girl? Margaret was out all day. Would Greta sit at home like a good little girl and twiddle her thumbs? "I *don't* think," said Charles. He gazed gloomily at a close-up of a glad-eyed heroine embracing a strong, silent hero. The embrace seemed to last an unconscionable time.

They came out into a fine drizzle of rain. Charles felt himself touched on the arm. He looked round and saw an old lady in a black cloak and an old-fashioned bonnet. She was holding up an umbrella, but she held it tilted sideways so that Charles could see her face. Under the meekly banded hair Miss Maud Silver's nondescript eyes looked at him.

For a yard or two they walked side by side. The umbrella was no longer tilted, but a small, old voice spoke from beneath it:

"Jaffray is just ahead of us—there, beyond the big man in the overcoat. I'd like you to follow him. He's going to meet someone."

Charles said, "All right," and looked round for the rest of his party. Archie was in the road waving to a taxi; Margaret and Greta on the kerb.

He reached Margaret, said goodnight hurriedly, and pursued the deaf man. It was easy enough to keep him in view without being remarked as long as the pavement was so crowded; one had only just to keep one's own place in the stream and move with it. Presently, however, there was no stream, and Charles fell back a little. Mr. Jaffray got into a Hammersmith bus, and as he went inside, Charles thought it as well to go outside.

At Hammersmith Broadway Jaffray got out and walked again. Charles kept the other side of the narrow street. It went on drizzling, but Jaffray had no umbrella, nor had Charles. He reflected that an umbrella was the best disguise in the world.

Jaffray walked on and on. Charles had been wondering whether the man was merely going home; but he passed the turning that led to Gladys Villas and kept on at the same steady pace. When he came to the Great West Road, he turned on to it and kept on walking. Charles began to wonder whether he meant to walk to Slough—or Bath. However, after a quarter of a mile Jaffray stopped, took out a watch, looked at it, and began to walk slowly up and down.

Charles felt at a disadvantage. There is no cover on the Great West Road. Pedestrians are sufficiently few in number to attract attention, and every inch of the roadway and the spaces beside it were continually lit up by the glare of passing headlights. The place was about as public as the middle of an empty ballroom, and almost as brightly lighted.

Jaffray walked up and down, and Charles lurked as far from the track of the headlights as he could. Ten minutes passed. Charles decided that he had no vocation for the life of a sleuth; it appeared to him utterably dreary, boring, flat, and dull. If it hadn't been so damp, he would have sat down, gone to sleep— and finished the night as a drunk at the nearest police station. This exhilarating thought had just occurred to him, when something happened.

A large Daimler coming from London slowed down as it passed him and stopped near Jaffray. It stopped at the moment that Jaffray was shaking out an unusually large white handkerchief.

Charles meandered slowly towards the car. It had a London number. He noted it. By the time he had done this, Jaffray was in the car, and the car was off.

One cannot pursue a Daimler on foot. Charles went home in a most disgruntled mood.

On Monday morning he visited Miss Silver. She had finished the grey stockings, and was knitting something small, white, and fleecy that looked like a baby's boot. She nodded to Charles and went on knitting.

"Sit down, Mr. Moray. Did you follow Jaffray?"

"Yes, I did."

"What happened?"

Charles told her what happened. She nodded again.

"Yes, I knew it would be the Great West Road and I didn't think my make-up was altogether suitable. Did you see who was in the car?"

"One man."

"Did you see his face?"

The busy needles stopped for a moment as she asked the question.

"He was wearing dark goggles," said Charles.

Miss Silver went on knitting.

"I wish you had seen his face—but it can't be helped."

"I've got the number of the car."

"So have I," said Miss Silver, "Jaffray bought it on Friday."

"*Jaffray* bought it!"

"Jaffray bought it from Hogstone and Cornhill. He paid for it in notes and took it away on Saturday afternoon to a garage in the Fulham Road."

"Who fetched it away?" said Charles.

"Jaffray did. He called for it about eight o'clock on Saturday evening."

Charles frowned.

"Jaffray called for it, but someone else drove it down the Great West Road and picked Jaffray up at eleven o'clock—"

"Of course I don't know," said Miss Silver; "but Jaffray probably parked the car somewhere, and the owner picked it up."

"Who is the owner?"

"I wish you had seen his face," said Miss Silver.

"You don't know?"

"No. I don't know. I have the numbers of the notes. I will try and trace them back." There was a pause. Then she said, "Have you anything to tell me, Mr. Moray?"

Charles said, "No," and then added, "I've things to ask you. I want to know more about the servants in the Standing household."

"Who do you want to know about?"

"All the men servants, I think—a footman called William in particular."

Miss Silver laid down her white fleecy knitting and took up the brown exercise-book.

"I have some notes about the servants here." She turned the pages and read; "'Pullen'—the butler's name is Pullen."

"How long has he been there?"

"A few weeks only. I was going to explain that to you—none of the servants have been there for more than a few weeks with the exception of the housekeeper, Mrs. Long, and her daughter, who is head housemaid. The house was shut up all the summer. Miss Standing was abroad for the summer holidays with her chaperone, Mrs. Beauchamp. Mr. Standing was not in town. Mrs. Long and her daughter act as caretakers, and Mrs. Long engages servants when Mr. Standing wishes the house to be opened. He came back for a fortnight in September, and was expected again next month. All the servants were engaged in September. Is that clear?"

"Quite."

"Pullen, then, is the butler. I have what the French would call his *dossier*. His last place was with the Dowager Lady Perringham at her place in Dalesshire." Miss Silver broke off and coughed gently. "Lady Perringham was fortunate enough not to suffer from the epidemic of burglary which took place in her neighbourhood last year."

"There were burglaries?"

"I thought perhaps you might have read about them. Most of the big houses in the neighbourhood suffered. The historic Dale Leston silver was stolen, and has never been recovered.

114

The Kingmore pearls were taken. Lady Perringham was fortunate. Pullen was with her for six months. Before that he was in Scotland with Mr. Mackay. Do you remember the St. Andrade burglary?"

Charles shook his head.

"I've been in the wilds."

"Mr. St. Andrade is a Brazilian millionaire—that is, he made his money in Brazil. His wife had a collar of emeralds which were reputed to be the finest in the world. They were stolen whilst Mr. St. Andrade was occupying a shooting-box about five miles from Mr. Mackay's. The thief was surprised, and the emeralds were dropped by him in his flight."

"I see," said Charles. "Go on."

"There are two footmen," said Miss Silver. "Frederick Smith—no, I don't think there's really anything of interest with regard to Frederick Smith—a coachman's son; very respectable; last character satisfactory, three years. The other footman is William Cole. He was for three months with Mrs. James Barnard, and left at the close of the season with a good character. The only curious thing about William Cole is this—I can't find out where he came from, or what he was doing before he went to Mrs. James Barnard."

"Did anything odd happen whilst he was there—to Mrs. Barnard or to any of her friends?"

"No," said Miss Silver. "No—not exactly, Mr. Moray. Of course there was the scandal about Mr. Barnard's nephew."

"What scandal?"

"It was hushed up. He was said to have forged his uncle's name. He has left the country, I understand."

There seemed to be a lot of tangled threads that led nowhere. Charles hesitated. Then he said,

"There is some connection between William Cole and Egbert Standing. I think Egbert Standing is Number Thirty-two of

115

Grey Mask's little lot. William is probably Twenty-seven—I'm not sure—it might be Pullen. I don't know about Pullen—he sounds a bit fishy. But I'm sure William is in it up to the neck, and I rather think he's Number Twenty-seven."

Miss Silver turned back the pages of the brown copybook.

"Twenty-seven came to report. You saw him. What was he like?"

"I saw his back—tallish—thinnish—bowler hat—overcoat. Any number of him walking about all over London."

"It might be William," said Miss Silver. "Pullen is the typical butler—a stout sedate person."

"It wasn't Pullen."

Miss Silver fixed her eyes upon him.

"Why do you think it was William?"

"I'm afraid I can't tell you that."

"You are not being very frank, are you?"

"Not very," said Charles with a disarming smile.

Miss Silver sighed. After a pause she proceeded to give the dull histories of housemaids, bootboys, and so forth.

"Any news of Miss Standing?" said Charles.

Miss Silver gazed placidly at him.

"Do you wish me to give you news of Miss Standing?" she said.

It was years since Charles had blushed; he did not blush now. He smiled delightfully.

"Or of Miss Langton?" said Miss Silver, still gazing.

She saw the dark colour come into his face. With a little nod she turned her attention to the white bootee.

Charles took his leave. He admired Miss Silver; but he became aware that he was a good deal afraid of her.

116

CHAPTER 22

Whilst Charles was interviewing Miss Silver, Miss Greta Wilson was writing to Stephanie Polson.

Oh, Stephanie, I've had the most thrilling adventures. I'm really having them still. It's frightfully exciting, and you'll be frightfully angry with me, because I can't tell you about them—at least I can only tell you bits, because I promised Charles and Margaret I wouldn't tell anyone the other bits—at least not till they said I could. So you'll just have to be frightfully angry. I'm staying with Margaret, and I can't even tell you her name or give you my address, because that's one of the bits I promised not to. Margaret is a dear, and so is Charles. Margaret has known him for years and years and years, but I do believe he really likes me best, because he took me out for the whole day yesterday which was Sunday, and he didn't take Margaret, though it's her day at home. She works in a hat-shop every day, and she doesn't get home till half-past six—so it would be very dull for me, only Charles says he will come and cheer me up. Archie would come too if he could. Archie is another friend of Margaret's. He and Charles are friends too. It's frightfully jolly everyone being friends, after having such a dreadfully dull time. Archie can't come and take me out like Charles can, because he has to go to his office. He says he is an oddment in a publishing firm. He says they only took him because his uncle was in it. He says he is rotten at it. But I think he is frightfully clever—he knows lots of quotations out of Shakespeare and other people like that. I don't know whether I like him best or Charles. Charles is an explorer, but he isn't exploring just now. He is the handsomest. He has grey eyes and a most frightfully romantic frown, but he isn't quite as tall as Archie is. Archie is five feet eleven and three-quarters, and he says if he hadn't been brought up frightfully strictly and simply made to tell the truth, he would call it six foot. He has got blue eyes, but not many eyelashes—just ordinary, you know. But Charles has a lot of black eyelashes and frightfully black eyebrows. They go all twisty when he is cross. I shouldn't like them to go all twisty at me.

Saturday was the first day I was with Margaret, and Charles and Archie came to tea, and we all went to the cinema and saw a most frightfully thrilling drama—only I can't tell you about it now. Archie came home with us, but Charles rushed off in a frightfully sudden sort of way as soon as we came out. On Sunday morning he came quite early with a car, and he said would I like to go down to Bognor, and I said I would, and we went. He didn't ask Margaret.

In the evening he and Archie came to supper. They brought their supper with them because Margaret said she hadn't any. Archie brought sardines and bananas, and Charles all sorts of exciting things—lots more than we could eat, so Margaret and I are eating them up— they are frightfully good. He brought chocolates too— really thrilling ones. I think I really do like Charles best. But I like Archie too. After supper Mr. Pelham came in. He is Margaret's stepfather, and I'm not sure whether I ought to have said what his name was, so don't tell anyone

118

and *tear my letter up*, because I sort of promised Margaret I wouldn't say anyone's name. But I think she's a bit of a fuss, don't you? It isn't as if you'd be seeing Egbert—is it? Margaret's stepfather is frightfully nice. They all call him Freddy. He said I could too. I've never called such an old person by their Christian name before, so I didn't do it at first—not till he seemed quite hurt and said didn't I like him. So of course I said I did, and then I called him Freddy, only I got most frightfully red when I did it, and they all laughed, and Freddy said he felt most frightfully flattered, and he said might he have the pleasure of taking me to a matinee, and what would I like to see, and could I come on Wednesday? But I said couldn't it be Saturday so Margaret could come too? And he said 'All right', and he asked Charles to come, and Charles said he would. He didn't like it when Freddy asked me, nor did Margaret. I don't know why they didn't. Archie couldn't come because he was playing a football match. Charles says he is very good at it.

I mustn't write any more, because I shall use all Margaret's paper, and I've only got a shilling to buy any more. When you've only got a shilling, there are hundreds of things you want to buy.

Margot

CHAPTER 23

Charles went back to Miss Silver next day.

"Do you know anything of one Ambrose Kimberley?" he inquired.

Miss Silver dropped a stitch and picked it up again before she answered:

"I know the name." Then, before Charles could say anything more, she spoke briskly: "There are some things I want to tell you, Mr. Moray. I should have telephoned to you if you hadn't come in."

"Go on," said Charles.

She took up the brown exercise-book.

"We'll take Jaffray first. He came back on Sunday. I haven't been able to trace the car yet."

"Or the owner?"

"Or the owner." She tapped the page with a knitting-needle. "So much for Jaffray. I really wanted to see you about William Cole. I have found out who he is."

"Is he someone?"

"He is Leonard Morrison."

Charles looked blank.

"I'm afraid that conveys nothing to me."

"Nonsense!" said Miss Silver. "Six years ago—the Thale-Morrison case—you must remember it."

Charles began to remember.

"You don't mean to say that William—"

"Is Morrison? Yes, I do. He'd have got a life sentence if it had not been for his youth. He was, I think, only just eighteen, and the Court took it into account."

Charles began to remember the case—a horrible one.

"Yes," said Miss Silver. She nodded, as if in answer to something which he had not said. "Yes, a most cold-blooded, dangerous young man and an astonishingly good actor. All through the trial he was acting, and the Court pronounced sentence on a dull backward lout of a lad. They never had a glimpse of the real Leonard Morrison."

Miss Silver fixed a direct look upon Charles Moray.

"Mr. Moray, I want to ask you very seriously what you're going to do."

"I don't know," said Charles.

"How long are you going to wait before you call in the police?"

"I don't propose to call in the police."

Miss Silver sighed gently.

"You will have to call them in in the end. How far are you going to let things go before you take a step which you ought to have taken at the very beginning?"

Charles set his jaw.

"Do you think they would have believed me if I had gone to them?"

"I don't know."

"I do. They would have said I was drunk, and I should have been told in quite polite officialese to go home and boil my head. Come, Miss Silver! Did you believe my story yourself?"

Miss Silver closed the exercise-book and sat back in her chair.

"Since you ask me, Mr. Moray, I was inclined to think you had been dining a little too well. You did not appear to me to be suffering from hallucinations. No, I must confess I thought you had been—shall I say—celebrating your return."

121

"And you still think so?"

"No," said Miss Silver.

"Well?"

"I believe that you stumbled upon a very dangerous set of people engaged in a criminal conspiracy. I believe Miss Standing to be in serious danger, and I ask you again—how far are you going to let matters go?" She coughed very gently and added, "You will not be able to screen Miss Langton indefinitely."

Charles was stabbed by a most acute and poignant fear. He mastered his voice and said coolly,

"What do you mean?"

Miss Silver shook her head.

"Now Mr. Moray, what is the use of our pretending any longer? I am going to lay my cards on the table, and you would be very well advised to do the same. I know perfectly well that Miss Standing has been staying with Miss Langton since Friday night. She left home at about six o'clock on Friday, and Miss Langton brought her back to her flat in a taxi at a quarter to eleven. I don't know what happened in the interval. Naturally, you do."

"Do I?"

"Oh, I think so. You helped Miss Langton to get Miss Standing upstairs—she was exhausted and hysterical."

"She had had a fright," said Charles, "nothing serious."

"I'm glad to know that. I don't ask you why you were not frank with me about Miss Standing's whereabouts." She coughed again. "I don't ask you, because I know."

"Well," said Charles pleasantly, "what do you know? Or shall I say, what do you think you know?"

Miss Silver took up her knitting. She had arrived at the toe of the little white bootee.

"I will tell you what I think. You stumbled upon a conspiracy.

You saw a number of people whom you did not recognize. They were men. Well, I think, Mr. Moray, that you saw another person whom you did recognize. I think this person was a woman—I think it was Miss Langton."

"What a remarkably vivid imagination you have, Miss Silver!" said Charles.

Miss Silver counted her stitches—three—four—five—six—seven. After a moment's pause she spoke again:

"I think so because I cannot account otherwise for your allowing Miss Standing to run so many risks. She should be under police protection. You know that, I think."

"She's under Miss Langton's protection, and mine."

Miss Silver looked at him sorrowfully.

"You have confidence in Miss Langton's protection?"

"Complete confidence. Besides, they don't know where she is."

"I'm afraid they do."

Charles was really startled.

"What makes you think so?"

"You mentioned a name when you came in, Mr. Moray—you asked me if I knew anything about Ambrose Kimberley. Why did you ask me that?"

There was a silence. Miss Silver broke it.

"Pray, Mr. Moray, be frank with me," she said. "In a matter as serious as this, I must warn you that concealment is a very dangerous policy for yourself, for Miss Standing, and, in the long run, for Miss Langton too." She coughed in her gentle ineffective way. "I will tell you about Ambrose Kimberley. I spoke of him yesterday; but not, I think, by name."

"Yesterday?"

"I told you that William Cole had been for three months with Mrs. James Barnard, and when you asked me whether there had been any trouble in the family during that time, I mentioned that a nephew of Mr. Barnard's had left the country in disgrace."

"What about it?"

"The nephew's name was Ambrose Kimberley."

There was a long pause. Charles stared at the bare wall in front of him, which was not bare to him; he saw pictures on it. He turned from the pictures to Miss Silver.

"Ambrose Kimberley called at Miss Langton's flat yesterday. He found Miss Standing alone there. By the way, as you know everything, you probably know that we thought it wise to change her name."

"To Greta Wilson—yes, I know that."

"Kimberley introduced himself as a friend of Miss Langton's. As a matter of fact, she met him twice last winter at dances. When was he supposed to have left the country?"

"I think it was in June. The affair was kept very secret, you understand. There were no proceedings. Mr. Barnard pocketed his loss, and only about half a dozen people knew that anything had happened. Now, Mr. Moray, I asked you just now whether you thought Miss Langton was to be trusted. Do you still think so after hearing what I have just told you?"

"Why not?"

"Who gave away Miss Standing's whereabouts?"

"Someone saw her, I suppose," said Charles.

"Someone? You have to remember how very few people know her by sight. She had not been in England for a year. She had not been photographed. She only came to Miss Langton late on Friday night."

"She was at a cinema on Saturday."

"In a hat that practically hid her face. I saw her, you know; and I should be hard put to it to remember her. Between that hat and her big fur collar there was very little to recognize."

Charles moved impatiently. Miss Silver went on:

"Ambrose Kimberley turned up on Monday. Do you believe that he came to see Miss Langton? Mr. Moray, you are playing a very dangerous game."

Charles Moray's face was cold and hard.

"You had better speak plainly," he said.

"I am speaking very plainly—I am warning you that Miss Langton is not to be trusted—I am warning you that Margot Standing is in serious danger."

"Not unless one of those certificates turns up," said Charles quickly. "They won't bother with her if she's illegitimate—why should they? Egbert Standing gets the money. That's all they want, isn't it?"

"They wanted him to marry her, didn't they? And she refused. Why don't you tell me what you know about that?"

Charles got up.

"Miss Silver—"

"You had much better tell me everything."

A bitter gleam of humour crossed his face.

"If I don't tell you, you find out. Is that what you mean?"

"It saves trouble."

"If I tell you—" He burst into hard laughter.

"Sit down, Mr. Moray."

Charles walked up and down.

"I'll tell you what she told us. You're right—you'd better know—I don't want to keep you in the dark. You're wrong about Miss Langton—utterly wrong. I've known her for years. She is incapable—"

"Of letting anyone down?"

The colour rushed violently into Charles Moray's face.

"Sit down, Mr. Moray," said Miss Silver.

Charles sat down, and told her Margot's story as Margot had told it to Margaret.

CHAPTER 24

When he had finished, Miss Silver laid her knitting in her lap.

"Just a moment, Mr. Moray. I think we want to get things clear. We have a conspiracy, and there are a number of persons whom we suspect of being involved in it. You have the advantage of having seen some of these people. I would like to go back to the night of October third and just see whether any of these people can be identified. You looked into the room where the man in the grey mask was transacting his business. You saw him—"

Charles shrugged his shoulders.

"I saw nothing that anyone could recognize. I can think of no one whom I suspect of being Grey Mask."

"I have come across him before," said Miss Silver "—not as Grey Mask of course; but in the last five or six years I have constantly come across small bits of evidence which have led me to suspect that there is one man behind a number of co-ordinated criminal enterprises. He pulls a great many strings, and every now and then I have come across one of them. Well—there was a second man sitting with his back to you."

"In an overcoat and a felt hat," said Charles.

"You didn't see his face?"

"Not a glimpse."

"You heard his voice?"

"A very ordinary one," said Charles, "no accent."

"What make of man?"

"Fairly broad in the shoulders. Not tall, from the way he was sitting."

"It might have been Pullen," said Miss Silver meditatively.

"It might have been ten thousand other people," said Charles with impatience.

Miss Silver went on in a placid voice:

"Then there was another man keeping the door. They alluded to him as Forty. Well, we know that Forty is Jaffray, who was Mr. Standing's valet and on board the yacht when Mr. Standing was drowned. You did not actually hear Mr. Standing's name mentioned; but you picked up a piece of paper with the last syllable of his name, and you heard one of the men speak of Margot. Grey Mask spoke of Forty having been at sea, and made a number of allusions to his connection with an unnamed man afterwards drowned. It is clear that the late Mr. Standing was meant. Now we pass to the fourth man—Twenty-seven. He came in to report. I think he was William Cole. And I think the man with no number was Pullen. A fifth man, who was described as a jellyfish and as being unwilling to marry the girl, is certainly Egbert Standing."

Charles nodded.

"I give you Egbert. But as to the rest, it's the very purest conjecture." He laughed. "You ask me when I'm going to the police. What do you suppose they would make of those surmises of yours? Pullen is secretary of a criminal conspiracy because Lady Perringham didn't lose her pearls whilst he buttled for her. You see? William Cole has been in prison; therefore he is Number Twenty-seven, with a roving commission to murder inconvenient heiresses. Good Lord! You ask why I don't go to the police? What sort of fool should I look if I did? I saw hats, overcoats, a muffler, a mask, and a shirt-front. I should be making a prize ass of myself, and you know it."

He laughed again. He was fighting desperately for Margaret, and fighting in the dark. They were lovers no more, and friends no more; but the instinct to fight for her survived both love and friendship; it rose up in him hard and stark. He plunged on:

"What beats me is why they should have pitched on my house as a rendezvous."

"Oh—" said Miss Silver mildly, "I think I can explain that. It is a point I was about to mention. You have a caretaker called Lattery. He is a married man. Do you happen to know Mrs. Lattery's maiden name?"

"No, I don't."

"It was Pullen," said Miss Silver,—"Eliza Pullen."

Charles exclaimed.

"Pullen!"

"Pullen the butler is her brother. It would be easy for him to find out just when the house would be empty; and a big empty house would make a very good meeting place. Your house offers peculiar advantages. Thorney Lane is not much frequented, and the alley-way by which access may be had to the garden is very dark and lonely."

Charles whistled.

Miss Silver waited a moment. Then she said,

"Yes, Mr. Moray. To continue—On the night of October third Miss Langton was in your house, and it would help me very much if you would be frank about this. I know that you were once engaged, and if Miss Langton's visit was, if I may say so, a *personal* one, it would of course alter the whole situation—No, Mr. Moray—a moment. I will say nothing that is not necessary; but if Miss Langton had come there to meet you, it would account for a good deal—it would account for your reticence and for your desire to keep the matter out of the hands of the police. It is even possible that Miss Langton was seen by Pullen or one of the others, and that this increases your apprehension on her account—it would be very natural, and, if I may say so, very pardonable."

She smiled a deprecating smile. Charles met it with a blank expression.

"And if Miss Langton *had* come to see me, would there have been anything very strange or compromising in that? She has been free of the house since she was a child. I have known her since she was ten years old, Miss Silver. Will you say there was any reason why we should not have met? Wouldn't it be perfectly natural in the circumstances?"

"Oh yes," said Miss Silver. Then she coughed. "You really tell lies very badly, Mr. Moray."

"Do I?"

"Oh, very badly indeed. It would have been better if you had been frank with me—much better. You see, you have told me what I wanted to know. I was not quite sure about Miss Langton."

Charles pushed back his chair.

"I think we won't discuss Miss Langton."

Miss Silver sighed.

"That is foolish of you. You see, I know now that you saw her with Grey Mask, because if you had not done so, you would certainly have denied my suggestion that she came to the house to meet you."

"Miss Silver!"

Miss Silver shook her head mournfully.

"You would have been very angry indeed if you had not thought I was offering you a way of escape. You know that."

"Miss Silver!"

"Mr. Moray have you ever asked Miss Langton for an explanation of what you saw?"

Charles was silent. He felt a sort of horrified fear of this gentle nondescript person.

"Mr. Moray, I am most earnestly anxious to help you. *Have* you asked Miss Langton for an explanation?"

"Yes," said Charles, "I have."

"Did she give you one?"

"No."

"None at all?"

"No."

"Will you now tell me where you saw Miss Langton, and in what circumstances?"

"She came into the room, walked up to the table, and put down a package. She said something, and Grey Mask said something. I couldn't hear what they said. She only stayed a moment. I didn't see her face."

"But you were in no doubt as to her identity?"

"No."

"I see," said Miss Silver. "Just one more question. Was she announced in any way?"

Charles did not answer. He heard Jaffray's voice, a little husky, pitched in a Cockney whisper: "Number Twenty-six is 'ere, guvnor."

Miss Silver asked another question:

"The men had numbers. Was Miss Langton designated by a number?"

Charles was silent.

Miss Silver was silent for a moment too. Then she said very gently,

"I see that she was, Mr. Moray. It must have been a great shock to you. I think it is probable that these people have been blackmailing her. I have come across indications of this sort of thing before. The man you call Grey Mask works by means of blackmail—only instead of money he demands service. That is his method. You see, it gives him a hold over his tools—they are bound to obey."

Charles lifted his head.

"In Miss Langton's case there could be no question of blackmail. There could be nothing—"

"There is often something that no one dreams of. Think, Mr. Moray! Go back four years. She broke her engagement a week before her wedding day. Does a girl do that for nothing? Did she ever tell you why she did it?"

Charles Moray turned abruptly and walked out of the room. The door shut behind him. The outer door shut behind him.

Miss Silver put away the brown exercise-book and took up her knitting.

CHAPTER 25

Having posted a letter to Stephanie on Monday, Greta wrote another on Tuesday:

My dear, I keep on meeting young men. It's really too thrilling. I must tell you about it. Oh, Stephanie, it *is* such fun not being at school, and having men simply glaring because you've just been polite to someone else. I think Charles must have a most awful temper really, because he glared in the *most* frightful way you ever saw. I've never seen anyone glare like it before, except on the films when they're just going to murder somebody, or the girl has been carried away by Bad Pete or someone like that. Of course Sheikhs glare nearly the whole time. I think Charles is awfully like a Sheikh really. He would look frightfully hand-

131

some in that sort of long nightgown thing they wear and the thrilling thing over their heads that looks like a sheet tied round and round with a twisty, knotty kind of rope. It would suit Charles like anything—only of course Archie *is* taller. But he wouldn't make nearly such a good Sheikh, because he's got rather a funny sort of face and he laughs a lot—and of course Sheikhs don't. Charles was a Sheikh about Ambrose Kimberley. I'd only *just* finished my letter to you yesterday, and was putting on my hat to go out and post it, when the bell rang. And when I opened the door, there was a most *awfully* good-looking man standing there. And he asked if Margaret was in, and I said she wasn't ever in till half-past six, and sometimes later. And he said wasn't that frightfully dull for me? And I said, yes, it *was*. He was frightfully nice. I think he is a little bit taller than Archie really, and he had the most lovely dark eyes and chestnut hair, and if he had been a girl, he would have had a lovely complexion. And he said might he go and post my letter with me, so we did. And then he said it was such a fine day, wouldn't I come for a walk? So we walked as far as Kensington High Street, and we looked at the shops. All the skirts are *quite full*. Ambrose Kimberley was frightfully nice. He said he didn't often meet a girl like me. And when I said why didn't he, he said "Because there aren't any more." He said a lot of other things too. It is frightfully nice to have people saying things like that and being most awfully admiring and respectful. He said, wouldn't I have lunch and go to the pictures with him? But I couldn't, because Charles was coming to take me out. He wasn't at all pleased about Charles, but I stood *firm*. I had one fright whilst I was out. I thought I saw Pullen across the road. He's Papa's butler, you know, and I don't want anyone to know where I am, and if it was Pullen, he'd tell Egbert—and I most particularly don't want Egbert to know. I do hope it wasn't Pullen.

When I got back to the flat, Charles was there in a most awful temper. He had seen Ambrose say goodbye to me at the corner, and he was ramping and tramping up and down like a tiger. His eyebrows were all twisty, and he sort of barked at me and said, *"Who was that?"* And I wouldn't tell him at first, not till we got up to the flat, and then he put on a most frightfully severe sort of voice, and lectured me like anything, and reminded me about Mr. Percy Smith, which was *mean*—only you don't know about *him*, and it's too long to tell—besides I don't want to—and I promised Margaret. Charles really made me cry, and then he was sorry and said I mustn't. Madame's scoldings were pretty fierce, but Charles was worse, only he said he was sorry afterwards, and of course Madame never did that. And he took me out to lunch, and we went to Hindhead in his car and had tea in Guildford, and didn't get back till after Margaret did. I don't think Margaret likes Charles to like me so much. She doesn't say anything. I think she doesn't like Charles very much really, though she's known him for simply ages. We're dining with Mr. Pelham tomorrow. It's frightfully difficult to call him Freddy. We're dining at his house, and we're going on to the theatre—instead of Saturday. Mr. Pelham came round last night and fixed it up. Charles is coming too. I don't know about Archie.

CHAPTER 26

Margaret came home a little earlier than usual. Business had been slack and she had got away punctually—a thing which did not very often happen. Greta came in full of conversation, full of Ambrose Kimberley, full of Charles and their run to Hindhead.

"Where is Charles?" asked Margaret.

"He wouldn't come in. But he's coming tomorrow, and he's going to teach me to drive his car. He did teach me a little bit today, only every time I met something I was so frightened I just threw the wheel at him, and he says his nerves won't stand the strain for more than about a quarter of an hour at a time. I said I didn't mind going on a bit, and he said it was frightfully brave of me."

Greta was looking alarmingly pretty. She glowed and shone in the little room. She made Margaret feel dingy and drab and old, with that dreadful sense of age which is only possible when one is under five-and-twenty. Everything had gone by her—home, friends, leisure, looks. She did not say to herself that she had lost Charles Moray; but perhaps this one loss included all the others.

She cleared away supper, made up the fire, and sat down with idle hands. Greta prattled on about Archie, about Charles, about whether Archie was better looking than Charles, or Charles better looking than Archie, or whether Ambrose Kimberley wasn't better looking than either of them, and did Margaret like blue eyes or grey ones best, or did she prefer brown?

"Yours are brown, so you ought to marry someone with blue eyes, oughtn't you?"—Greta's voice was earnest—"or grey ones. Archie has blue eyes—hasn't he? Of course they show a lot because of his not having very bushy eyelashes. Now Charles—what colour would you say Charles's eyes were?"

"Grey."

"I thought they were. I said so in my letter to Stephanie, but afterwards I thought perhaps they weren't. His eyelashes being so black makes it sort of confusing. You're sure they're grey?"

Margaret looked into the fire.

"Quite sure."

She saw Charles's eyes looking into hers, looking smilingly, teasingly, earnestly; looking love—all gone—all past—all dead—never to come again.

Greta went on in her soft childish voice.

"I do like dark eyes—in a man. Don't you? No, you wouldn't, because yours are dark. Margaret, have you ever been engaged?"

Margaret got up.

"What a lot of questions!"

"It must be such fun," said Greta. "I should like to be engaged a lot of times before I got married, because you can't ever go back and get engaged again—can you?"

Margaret's eyes stung.

"No, you can't go back."

"So you might just as well be engaged to plenty of people while you can. Do you think Charles would be nice to be engaged to?"

"Quite," said Margaret. She was standing with her back to Greta arranging the music in a little stand.

"That's what I thought. I don't think I should mind being engaged to Charles. You see, he's got a car, and he could teach me to drive, and I think that's rather important—isn't it?"

135

"*Essential*," said Margaret, in an odd dry voice.

"Of course I think he'd be simply terrifying to be married to. Don't you?"

Margaret lifted the parcel which she had brought from her old home on the night she first met Margot Standing. She held it stiffly at arms' length. She spoke a little stiffly too:

"Has he asked you to marry him?"

Greta giggled.

"Oh, not yet. Archie hasn't either. I want to have lots of fun first. Florence, one of the girls at school, says her sister has been engaged fifteen times. She's a simply *frightfully* pretty girl called Rose Lefevre, and she says Rose always says it's a great mistake to let them rush you, because really the most amusing time is just before. Rose says they get uppish almost at once after you've said 'Yes.' And she says if they're like that when they're engaged, what will they be like when you're married to them? That's why she doesn't ever stay engaged very long. She says about three weeks is enough really. But Florence says once it was only three days—only then there *was* a row, and her father said he wouldn't have it and Rose was a scandal. But she's been engaged a lot more times since. Which do you think would be the most fun to be engaged to—Archie, or Charles?"

Margaret came over to the table. She put her parcel down on it and began to remove the paper wrapping.

"I shouldn't get engaged to either until you're quite sure."

"Oh, but I *want* to be engaged! I want to have a ring and write and tell all the girls. I don't want to wait. You see I could easily be not engaged if I didn't like it—couldn't I? You didn't say if you were ever engaged. I expect you must have been. What sort of ring did you have? I just can't make up my mind about the ring. Sometimes I think a sapphire, and sometimes I think all diamonds. I don't think fair girls ought to wear rubies. Do you?"

Margaret folded up the paper which she had taken off the parcel. It crackled a good deal. She put it away in the bottom drawer of an old walnut bureau before she spoke. Then she said,

"Wait till you've quite made up your mind."

"Oh!" said Greta; it was a quick, sudden exclamation. She jumped up, ran to the table, and caught with both hands at the desk which Margaret had just unpacked.

"Margaret! Where did you get it from?"

Margaret turned in astonishment. Greta was flushed and excited.

"Margaret, where did you get it?"

"It's mine—it was my mother's."

"Oh!" said Greta. She looked down at the desk. "It's—it's—do you know I thought it was mine—I did really. And it gave me a most frightful start, because I couldn't think *how* you'd got it."

Margaret came up to the table. The desk stood between her and Greta. It was covered in green morocco with a little diagonal pattern stamped on it; the corners were worn shabby; there was a brass handle over a sunk brass plate; and between the plate and the front of the desk were the initials E. M. B. in faded gold.

Greta touched the leather.

"I thought it was mine! It's—it's exactly like mine."

"All these old desks are alike."

"They don't all have the same initials on them. Mine—no, how silly of me!—mine has M. E. B. on it—not E. M. B.—but it's awfully, awfully like this one." She slid her finger to and fro over the initials. "Is this your mother? What was her name?"

"Mary Esther Brandon."

Greta gave a little shriek.

"Esther Brandon? Margaret—not *really*! Oh, Margaret, how *thrilling*! Weren't you frightfully, frightfully surprised when you asked me what my name was, and I said it was Esther Brandon? Margaret—is *that* why you brought me home? Oh, Margaret, do you think we're relations?"

Margaret had a most curious sense of shock. Greta with both hands on the desk, leaning towards her, talking nineteen to the dozen—asking if they were relations. She felt afraid. She said quickly,

"You told me you called yourself Esther Brandon because you found a bit of a torn letter with my mother's signature. It may have been written to your father or mother."

"It was signed Esther Brandon."

"That was my mother's name before she married my father."

"You said Mary Esther."

"She never used the Mary."

"But it was her initial—she was M. E. B.?"

"Yes, of course."

"But that's what there was on my desk—there was M. E. B. in gold. This is E. M. B." she prodded the E with a little vicious dig. "This is E, Margaret—E. M. B. It's mine that's M. E. B.— not yours."

Margaret gave herself a mental shake. It was like a ridiculous argument in a dream. It meant nothing; it could not possibly mean anything. She laughed a little.

"I don't really know which of her names came first; but these are her initials, and this is her desk."

"What's in it?" said Greta.

"It's empty. I'm going to put it away."

"Margaret, do open it! I want to see if it's like mine inside. Mine opened like this."

She slid the lock to one side, and the lid came up as she pulled at it.

Margaret came round the table.

"There's really nothing in it, Greta—just a pencil or two."

138

The pencils were plain cedar pencils. Only one had been cut. Margaret lifted out the tray.

"You see, there's nothing more."

Greta bent closer.

"Mine had a little drawer down here—a little thin drawer, in under the place where the ink goes. That's where my letter was—the bit with Esther Brandon on it, you know. I shouldn't have found my little drawer, only I dropped the desk carrying it down, and a bit of the wood broke, and I saw there was a drawer. And I hooked it out with a hairpin, and there was a tiny little scrap of scrooged-up paper wedged in under it. It came out when I got the drawer out. Margaret, yours *has* got a drawer there too—I can feel it wobble! Ooh! It's coming out! Margaret, there's something in it!"

Margaret pushed her aside. The little drawer had started from its place. There was a folded paper in it. She pulled the drawer right out.

The paper was a long envelope, doubled to fit the drawer. The minute her fingers touched it, the fear came back. She stood looking at the wrong side of the envelope, dreading to turn it round.

"What is it? said Greta. "Margaret, do look—do look quickly!"

Margaret Langton turned the envelope. It was of thick yellowish paper. It had a long crease down the middle, and three creases running across it. At one end there was an endorsement in a bold, clear hand:

"Our declaration of marriage.
E. S."

"Oh!" said Greta. She pinched Margaret violently. "Oh,— Margaret! How thrilling!"

Margaret frowned at the bold, clear writing. It was utterly strange to her. Who was E. S.? Esther Brandon had become Esther Langton, and then Esther Pelham. Who was E. S.? It wasn't her mother's writing at all. She hardly felt Greta's clutch on her arm.

"Margaret—Margaret! It's my father's writing!"

She said "Nonsense!" in a deep, loud voice that filled the little room and made an echo there.

Greta let go of Margaret's arm and snatched the envelope.

"It is! It is! It's poor Papa's very own writing. It is really! And it's his initials too—E. S. for Edward Standing."

Margaret put a rigid, steady hand on the paper.

"Give it back to me, please."

"It says 'Our declaration of marriage.' Margaret, it's my father's writing! Open it—open it quickly! Don't you see how frightfully important it is? It's what Mr. Hale was looking for. It really is Papa's writing. Do—*do* open it!"

"Hush," said Margaret.

Greta flung her arms about her; and it was only when those warm arms touched her that Margaret knew how cold she was. She was very cold, and very much afraid.

Greta hugged her.

"Oh Margaret *darling*, it was in your mother's desk! Oh, Margaret, wouldn't it be *thrilling* if we were sisters?"

Margaret pushed her away with violence.

"You little fool! Hold your tongue!"

Greta stared, most innocently aggrieved.

"Why, I'd love to be your sister. Do—*do* open it!"

Margaret lifted the flap of the envelope. It had been stuck down, but only very lightly; the flap came up without tearing.

The envelope was empty.

CHAPTER 27

"Margaret, why do you look like that?"

"There's nothing in it—the envelope's empty."

"Are you *sure*?"

"Look for yourself."

Greta held the envelope up to the light, turned it over, shook it. There was nothing inside.

"What a funny thing! It *is* Papa's writing, you know—and his initials, and—look here! Something's been rubbed out! Look—under the E. S.! Can't you see the paper's all rubbed?"

She pressed against Margaret, pushing the envelope into her hand, pointing with a plump pink finger. Under the initials E. S. the paper was roughened as if it had been scraped—very carefully and lightly scraped.

Margaret held it close under the light. Something had certainly been erased—initials? As she turned the paper, a faint marking just showed here and there. Two letters had been written and then erased. Of the first initial she could make nothing. The second—no, there was nothing to be made of that either. No one could make anything of those faint marks. Why should she think that the second letter was a B?

She went over to the walnut bureau and unlocked one of the drawers. And then, as she stood there with her back to Greta, she had a moment of sudden, vivid memory. The endorsement on the envelope caught her eye, and instantly that flash of memory followed. She was a child of five or six pushing open the door of a room. The open door showed the sun streaming

141

in from a long window. The light fell across her mother's white dress. The picture was quite extraordinarily clear—Esther Langton in a white muslin dress that swept the ground and was edged with little gathered frills; she had a black velvet ribbon at her waist, and a bunch of clove carnations where the muslin fichu crossed her breast; she was bare-headed; the sun shone on her black hair. There was another woman in the room, little and plump in a lilac dress. They did not see Margaret. She pushed the door, and she heard her mother say, "It was marriage by declaration." She did not know what the word meant, but she liked the sound of it. She said it to herself like a song, accenting it very much: "Declaration—declaration." The child's pleasure in the rhythm came back sharply. Then her mother said, "Lesbia—the child!" and they saw her.

There was no more of the picture than that. It did not come back to her in words, but as a single momentary impression. It came, and went again even as she put the envelope into the drawer and locked it away.

The bell rang, and she turned to find Greta's attention distracted.

"I expect it's Archie. He said he'd come round. I was just thinking he wasn't coming, and wishing he would—only I shan't tell him that."

Margaret went to the door. On an impulse she shut the sitting-room door behind her and took half a step on to the landing to meet Archie Millar.

"Archie, you have read all sort of books. I'm being teased by something I don't know the meaning of—you know how bothering it is. I heard it somewhere, and I want to know what it means."

Archie stared.

"Why this sudden thirst for knowledge? And why out here in the cold? Isn't it fit for the child's young ears?"

"Don't be silly!" Margaret managed to laugh. "It just came into my head."

"What is it?"

"Declaration. What's marriage by declaration?"

"Scotch marriage by declaration. The old Gretna Green business—only nowadays you have to have a Scotch domicile. Beautifully simple arrangement—no parsons—no relations—no fuss."

"What does it *mean*?"

"Are you thinking of doin' it? You can't in this benighted country. Most inferior place, England."

"I'm Scotch too, every bit as much as you are. My mother—" Margaret's voice failed suddenly. She forced it and asked another question: "Is it legal?"

"Oh, perfectly. Not exactly smiled on, you know, but perfectly legal."

The sitting-room door opened. Greta appeared.

"What *are* you doing?"

"Discussin' the Scotch marriage laws," said Archie. "I'm all Scotch, and Margaret's half-Scotch; and when Scot meets Scot, it's about ninety-nine to one that they're talkin' about law or theology. We were combinin' them."

Greta giggled and then pouted.

"I don't know any theology. Must you talk it to me?"

"You're not Scotch."

"Oh, but I *am*—at least poor Papa was. Margaret, aren't you frozen? Can't we shut these doors?"

As they went into the sitting-room, Margaret said in a startled voice;

"Was your father Scotch? I thought you said you didn't know where he came from."

"I know he lived in Scotland when he was a boy, because once when I said how cold it was, he said, 'Ah! You ought to have been brought up in Scotland like I was.' And I said, 'Oh, were you?' and he wouldn't say any more. But I'd rather not be Scotch if I've got to know about frightful things like laws."

"We'll talk about anythin' you like," said Archie.

"I'd like to talk about cars. Have you got a car? And will you take me out in it? Charles took me out today, and I can very nearly drive."

Archie cocked his eyebrows up and sang through his nose:

"Don't you ever take your sweetie in an auto!
Don't you ever take your girlie in a car!
    When she gently murmurs Charlie,
    You tread on the gas, and then—finale!
So don't you take your sweetie in a car!"

Greta uttered a shriek of delight.

"What a lovely one! Do you know any more? Have you got a ukelele? Can you play it? Will you teach me? Oh, *do* say you will! I want to have one most *frightfully*, and Mrs. Beauchamp said they weren't ladylike, and Madame wouldn't let anyone have one at school, though we simply *pined*."

Margaret lost Archie's answer. She put the old desk away in a corner and then sat down at the bureau and began to sort and tidy the pile of miscellaneous papers. Her thoughts frightened her. The picture of her mother standing in the sunlight kept coming back. It was astonishingly clear and distinct, astonishingly full of light and colour. Esther Langton's black hair and brilliant bloom; the white dress; the red carnations; and the sunshine. The little lady in the lilac dress whose name was Lesbia. Her mother's voice saying, "It was marriage by declaration."

She tore up a couple of letters and dropped them in the wastepaper basket. Words and sentences kept forming in her mind— Our declaration of marriage. E. S.—It's poor Papa's writing—it

144

really is—and his initials—He was brought up in Scotland!—I thought you didn't know where he was brought up—Of course you have to have a Scotch domicile—I am half Scotch because of the Brandons—My mother had a Scotch domicile—Our declaration of marriage. E. S.—It was marriage by declaration."

Margaret's hand shook so much that the letter she was holding dropped from it. Why should she have thoughts like these? What had come over her? She tried to stop the thoughts, to fix her attention on the letters that had to be sorted. She tried to listen to Greta's chatter.

Greta and Archie were sitting very close together, Greta gazing earnestly into his face.

"Charles has a moustache," she said. "Why haven't you got a moustache?"

"Poor old Charles looks better when a good bit of his face is covered up."

"He *doesn't*!"

"How do you know? I know, because we played together in infancy, I knew the lad when he had a chin not yet enriched by one appearing hair—misquotation from Shakespeare."

Greta giggled.

"What a frightful lot of Shakespeare you know! I don't know any except 'Friends, Romans, Countrymen'; and I always get that wrong after the first three lines. I do think Shakespeare's silly. Don't you?"

"Poor old William!"

"*Frightfully* silly," said Greta.

The words reached Margaret; but it was just as if Greta and Archie were a long way off—people in a play, talking about things which hadn't anything to do with her. She thought strangely, passionately of her mother. It came over her how little she knew of her early life. What she remembered was Esther Pelham; and Esther Pelham never spoke of the time when she

145

was Esther Langton or Esther Brandon. There seemed nothing strange about it. If Esther Pelham had never looked back into the past, it was because she was so abundantly satisfied with the present, a life full of enthusiasms, always offering fresh zest, colour, interest, new worlds to enjoy and conquer. Why should any woman with all this before her turn a remembering glance backwards? The one inexplicable thing in Esther Pelham's life was poor little Freddy. That he should be the most devoted of her adorers was quite natural. But that she should have chosen him as a husband—he adored, and for seventeen years she had contentedly accepted his adoration. Margaret could never remember a break in this strangely happy relationship.

Presently, when Freddy came in, she looked at him with puzzled eyes. One got fond of Freddy. But there was nothing romantic about him; and Esther Pelham had breathed and diffused romance.

Freddy was cheerful and affectionate.

"Well, well, it's very nice to see you—and Miss Greta. No, no—I must remember my privileges. It's Greta, isn't it? And you're remembering to call me Freddy, I hope. What? Nonsense! You must, or I shall think I'm getting old—and that won't do—will it? Now, there's Morley Milton—Margaret, you remember Morley Milton—five years older than me and getting fat. Well, no one can say I'm getting fat. Well, old Morley's just gone and got engaged to an heiress—done uncommon well for himself too, I heard—a Miss Gray—or is it May, or Way? I've got a shocking head for names. Why, only yesterday I met Jack Crosbie, and said to him 'How's Polly?' and I give you my word he looked glum. And then I remembered Polly jilted him, and I took a plunge and said 'No—of course—of course—I mean Sylvia—how's dear little Sylvia?' And he looked—oh, dreadfully annoyed and walked away, and the next man I met told me he and Sylvia don't speak. But there, I hope he won't bear malice, for I wouldn't hurt anyone's feelings for the world—now would I?"

Freddy flowed happily on. He paid Greta flowery compliments, and told endless pointless stories about people whom the others had never heard of, and in whom no one could possibly have taken any interest. Margaret had not seen him so like himself since her mother's death. When he got up to go, she drew him on one side and asked the question which she had been waiting to ask.

"Freddy, did Mother ever have a friend called Lesbia?"

Freddy wrinkled his brow.

"She'd such a lot of friends. I don't think I ever knew anyone who had so many friends as Esther did."

"Yes, she had. But I remember someone called Lesbia when I was a little girl."

"What about her?"

"Nothing. I just wondered who she was."

"Lesbia?" said Freddy. "Lesbia? You're sure it was Lesbia, and not Sylvia?"

"Quite sure."

"Because there was Sylvia Flowerdew who married Nigel Adair. No—no, that's wrong, because Nigel married Kitty Lennox, so it must have been Ian who married Sylvia. Only I seem to remember Ian being married to a dark girl with a bit of a cast in her eye—and of course some people admire it, but I don't myself, and Sylvia—"

"It wasn't Sylvia—it was Lesbia."

Freddy brightened.

"It wasn't Lesbia Boyne?"

"I don't know. Who was Lesbia Boyne?"

"She was Esther's great friend about the time we married. But I think she went out to America—yes, I think so."

"I never heard of her."

"She used to write—yes, yes, it all comes back—she used to write. And then she stopped writing—these things drop off, you know. Now there was Janet Gordon about the same time, always writing to Esther. No, not Janet—Joan—Jean—Jane—hanged if I can remember the girl's name! But I'll swear it began with a J. No—Elspeth—that's it—Elspeth Gordon! Or was it Campbell? Bless my soul. I can't be sure. But she used to write a dozen times a week, and now I can't even remember her name."

Archie was saying goodnight to Greta. He whispered something, and Greta blushed and dimpled. Freddy turned on them, shaking a finger.

"Don't you believe a word he says, I don't know what he's saying, but don't you believe it. Young men are all alike. Don't forget you're all dining with me tomorrow."

Archie was quite unabashed.

"Am I dinin' too?"

"Didn't I ask you? D'you want to come? The more, the merrier—what? Half-past seven, and don't be late. Goodnight, everybody. Goodnight, Greta." He pressed Greta's hand and held it for a moment. "Aren't you going to say 'Goodnight, Freddy'?"

Greta giggled, caught Archie's look of disfavour, and gave Freddy a beaming smile.

"Goodnight, Freddy," she said.

CHAPTER 28

"I've never been to a dinner party before," said Greta. "I'm frightfully excited. I was afraid we were going to be late, because Margaret was kept hours over time at her horrid shop. She had simply to whisk into her dress in about three minutes. I'd been quite ready for half an hour before she ever came in."

Freddy Pelham beamed on his arriving guests.

"Your first dinner party? And my last in this house."

"Your last?"

"Didn't Margaret tell you I was going?"

It was Charles who said, "Yes, she told me, but I didn't know you were off so soon."

Freddy looked pathetic.

"What's the good of my staying on? I can't bear it, and that's the fact."

"You're not selling the house?"

"No, I'm taking a leaf out of your book. I shall just lock it up and leave it standing, and then if I want to come back, I can. This is a little farewell party, just to keep me company my last night."

Even Margaret looked surprised.

"I thought you weren't going till the end of the month."

"I'm moving over to my club tomorrow—letting the servants go and all that. And I may pop off any day without saying goodbye. Hateful things goodbyes. I shan't say any—I shall just pop off, and the next you know you'll be getting picture postcards of Constantinople or Hong Kong—what? And now let's enjoy ourselves."

He turned to Greta.

"Your first dinner party? Now just think of that! I didn't know I was to be so much honoured. And Margaret was late? That's too bad! Well, I haven't got to introduce anyone to you—have I? That's splendid! And am I allowed to pay you a compliment on the very charming frock you have on?"

Greta giggled.

"It's Margaret's. I haven't got any of my own things, you know."

"Haven't you? Haven't you really? That's too bad!"

Margaret slipped her hand inside Greta's arm and pinched it.

"Come and look at this bit of jade. Isn't it pretty? I used to love it when I was a little girl. Look—you can see the light through the grapes if you hold it in front of the lamp."

Greta's attention was diverted. As she went in to dinner on Freddy's arm, she appeared to be occupied with the momentous question of whether green, "bright green like that funny bunch of grapes", would really suit her. Did Freddy think it would? "Only I ought really to be in mourning for poor Papa."

Margaret saw Charles's eyebrows go up. He made a valiant attempt to distract Greta from what was due to "poor Papa".

"You should always wear white. I'm all for the good old-fashioned heroine in white muslin and a blue sash. You know where you are then. If she's got on white muslin and a blue sash, she's the heroine, and you're not kept all worked up wondering whether she's the vamp in disguise."

"Very nice," said Freddy—"very nice indeed. I always did like to see a pretty girl in a white frock. Now your mother—" he turned to Margaret—"your mother was wonderful in

150

white. I remember her telling me she wanted to wear a coloured dress when she had her miniature painted, and the lady who did it wouldn't hear of it. Bless my soul, I can't remember her name! It wasn't Tod—no, it wasn't Tod. And it wasn't Mackintosh. Now that's really very stupid of me, for your mother used to talk about her quite a lot and say what a pity it was she married that cousin of hers and went out to British Columbia with him and never touched a brush again. Nina—yes, it was Nina—No, it wasn't McLean. Dear me, it's very stupid of me! She painted uncommonly well, and exhibited every year at the Scottish Academy. But I can't remember her name."

"Wouldn't it be on the miniature?" suggested Archie.

"Yes, yes, of course. We'll have to look at it afterwards. Now you must all have some of this entree, because it's uncommonly good. Margaret, you're not eating anything. My dear, I must really insist. By the way, that old desk of your mother's—dear me now, I've forgotten what I was going to say about it, but there *was* something I was going to say. Now what was it?"

"When did Mother have it?" said Margaret.

"I don't know. It's an old thing—not worth your taking away, my dear."

"Oh, but it *was*," said Greta. "It was *frightfully* exciting when we found the little drawer."

"A drawer?" Freddy's voice was vague and puzzled.

"A little secret drawer just like my own had, underneath the place for the ink. And Margaret wouldn't ever had found it for herself—would you, Margaret? And I shouldn't have found it either, only my desk was just like this one and I dropped it carrying it down from the attic and a little bit got broken, so I could see there was a drawer there. And when I saw Margaret's, I thought perhaps it would be the same. And it *was*." Greta's tone was triumphant.

151

The white frock, which Margaret had had in the spring and only worn once, was extravagantly becoming to Greta. The shaded lights touched up the gold in her hair. She leaned bare elbows on the dark polished table and talked with a child's excitement.

"Wasn't it funny Margaret's desk being the same as mine? It was frightfully exciting when the little drawer came out and *there* was the envelope about the certificate."

The table was a round one. Freddy Pelham had Margaret on one side of him and Greta on the other, Archie next Margaret, and Charles next Greta. As Greta said the word certificate, a manly heel came down hard upon the toe of her satin shoe. She blinked and said "Oh!" blinked again, and turned indignantly on Charles.

"You trod on me!"

Charles smiled a charming smile.

"My dear child, what do you mean? I never tread on people."

"Then it was Archie. I think the front bit of my foot's broken. Archie, why did you tread on me?"

Archie made an indignant denial. Freddy was full of fussy concern.

"You're not really hurt? I do trust you are not really hurt— and just as you were telling us such an exciting story too. Did you say, you had a desk like Margaret's, and that you actually found something in a secret drawer?"

"All scrooged up," said Greta, nodding her head. "It was *frightfully* exciting. But I don't think I'd better tell you about it, because I've just remembered I promised I wouldn't, so it's no good your asking me really. And I expect that's why Charles trod on me—only he needn't have done it so hard— it hurt frightfully."

She turned reproachful eyes on Charles, who burst out laughing.

"Greta, if you don't stop being an *enfant terrible*, I shall do something worse than tread on you—I shall take you back to the flat and lock you in."

"How horrid of you! Freddy, isn't he horrid?"

"He's a tyrant," said Freddy. "He's been travelling amongst savages, and he's forgotten how to behave. Don't take any notice of him. We were all getting most excited about your discovery. Don't take any notice of Charles. Did you say you found a certificate? What sort of a certificate?"

Greta shook her head.

"I did really promise I wouldn't tell, so I won't. I couldn't when I'd really promised—could I? But I'll tell you something I didn't promise about, something simply frightfully exciting that only happened this evening, and that no one knows anything about but me."

"Bless my soul!" said Freddy.

Charles leaned back in his chair. He looked at Margaret; but Margaret was looking at Greta with an air part startled, part weary. The weariness was uppermost. He thought she looked worn out, as if she were neither sleeping nor eating. The hastily-put-on black dress made her seem paler still. Why did she look like that? Her eyes had no fire left in them; they were tired—tired and hopeless.

Greta had begun her story. He reflected that one might just as well try to stop running water.

"It's frightfully exciting—it really is. And even Charles doesn't know about it, because it happened *after* he brought me home, and *before* Margaret came home."

"What happened?" It was Margaret who asked.

"Well, Charles brought me home, and—Oh, Freddy, do you know, I really can drive—can't I, Charles? I drove two miles, and Charles never touched the wheel once."

"What happened after you got home?" This was Archie.

"Well, I thought I'd write to Stephanie and tell her I could drive. So I did. And then I thought I would go out and post it. So I went out, and there was a big car standing just opposite, and the chauffeur walking up and down. And I stopped under the lamp-post just to see if I had stuck my letter down properly, and then I went along to the letter-box. And when I got to the dark bit where the gardens are, I looked back because I heard something, and I saw the car coming along ever so slowly—just crawling, you know. And I thought it was going to stop at one of the houses, and it did! And I ran on to the pillar-box and put my letter in and started to come back. And it was still there."

Greta's words came faster and faster, and her cheeks got pinker and pinker. She made Margaret look like a ghost.

"Not very exciting so far," said Charles drily.

"It's going to be. You *wait*. When I got up to the car I did get a fright. The chauffeur spoke to me. He had a sort of growly voice, and he said, 'Get in quick, miss.' And I said, 'It's not my car.' And he came after me, and he said I must come quickly because Egbert wanted me to."

"Oh, Lord!" said Charles to himself.

Freddy said, "Egbert?" in a mild puzzled way.

"Oh, I oughtn't to have said that! But you won't tell anyone—will you? And Archie won't. And I really didn't mean to say his name, but it's so frightfully difficult to remember all the things I mustn't say. You'll be frightfully nice—won't you, and forget about my saying Egbert—won't you?"

Freddy assured her that he had already forgotten.

"The fellow spoke to you—dash his impudence! And then what happened?"

"He said my cousin wanted me. It'll be all right if I say my cousin, won't it? I needn't say his name."

154

"What happened?" asked Archie.

"I simply ran, and I gave a sort of scream. And he said, 'Don't make a noise.' And I made a louder scream and simply ran like anything. And he caught my arm. Wasn't it *frightful*? Only just then two cars came along out of that little crescent, and that frightened him, and he let go, and I never stopped running till I got home. Wasn't it a *frightful* adventure?"

CHAPTER 29

Dinner was over at last. Charles had never endured forty minutes more crowded with indiscretions. He was reduced to a condition of exasperated resignation. After all, neither Freddy nor Archie mattered; but unless one locked the creature up, she would prattle in the same artless way to anyone she met. He thought of uninhabited islands with yearning, and of Margaret with rage. If it were not for Margaret he would not be mixed up in this damned affair at all.

The girls went upstairs to put on their coats. Freddy fussed away to see if the car had come round. Archie turned a reproachful eye on Charles.

"Why teach an innocent child to practise concealments?"

Charles had no reply but a frown.

"Why keep me out of it anyhow? Why pretend?"

"What are you driving at?"

"Well, she's Margot Standing, isn't she?"

"You guessed when she said 'Egbert'?"

"I guessed the second time I saw her," said Archie. "She

wants a whole heap of practice before she can conceal anything. Does Freddy know?"

"I expect he does by now. Egbert isn't the sort of name most
fellows would be seen dead in a ditch with. Look here, Archie,
I want to talk to you. What about after the show? We can
take the girls home, and then you come round to The Luxe
with me."

Archie nodded, and Freddy came back into the room.
Upstairs Greta clutched Margaret by the arm.

"He never showed us the miniature. Margaret, I *do* want to
see your mother's miniature so badly."

"Why should you want to see it?" Her tone said plainly, "It
has nothing to do with you."

"I want to see it *frightfully*. When I saw Esther Brandon
written on that bit of paper, it gave me a most frightfully
excited sort of feeling. I simply *must* see her miniature. Where
is it? Can't you show it to me?"

"It's in Freddy's study," said Margaret in a slow, flat voice.

"Show it to me quickly! Oh, do put on your coat and come
and show it to me!"

She fairly danced down the stairs, looking back over her
shoulder and urging Margaret to hurry.

The study was one of those built-out rooms half-way down
the stair—a fussy, untidy place full of photographs, pipes,
guns, fishing-rods, stamp-albums, old bound magazines, and
a chaotic muddle of letters and bills.

"Freddy's hopeless," said Margaret.

"Where's the miniature?"

"On his writing-table." She moved *The Times* and two picture papers as she spoke. Under the papers was a tall old-
fashioned miniature case. It had folding doors that could be
locked. The doors were shut.

"Oh!" said Greta. She caught at the table and leaned

156

on it. "Oh, it's Papa's! Oh, Margaret, it's Papa's!"

Margaret just stood and looked at it.

"Margaret, it *is* Papa's! Oh, do open it!"

"What are you talking about?" said Margaret very slowly.

"Papa had a case just like this. It stood on his table. I told Mr. Hale about it. I only saw inside it once—just a peep. Oh, Margaret, do open it—*do*!"

Margaret put her hand on the case.

"It's locked, Greta."

"Get him to open it. Oh, I *do* want to see what's inside!"

"I can't do that."

"Papa's had diamonds all round it. Has this one got diamonds all round it?"

"No, it's quite plain—just a picture of my mother in a white dress."

"My mother had a white dress too. It must have been my mother. Don't you think so? There were diamonds all round. They sparkled like anything."

"Greta! Margaret! Hurry up!" Freddy was fussing in the hall; his voice sounded querulous.

Greta gave a little shriek of dismay:

"Oh, we'll be late! We mustn't be late! We're coming," she cried, and ran out of the room.

For a moment Margaret stayed behind. She put both hands on the case and opened the little doors. The case opened quite easily. Esther Brandon looked out at her. She wore a white dress. She smiled serenely. The world was at her feet.

Margaret shut the case and went slowly out of the room.

The show was a great success as far as Greta and Freddy were concerned. There was singing, there was dancing; there were coloured lights and gorgeous scenes quite unlike anything except a stage land of dreams.

Greta was in the seventh heaven. She sat between Freddy

and Archie, and at intervals she murmured, "How *frightfully* clever! How *frightfully* sweet!" and "Oh, isn't he *wonderful?*"

Archie's comment, "Revoltin' fellow," was received with intense disfavour.

"He's lovely! His eyelashes are longer than Charles's. I think he's simply *sweet*."

This was in the interval.

Archie made a face and hummed just under his breath.

"Oh, you do need
Someone to watch over you—misquotation from *Oh Kay*."

"You've got it all wrong. It says,

'Oh, I do *need*
Someone to watch over *me*.' "

"That's what I said. Or, in the plain words of everyday life, you want someone to look after you."

"I *don't*! I can look after myself. I'm eighteen, and I was leaving school at Christmas anyhow. Of course you're older than me. But I'm grown up, and that's what matters. How old are you, Archie? Are you frightfully old?"

"Frightfully. Poor old Charles and I are just hangin' on."

"How old *are* you?"

"Twenty-seven," said Archie. "But Charles was twenty-eight a week ago, so I'm one up on him."

"It must be simply frightful to be twenty-eight," said Greta with conviction. She snuggled up to Archie and whispered, "Is Margaret awfully old too?"

"Ssh! She's twenty-four. Pretty bad—isn't it?"

Greta considered.

"I shall be married years and years before I'm twenty-four. It's *rather* old, but I do love Margaret all the same."

158

When the curtain had fallen for the last time, they came out into a windy night. It had been raining; the pavements were wet, and the wind was wet.

Freddy shepherded his party briskly.

"We'll just go along to the corner and cross over. Archie can get us a taxi quite easily there. Much better than waiting in this crush. Rather nice to get a breath of air—what? Lucky it's not raining—isn't it? Now I remember once—" he addressed himself to Greta; fragments of the anecdote that followed reached Charles as he walked a yard ahead . . . "and I said I'd give her a lift because it was so wet . . . too bad, wasn't it? . . . me, of all people in the world . . . and I think her name was Gwendolen Jones, but I can't be sure . . ."

They crossed to an island in the middle of the road. Archie made a rapid dash and got to the farther side. Freddy was fussing over Margaret and Greta.

"Now, my dear, take my arm. Margaret, perhaps you'd better take Charles's arm."

Charles heard Margaret say, "I don't want anyone's arm," and at the same moment the people on the island began to flow across. He saw Margaret and Greta together, Freddy next Margaret; and then, when he was half-way over, he heard Greta scream. He turned. It was a scream of sharp and anguished fear. He looked, and could see only a crowd and a confusion. There was a bus standing still.

He pushed through, and saw Greta just not under the bus. She was lying as she had fallen, her hands spread out, her fair hair splashed with mud, her face splashed with mud. Freddy and the bus-conductor were picking her up, and as Charles arrived she was beginning to cry. He looked round for Margaret, and saw her standing straight and still. The light from the arc-lamp was on her face.

Charles felt his heart turn over. The whole thing had happened in a moment, and in a moment it was past. The driver of the bus was saying loudly and dogmatically, "She ain't hurt, I tell you. She ain't touched I tell you"; and this was mixed with Greta's sobs and Freddy's "Very careless—very careless indeed! The young lady might have been killed."

Charles said, "What happened?" and the sound of his own voice startled him. It seemed to startle Greta too. She gave a much louder sob and flung both arms round his neck with a wail of "Take me home! Oh, Charles, please take me home!"

It was at this moment that the policeman arrived.

Freddy was in his element at once.

"Most unfortunate, constable—the young lady might have been killed. We were all going across together, my daughter and this young lady and I, and she slipped—Didn't you, my dear? Dear me, we ought to be very thankful she isn't hurt. She slipped and fell right in front of the bus. Now, my dear, you're quite safe. No—don't cry. You're not hurt, are you?"

"She wasn't touched," said the driver of the bus in the same loud aggressive voice.

"Are you hurt, Miss?" inquired the policeman.

Charles had removed Greta's arms from about his neck, but she still clung to his shoulder. In spite of the splashes of mud on her face she managed to look pretty and appealing.

"I might have been killed," she said.

"Are you hurt, Miss?"

"I might have been killed," said Greta with a sob. "Someone pushed me, and I fell right under that horrible bus."

"Any injuries, Miss?"

"No—no," said Greta. She gazed down at the drabbled white skirt which her open coat disclosed. "Oh, my frock's spoilt!"

It was like a nightmare. When Archie came up with a taxi, Charles felt as if the whole thing had been going on for years and would continue to go on for ever. The interested crowd; the voice of the bus driver; Greta's hysterical sobbing; and

160

the policeman writing things down in a notebook. Just outside all this, Margaret standing under the arc-light. She had not spoken a word or moved to come to Greta.

Charles touched her on the arm.

"Come along—we want to get out of this. Freddy says he'll walk, and Archie's going the other way. I'll take you home."

When he had put the girls into the taxi, Charles spoke for a moment to Archie Millar:

"I'll fix up a talk some other time—tonight won't do."

It was only afterwards he thought it strange that Archie turned away without so much as a word.

CHAPTER 30

Greta talked the whole way home:

"Wasn't it a frightful thing to happen? Didn't I have a most frightfully narrow escape?"

"How did it happen?" said Charles.

"Margaret and I were going across, and Freddy was going with us, and I heard the bus coming and I said, 'Oh!' And Margaret said 'Don't be silly', and I started to run. And someone pushed me frightfully hard, and I fell right under the bus."

She held Charles tightly by the hand; her fingers were warm and clinging. She went on talking:

"I always did hate crossings, but now I shall hate them more than ever. Charles, it was frightful. Someone pushed me right under the bus."

"You must have slipped," said Charles.

He tried to draw his hand away, but she held it tight.

"No, I didn't—not till I was pushed. I was just beginning to run, and someone pushed me hard."

"Someone knocked against you in the crowd."

"They knocked me right down," said Greta indignantly. "And I've got mud all over my face, and Margaret's white dress that she lent me is simply ruined. Margaret, your white frock is quite spoilt. Isn't it a pity? But it's not my fault—is it?"

She talked so much she did not even notice that Margaret did not speak at all. It was Charles for whom this silence came to be one of those unbearable things which have to be borne.

Greta exclaimed with pleasure when, having paid the taxi, he came upstairs with them. Her fright was wearing off; she was now merely excited and pleased at having Charles to talk to. She was not at all pleased, however, at being told to go to bed.

"I don't want to. I want to sit up and talk—oh, for hours. Margaret, can't we make coffee and have supper, just you and Charles and me? I'm frightfully hungry."

Margaret was standing over the dead fire. She spoke now without turning round. Her voice sounded as if her lips were dry.

"There isn't any coffee. You'd better go to bed."

"Oh!" said Greta in a disappointed tone.

Charles put his hand on her shoulder and walked her to the door.

"Run along—there's a good child. Wash your face and go to bed. I want to talk to Margaret."

"Oh!" said Greta again. She pouted, looked at him through her eyelashes, and then suddenly showed all her very pretty teeth in a yawn.

"Off with you!" said Charles, and shut the door.

He came back to the hearth. Margaret had not moved, and for a long heavy minute Charles stood looking at her in silence. One arm lay on the mantelpiece. Her head was bent; she was looking down at the ashes of the fire. Her left hand hung straight at her side. The third finger would not have held his emerald now; the hand was thinner, whiter than it had been four years ago; it looked very white against the black dress.

Charles stood there. Three things said themselves over and over in his mind: "A street accident would be the safest way"; "Someone pushed me"; and, "All the perfumes of Arabia."

He looked at Margaret's hand—Margaret's white hand, hanging there as if all the life, all the strength had gone out of it.

"Someone pushed me frightfully hard": "A street accident would be the safest plan"; "All the perfumes of Arabia cannot sweeten—"

Margaret lifted her head.

"It is late," she said.

"Yes."

She looked like Margaret carved in stone; there seemed to be no colour, no feeling, no emotion. She said, "Aren't you going?" and Charles shook his head.

"No—I want to talk to you."

"Yes, there was something I was going to say—but it's so late."

"What were you going to say?"

She had not looked at him at all; she did not look at him now. He could not see her eyes. She spoke in a dull voice:

"When are you going to take her away?"

"Do you mean Greta?"

"I mean Margot Standing. When are you going to take

163

her away? You had better take her away quickly."

At the first sound of her voice Charles became once more master of his own thoughts. The obsession of those three terrible sentences was gone. He said perhaps the last thing that she expected, and said it in quiet everyday tones:

"Why did you break off our engagement?"

She had been still before; but it seemed as if a hush came upon the stillness like the glaze of ice upon still water. There was a pause, so deep that very far off sounds came near and clamoured at Charles's ears—a footstep a long way down the street; a motor horn two roads away; the sound of wet branches rubbing against each other from the tree whose yellow leaves he had watched falling—he could almost have heard them falling now.

Then Margaret said slowly,

"Do you want me to tell you that?"

"I think so—I think it would be better if you did."

She moved her head a little. The movement said "No." Her voice came faintly:

"It won't do any good."

"I want to know. I think you must tell me."

"Yes," said Margaret, "I must—now. But it won't do any good. Nothing will do any good. Only you must take her away. I can't have her here. You'll take her away tomorrow—won't you?"

Charles looked at her with a set face.

"Tell me why you broke off our engagement."

Just for a moment she stood where she was. Then she sat down in the nearest chair. It was the armchair affected by Greta; a novel lay on the floor beside it. Margaret sat down in the chair. She leaned forward, her elbows on her knees, her face screened by her hands.

Charles remained standing.

"Something happened to make you break our engagement. I want to know what it was."

"Yes—something happened." She paused. "It's very difficult to tell."

"Something happened after you got home from our dance that night, for I'll swear—" He checked a rising note of passion, the memory of how they had parted.

"Some of it happened before. I didn't know it was happening—I didn't know what did happen. It was that morning. I was in a hurry. I went into the study for something. You know Freddy used to write there before breakfast—those long letters he loved to send people. He always wrote them in the study before breakfast. No one was allowed to disturb him. It was a regular family joke. Well, I thought he must have finished, and I went in. He was standing on the other side of the room with his back to me, and—Charles, there was a hole in the wall."

"What!"

"It was a safe. You know, lots of people have them; only I didn't know there was such a thing in the house. He had taken down a picture that covered it. And he was rustling some papers, so he didn't hear me come in. I came right up to the table. And he didn't hear me, so I stood there and waited for him to turn round. I wanted to ask him something—I forget what it was. I waited. I was rather curious too. There was a letter lying on the table—it caught my eye. You know, one wouldn't ever think of *Freddy's* letters being private—he used to pass them round. I noticed this one because it was written on such funny paper, like wrapping paper. I only saw one sentence, and I thought I had better not go on looking at it, so I moved back. And just then Freddy turned round. He was awfully startled. He thought he had locked the door, and he kept on saying how careless he was, and that it might have been one of the maids, and what was the good of a secret

165

safe if everyone knew where it was? And he said would I promise not to tell anyone? And then I went away. I think perhaps he'd forgotten I was going to be out all day, because he said afterwards he tried to find me—I *was* out, you know, all day."

Charles knew. They were together on the river—a cloudless day that neither of them guessed was to be their last.

Margaret went on. The words were coming more easily now. It was as if some frightful pressure of silence was at last finding relief.

"I only just had time to dress. Freddy seemed quite pleased all the evening. But when we got home, he let Mother go upstairs and he said he wanted to speak to me. I went into the study with him, and he began to cry. It—it was dreadful. I'd never seen him anything but cheerful before. I'd never seen a man cry. He sat down at the table and put his head in his hands and burst out crying."

She made a little pause; but Charles did not speak. She drew in her breath with a shiver and went on:

"It was about my mother. He told me she was very ill. He said she did not know it herself. He said if she had any trouble or anxiety, it would kill her. And then he put his head in his hands and groaned and said he was her murderer." Again the pause, the shivering breath. "I couldn't understand what he meant. And all of a sudden he began to talk about my coming into the study that morning. He asked me if I had noticed a letter lying on the table. I had almost forgotten all about it. He kept on asking whether I had read any of it, and how much I had read. And I told him I had only seen one sentence and a name. And I asked him if it was the name of a racehorse." Her voice sank and ceased.

Charles stood dark and frowning above her. He spoke now, sharply.

"What did you see?"

Without looking at him and without answering, she took her hands from her face and spread them to the cold unlighted fire.

Charles repeated his question:

"What did you see?"

"I can't tell you—I mustn't—I promised."

"What name did you see?"

"I didn't know it was a name—I didn't know what it was."

"You saw a name. What was it?"

"Grey Mask," said Margaret in a whisper.

After a moment Charles said, "Go on."

"He was dreadfully upset. He cried. After a bit he told me that when he was a boy he had got mixed up in a secret society. You know he lived abroad with his mother and never went to school or college. He said he got into bad company." For the first time she looked at Charles. It was a look of appeal—for Freddy, not for herself. "You can imagine how it happened—you can imagine what Freddy was like as a boy."

Charles had nothing sympathetic to say about Freddy. He said nothing.

"He joined this secret society. He didn't tell me what it was for. He said it was political; but he said everyone who joined it signed a statement that implicated them in something they could be sent to prison for—they had to take an oath, and they had to sign a statement that they had committed some crime. It was all very carefully worked out. The things were things they could have done. It was to make it quite safe for the society. Freddy said he joined it when he was only seventeen—you know how a boy of that age will join anything that's exciting. Well, he said after a few years he came over here, and he forgot all about it. And then he came into money, and they began to bother him. And he said he was in love with my mother, and he did foolish things to keep them quiet, so that they got a fresh hold on him. It was idiotic of him, but I don't suppose Freddy could help it—I mean he's like that. Then after he married Mother it got worse. I don't know what they made him do—things he hated, and things that frightened him. He'd had a rotten time, he said."

"Why did he tell you all this?"

"Because I had read that bit of the letter. He said they knew."

"How could they know?"

Margaret looked up and then down again. Charles's face was like a flint, all the features sharpened, the brows a black line.

"I'm afraid Freddy must have told them."

"Go on," said Charles in an expressionless voice.

Margaret hurried a little.

"He was afraid of them. He had been afraid of them for so many years he did not seem to have any will of his own. He told me the only thing I could do was to join them."

"So you joined them." His tone was quite polite and casual. It touched some secret spring of pride in Margaret; for the first time a little warmth came over her, a spark of the old fire showed in her eyes.

"I said what you would have said—what anyone would have said. I told him to be a man and stick it out. And he said it would kill Mother. I think we talked nearly all night. He told me some things I can't tell you. They could have sent him to prison—he said they would if I refused to join. And he said it would kill Mother." Margaret lifted her eyes to that hard face above her. They were very desolate, very tired; but the fire still burned. "It would have killed her—you won't deny that—it would certainly have killed her."

Charles did not speak.

"In the end I gave way. Freddy said it would be a form, just

168

to make them feel safe. He had the statement all ready for me to sign." Her lip lifted for an instant in the ghost of a smile. "I signed the statement, but I would not take any oath. I told Freddy it was no good—I wouldn't do it; but if they would be satisfied with knowing they could ruin me if I talked, I'd give them that. I think I confessed to pilfering jewellery when I went out to dances. There were some of my friends' names in the statement. It was frightfully cleverly done—the things really had been lost, and I could very easily have taken them. That frightened me afterwards, because I saw how clever they were. I saw how difficult it was for Freddy." She stopped. There was a dead silence. When it had lasted an unbearable time, Charles said, still in that easy voice:

"Aren't you going on?"

Margaret started a little. The cold and the silence had closed in upon her.

"There isn't anything more."

"I should have thought there was."

"I've told you." Her voice was very tired.

"You haven't told me why you broke off our engagement."

"How could I go on with it?"

"I'm afraid I don't quite understand."

"How could I? I'd got into this awful tangle. I couldn't let Freddy down. Even if I'd refused to join, it would have come to the same in the end for—for us—if there had been a scandal, if Freddy—I couldn't have married you—could I? I couldn't have dragged you into it. I couldn't marry you when I knew there might be some awful smash one day. I looked every way, and there wasn't any way out." Her voice trembled into passion. "Do you think I wouldn't have found a way out if there had been one to find? There wasn't any way out. There wasn't anything I could do to save—us." The last words faltered.

169

Margaret bent her head upon her hands. She was colder than she had ever been in her life. If only Charles would not hate her so! Nothing hurt her any more—she was too cold for that; but all the strength went out of her before this implacable resentment, and though everything in her failed, she had still to go on to the end. If he would understand a little and forgive! He did not love her any more; he was falling in love with Margot Standing. Why need he go on hating her so much?

"Thank you. It comes to this—you sacrificed yourself—me—everything, because Freddy had played the fool." His tone was coldly amused.

Margaret did not answer. "I must confess I thought I'd been cut out by something a little more romantic than Freddy." He paused, laughed, and repeated, "Freddy! Good Lord! *Freddy!*" Then, quite suddenly a violent passion came into his voice. "By heaven! I'll never forgive you!" he said, and went out of the room and out of the flat.

CHAPTER 31

At eight o'clock next morning Charles Moray, calm and cheerful, rang the bell of the flat. It may be said that he was the last person in the world whom Margaret expected to see. He greeted her without any sign of embarrassment.

"Morning, Margaret—thought I'd catch you before you went off. I suppose Greta isn't up. You might just tell her to hurry and pack anything she's got—no, she hasn't got anything—has she? But perhaps you won't mind lending her what she wants for a day or two."

"You're taking her away?"

It was dark in the tiny passage. The early morning cold chilled everything. He could not see her face; she was just a black shadow. A chink of light showed through the unfastened sitting-room door.

"Yes—I thought I'd better let you know before you went off."

"Where are you taking her?"

"D'you know, I hadn't thought of telling you that," said Charles. He spoke with the extreme of deliberate cruelty. He had one thought only—to strike hard, to strike deep, to break her pride.

Margaret had no pride left to break; it was all broken, and her heart too. She made no answer, only turned and went away from him into the sitting-room.

He came in after her and shut the door. His manner changed.

"Will you tell me that it is safe for you to know where she is? Will you tell me that? Is it safe?"

Margaret faced him, and faced the light. She could do that. Words that he had not planned rushed to Charles's lips:

"Who pushed her yesterday? She said she was pushed. You heard her. I want to know who pushed her."

A curious faint tremor touched Margaret. It made a change in the pale set of her mouth; it altered her. It was as if something horrible had touched her for an instant.

"Who pushed her?" said Charles in a low, hard voice.

The tremor came again. This time the horror was in her eyes.

"It wasn't—no—Charles—no!"

"What are you saying?"

"He was the other side of me," said Margaret in a shaken whisper.

"I didn't mean Freddy," said Charles. Then, as he said the name, he almost laughed, *"Freddy!"*

"Who did you mean? Charles—it was an accident. You don't think it was anything else?"

"It would have been a very convenient accident. I'm going to tell you something. Perhaps you know it already. I told you once before that I watched a meeting of this society of yours. I heard them speaking about Margot. Grey Mask said that if a certain certificate were found, she would have to be removed. He said a street accident would be the safest way. Last night Greta—Margot—babbled at dinner about having found a certificate. Less than three hours later the street accident happened. It didn't quite come off—I don't know why."

"Ask her why."

"No—I'll ask you—you must have seen what happened."

"She slipped."

"Why did she slip?"

The horror touched her eyes again.

"I don't know. Charles—I *don't* know."

"I do. She slipped because she was made to slip, because she was pushed. I want to know who pushed her."

She met his eyes.

"Did you think I knew?"

Charles did know what he had thought. He had endured a horrible nightmare in which anything was possible, an hour in which everything had gone adrift in a mad storm of evil. He was not sure of what he had thought in that hour. He looked at Margaret, and woke up.

The relief was so overwhelming that it carried him away. He did not know that his face was changed. But his mood had changed so much that he did not care where it was taking him. He said,

"You didn't see anything then?" And as Margaret shook

172

her head, he went on, his voice fallen to a tone of confidence. "You see what it means—they know where she is—they know where to find her. Look at the attempt to get her away last night. And then this accident. You see what it means?"

The change was so sudden that it came near to breaking Margaret's self-control. He did not wait for an answer. He was the old Charles asking for her help.

"We've got to put a stop to it. It can't go on. Can't you help me? If you'd just tell me the whole thing."

"But I have."

"You said you joined. What happened after that? Did you meet any of these people? Did you do anything? Did they make you do anything?"

"I went two or three times to meetings."

"What happened?"

"Nothing. The first time I just went. There were two men in the room. They both wore masks. They gave me a number—twenty-six—and I came away. I went again about a year later. They asked me to sign another statement. I said I wouldn't at first; but in the end I did."

"Did Freddy go with you?"

"No, I went alone. The last time was the time you saw me. Freddy was ill. He said there was a meeting, and he gave me some papers to take. I gave them to Grey Mask and came away."

"He spoke to you."

"He asked if Freddy was really ill. He didn't use his name, you know—only a number."

"The other man"—Charles spoke eagerly—"the one at the table? He had his back to me, but you must have seen his face."

"No—he had a mask. I never saw anyone's face—only masks."

173

He made an exclamation of disappointment.

"Well, you see I must get her away. I knocked Archie up after I left here last night, and he says he'll take her along to his cousin, Ernestine Foster. He says she'll take her in all right. Of course she won't know who she is."

"Until Greta gives herself away."

"Greta must be told not to give herself away."

Margaret's eyebrows went up.

"I know," said Charles. "But I shall put it across her. She's not to mention Egbert, or poor Papa, or that blighted school of hers."

Greta put her hand round the door and uttered a cry of rapture.

"Oh, Charles! How lovely! Have you come to take me out? Is it fine? Where are we going? I want to drive the whole way today. But you'll have to wait—I'm not dressed."

"So I see."

Greta came farther into the room. She wore a pale blue kimono; her feet were bare.

"This is Margaret's dressing-gown. Isn't it pretty? It's one she had ages ago in her trousseau—Isn't it, Margaret? She wouldn't quite say it was; but I'm sure it was really, and she didn't say 'No'. Of course the colours were brighter before it was washed. I'm going to have one just like it."

"Go and dress, baby," said Margaret. "Charles has come to take you away."

Charles found the light words tragic. The tragedy was in Margaret's voice and eyes.

Greta gave a little scream.

"Where are we going, Charles? Where are you going to take me? Are you going to take me right away?"

She held his arm, tugging at it as a child might have done.

"I'm not going to take you like that. Go and dress. You're

174

going to stay with a cousin of Archie's for a bit."

"How frightfully exciting! But I don't want to go away from Margaret. Won't she have me any longer?"

She left Charles and flung her arms round Margaret.

"I don't want to go away. Even if it's a little bit dull all the time you're out, I'd rather stay here—I would really. Why are you sending me away? Are you angry?"

Margaret shook her head. Just for a moment she could not speak.

"Charles, ask her to let me stay!" The bare arms were round Margaret's neck. "Margaret, I do love you! And you saved my life yesterday—Charles, she really did. So she ought to keep me. I should have been right *under* that horrible bus if she hadn't simply clutched me."

"What?"

"She clutched me and pulled me back. I told you someone pushed me. And if Margaret hadn't grabbed me, I should have gone right under the bus—I know I should."

Charles did not look at Margaret. He experienced some tumultuous emotions. He heard Margaret say, "I must go, or I shall be late. Greta, go and dress."

"You haven't had any breakfast, Margaret."

"I can't stop."

"Oh—" said Greta.

Margaret had detached herself and was at the door.

"Go and dress," she said, and went out.

CHAPTER 32

The sun came out later on; the October air glowed in an enchanting mixture of warmth and freshness. It was strange to see the trees hung with yellow instead of green.

Margaret had a busy morning. Women buy new hats when the sun shines. A stout lady with red hair bought six hats one after the other. She did not try them on—that was Margaret's business; she had to present Mrs. Collinson Jones with a pleasing picture of the hat she meant to buy. If it looked well on Margaret, she bought it with a magnificent disregard of her own contours and complexion. All the hats were very expensive.

When Mrs. Collinson Jones had departed, Margaret had a helpless bride and her still more helpless mother on her hands. Neither Mrs. Kennett nor Miss Rosabel Kennett had the very slightest idea what they wanted. They were both pretty, fair, fluffy, and ineffective. Rosabel tried on eighteen hats, and Mrs. Kennett always murmured *"Sweet!"* But in the end she and her daughter departed without having made a purchase.

The Kennetts were succeeded by Miss Canterbury, who wanted something which neither Sauterelle nor any other modern shop was likely to have.

"I don't care about these hats that hide the ears—they swallow you up so. I remember a most charming hat I had before the war, trimmed with shaded tulle and ostrich feathers. I wore it to the Deanery garden-party, and it was *much* admired."

Margaret tried to picture the tiny bent creature in a cart-wheel hat weighed down with trimming. She offered a neat small velvet shape.

"Would madam care to try this?"

"Feathers," said Miss Canterbury peevishly.

"If madam liked, she could have a feather mount at the side."

Miss Canterbury waved the shape away.

"Too small—too trivial. No, that one's too large for me. No, I don't care for velvet. The hat I was telling you about was made of the most charming crinoline straw, and the tulle was put on in big bows under the ostrich feathers—a most charming effect."

"Perhaps we could make you a hat, madam?"

"No—I shouldn't care for that. It's really very disappointing not to be able to get an ordinary black hat with feathers in Sloane Street."

After Miss Canterbury, a charming round-about little lady with plump rosy cheeks and crisp grey hair.

"Can you match this in a velour?"

Margaret took the scrap of crimson velvet ribbon. "I'm not sure, madam. I'll show you what we have."

As she crossed the room, one of the other girls spoke to her.

"Miss Langton, there are some new velours just come in."

She came back to the little plump lady, and found herself scrutinized. The red hat was tried on; but the little lady's attention seemed to wander.

"Very nice—yes, very nice indeed. Yes, I'll take it. Did I hear someone call you Miss Langton just now?"

Margaret smiled and said, "Yes."

The little lady hesitated and dropped her voice.

"Is your name Margaret? No, it can't be. But the name— and I thought I saw a likeness—I used to know—"

"My name *is* Margaret Langton."

"Not Esther Langton's daughter! Oh, my dear, I'm so pleased to meet you. Your mother was a very great friend about a hundred years ago when we were all very young and foolish—oh yes, a very great friend. Only you won't ever have heard of me, I expect. My name is Mrs. Ravenna, but I used to be Lesbia Boyne."

Margaret was so much startled that for a moment she wasn't in Sloane Street at all. The hats, the showroom, weren't there any more. She was standing at the door of another room, a very long-ago room indeed. Her mother was there, and a little lady in a lilac dress. Her mother said, "Lesbia—the child!"

She shut her eyes for a moment and opened them to see Mrs. Ravenna looking at her with an air of concern; she held her head a little on one side, and had the air of a plump, kind bird.

"I startled you—I'm afraid I startled you."

"A little," said Margaret—"just a little—because I have heard of you—my mother spoke of you—when I was a child."

"Not since then? Now that's too bad! But we must make up for lost time. I'd like to have you come and lunch with me, right away if you can. Can you manage it? You're not engaged?"

Margaret shook her head.

"Then I'll go and speak to Madam. Just you wait."

She went off smiling, and in a minute was back again.

"I've made love to her very successfully. I told her it was a very romantic meeting, and she says you may take an extra half-hour. So we can have a real, good talk. We'll come along to my hotel. I'm at The Luxe."

Mrs. Ravenna was very comfortably installed at The Luxe, with a private sitting-room.

"My dear, you look starving," she said to Margaret. "Now tell me, are you working too hard? Is that it? Serving tiresome women with hats they don't really want? I'm one of them, and my conscience pinches me. You've no business to look so pale. I remember a little girl with a very nice bright colour."

"I was late, and I hadn't really time for my breakfast," said Margaret.

Mrs. Ravenna was most dreadfully shocked.

"You lean right back and close your eyes, and don't you say a single word till you've had some soup. You look positively frozen."

The soup was deliciously hot. When Margaret had drunk it and was eating fish which tasted like some pleasantly new variety, Mrs. Ravenna removed the embargo on conversation.

"That's better! I couldn't talk to someone that I was expecting to faint all the time."

Margaret laughed.

"I never faint."

"I should faint in a minute if I didn't have my breakfast. It would be very good for my figure, but I couldn't do it—I don't bother about it any more. If I bothered, I shouldn't be so plump. But I can't do with being bothered—it's so worrying. And I'd rather be plump than have my face all over lines. Why, I know women that spend every morning in a beauty parlour, and they've got twice as many lines as I have. Of course it's lovely if you can have it both ways—no lines and a willowy figure. But that's only for the very, very few. Now your mother—"

Margaret laid down her fork.

"Yes, do tell me about my mother."

"Oh, she was looking very well. Of course I only saw her for a moment."

"Mrs. Ravenna!"

179

"Yes?" The little lady put her head on one side.

"Please—what did you say?"

"I said that Esther was looking very well—and so she was. My dear, what's the matter?"

"You haven't heard—" Margaret had to force her voice.

Mrs. Ravenna was plainly startled.

"What! You don't *mean*! Oh, my dear girl! *When?*"

"Six months ago."

Mrs. Ravenna sat up straight.

"Margaret Langton, you're not telling me your mother died six months ago?"

Margaret said, "Yes."

"Your mother—Esther Langton—Esther Pelham?"

"Yes."

"But I saw her."

"Where did you see her?"

"It was only for a minute, but I made sure. My dear, you don't know how you've shocked me. I did see her."

Margaret held the arms of her chair.

"Mrs. Ravenna—won't you tell me—what you mean?"

"I thought I saw her—and you tell me—six months ago? Impossible! Oh, I can't believe it! She looked so well."

Margaret shut her eyes for a moment. The room was turning round. Mrs. Ravenna's voice came from a long way off.

"My dear, how cruel of me! But I didn't know. I certainly thought I saw her."

She opened her eyes.

"My mother died six months ago in Hungary. They were travelling—for her health—and she died." Margaret's voice was slow and low.

Mrs. Ravenna gave a little sharp cry.

"Six months ago? But I saw her! My dear, I saw her, only a fortnight ago in Vienna."

"I—Mrs. Ravenna!"

"My dear, I *thought* I saw her."

"Did you speak to her?"

"I hadn't a chance. I was ever so vexed. You can't think how vexed I was. My train was just starting. I was leaning out of the window waving goodbye to the friend I'd been staying with, and I saw Esther in the crowd."

Her grief closed down on Margaret's heart.

"It was a mistake."

"I suppose it must have been. But, my dear—such a resemblance. She was standing looking up with the light shining on her. I thought how little she had changed. I waved to her, and I called out, and I thought she recognized me."

Margaret made a little sound of protest.

"It was a mistake."

"I thought she recognized me. You know how a person looks when they know you—she looked like that. And then I was ever so disappointed because she didn't wave to me or anything—she just turned and walked away. I was ever so disappointed."

"It was somebody else," said Margaret, with sad finality.

CHAPTER 33

Charles did his duty by Miss Greta Wilson for a couple of hours. He let her drive and entertained her to the best of his ability. She talked continuously.

"Margaret was rather odd this morning. Charles, didn't you think Margaret was rather odd this morning? I did. Do you think she was angry because of my going away?"

"I think she'll be able to bear up without you."

"What a frightfully horrid thing to say! I don't like you a bit when you say things like that. Archie never says things like that." She giggled and swerved dangerously right across the road. "Charles, why does it do that?"

Charles kept a steadying hand on the wheel.

"Keep your eye on the road," he said sternly.

"I only looked at you," said Greta in an injured voice. "Archie likes to have me look at him. Yesterday, when I looked at him, he said I'd got eyes like blue flowers—he did really."

"You weren't driving a car. You keep your eye on the road."

"I am keeping it on the road. Archie likes me to look at him. He did say that about my eyes. Are they like blue flowers, Charles?"

"You keep 'em on the road," said Charles firmly.

Greta recurred to Margaret.

"You didn't answer about Margaret. Shall I like Archie's cousin? Is she like Archie? I don't think Archie would make a pretty girl. Do you? Do you think Margaret is pretty?"

"No," said Charles.

He had often thought her beautiful.

"You've known her a frightfully long time, haven't you? You know, she won't tell me whether she was ever really engaged or not. But I think she must have been. Don't you? Of course I was only teasing her about the blue dressing-gown. But I think she must have been engaged really, and perhaps there's some frightfully romantic reason why she isn't married. Sometimes I think it's rather ordinary to get married, and that it would really be more romantic to have a hopeless attachment. Perhaps Margaret has got a frightfully romantic hopeless attachment. Do you think she has?"

"Among the Drastik Indians women who ask questions are buried alive," said Charles.

Greta gave a little shriek and did another swerve.

"Charles, it did it again! *Why* does it do it?"

"Because you look round at me. I'm going to drive now, and then you can look at me as much as you like."

When he had handed her over to Ernestine Foster, he went rather reluctantly to call on Miss Silver.

She was knitting an infant's pale blue woolly coat. A white silk handkerchief lay in her lap. When she saw Charles, she wrapped the pale blue coat in the handkerchief and dropped it into her knitting-bag. She said "Good morning," and then in the same breath,

"I'm very glad you've come."

Charles was wishing the interview well over; he was wishing he had never come at all. Every time it got more difficult to steer a course between Greta's safety and Margaret's.

Miss Silver took a sheet of paper out of a drawer and handed it to Charles.

"I thought you might come in, so I prepared this for you. I should like you to read it. It is a list of the cases in which I believe Grey Mask to have had a hand. In the ones marked with an asterisk the evidence is strong; in the others it is of a slighter nature; in the two last in the list it really amounts to nothing more than suspicion. You may remember some of the cases."

Charles looked at the list. Miss Silver was right; he remembered some of the cases. What he remembered about them appalled him. His brows drew together as he read:

" 'The Falny Case'—Good heavens! 'The Martin Case'—Martin got twenty years for that." The words came out just above his breath.

Miss Silver answered them.

"Yes. But Grey Mask was behind him, and Grey Mask went scot free. I knew Martin's wife. She told me things—nothing, you understand, that could have been used in evidence. You know what I mean, Mr. Moray—'The little more, and how much it is; the little less, and what worlds away.'"

Charles went on looking at the list. Names—a date or two— an occasional curt comment: "No arrest ever made"; "Smith arrested, but died before trial"; "Jewels never traced." When he had read to the end, he gave the paper back with a "thank you."

Miss Silver locked it up again.

"Do you feel quite comfortable about Miss Standing?"

"No," said Charles.

"She had a narrow escape last night, Mr. Moray."

Charles looked at her without speaking.

"It is not at all prudent for her to go to the theatre or to appear in public as she is doing."

"Do you suggest that I should lock her up?"

Miss Silver coughed. Charles leaned forward.

"You speak of her having had a narrow escape. What do you mean?"

"Well, Mr. Moray, it was a narrow escape—wasn't it?"

"How do you know about it?"

"I was following you."

"You saw it happen?"

"Unfortunately, no. I saw Miss Standing and Miss Langton step off the kerb, with Mr. Pelham a little behind them on Miss Langton's right. Then two men passed in front of me. I heard Miss Standing scream, and then I saw her lying on the ground. I waited until you took her away. What is her account?"

"She says that someone pushed her, and that Miss Langton saved her from going under the bus."

Miss Silver looked at him mildly.

184

"Miss Langton saved her—she says that? Does she know who pushed her?"

"No, she doesn't. Miss Silver—the two men you spoke of—were they near enough?"

"I am not sure. I spoke to them afterwards, but they declared they had not seen anything—they said they were talking. The policeman took down their names and addresses. They were quite genuine—two young clerks in a shipping office."

"Something else happened last night," said Charles. He gave Greta's account of the car that had followed her.

"Was it the Daimler?" said Miss Silver.

"She doesn't know a Daimler from a wheelbarrow," said Charles. "And she can't give any description of the chauffeur. The only thing she's sure about is that he said her cousin wanted her to come at once."

Miss Silver frowned.

"You are sure she said her cousin?"

"Perfectly. Her cousin Egbert Standing. It's the only thing she is sure about. By the way, she has left Miss Langton and is now staying with Mrs. Foster, whom I think you know."

Miss Silver did not reply. A small puzzled frown drew her brows together.

"What about Jaffray?" said Charles. "Anything more?"

"Jaffray has returned to his lodgings. I traced the car to a West End garage, but it was taken out late yesterday afternoon."

"By Jaffray?"

"No, not by Jaffray. It was not brought there by Jaffray either. The same man brought it and took it away. The only thing the people at the garage appear to have noticed about him was that he had red hair."

"Red hair?"

185

"So they said. If it is the man I suspect, the red hair is merely assumed. It makes a very good disguise, you know, just because everyone notices it."

"Who do you think he is?"

"I am not prepared to say. Your story doesn't fit in. I must follow it a little farther. You are quite sure Miss Standing said that it was her cousin Egbert who tried to carry her off?"

"She didn't see him," said Charles; "she only saw the chauffeur."

Miss Silver coughed.

"I think I had better see Miss Margot Standing," she said.

CHAPTER 34

Mrs. Ravenna drove Margaret back to Sauterelle's.

"I'm only in town for two days, and I simply must see you again. I kept tonight for a cousin whom I haven't seen for eighteen years; but she's wired to say she can't leave her husband, so I'd like to have you come instead if you will. Will you, my dear? If you don't, I shall think you've not forgiven me for having startled you with my stupid mistake."

Margaret accepted. She had no wish to spend the evening alone hearing the silence of her little room give up an echo of what Charles Moray had said. She looked at the old green desk as she stood waiting for a minute or two before walking to the corner to catch her bus. The room *was* silent; she missed Greta's chatter and Archie's laugh. She looked at the old green desk, and remembered the envelope that Greta had found. It was in her mind that she would ask Mrs. Ravenna about the words which she had overheard as a child.

She waited until dinner was over and they were sitting on either side of a pleasant blazing fire, with coffee set out on a small table between them. She helped herself to candied sugar and said:

"Mrs. Ravenna—"

"Yes, my dear? What is it?"

"I remember something—I want to ask you about it—something that happened when I was a child. I remember it quite clearly, just as if I was seeing a picture. You and my mother were in a room together. My mother had on a white dress—the sun shone across it—she had a bunch of carnations here." Margaret's hand went up to her breast. "She was standing by the window, and you were sitting at a round table that had books on it. You had a lilac dress. I was about six years old. And I pushed open the door and saw you, and I heard my mother say, 'It was marriage by declaration.' And then she saw me and said, 'Lesbia—the child!' "

Mrs. Ravenna's face showed the most lively interest.

"Fancy your remembering that old lilac dress of mine! I must say it was a very pretty one, and I always thought it suited me very well. But just think of your remembering it! It's all *I* can do to remember dresses I had eighteen years ago."

"Mrs. Ravenna," said Margaret, "what did my mother mean?"

"What did she say?"

"She said, 'It was marriage by declaration'. What did she mean?"

Mrs. Ravenna put her head on one side.

"Well, d'you know, Margaret, I'm not so very sure that I've any business to tell you."

"Mrs. Ravenna—if you *could*!"

Lesbia Ravenna hesitated. The hour, the firelight, the comfortable after-dinner mood, all prompted her to an interesting indiscretion. On the other hand she had held her tongue for eighteen years—yes, but all the people concerned were dead— still, a promise is a promise—well, but there wasn't any actual promise, and it's only to Esther's own daughter.

"Mrs. Ravenna—can't you tell me?"

"I can. I'm just not very sure whether I ought to. I don't see that I should be doing any harm, but—" She caught Margaret's look. "Well, I don't see why I shouldn't tell you after all these years, and when they're all dead—it's not as if it can hurt anyone now. Of course I don't know how much you know already."

"I don't know anything."

Mrs. Ravenna shot a quick bird-like glance at her. She did know something, or why had she such an anxious look? She hadn't her mother's bloom—she was far too worn for her age. But what a fine head!

"Well, my dear," she said, "very few people knew anything. I've always wondered how these things can be kept secret— but people manage it somehow. It all happened in Edinburgh. I only knew Edward Standing *very* slightly myself. He didn't come to the house, you understand. Old Archie Brandon wouldn't have had him—he was just a bank clerk. It only shows you never can tell—I see he died a millionaire. But nobody could have dreamed of such a thing then. I met them together once, walking up and down in the twilight, and she asked me not to mention it to her uncle—he was rather a savage old man, and she had to do as she was told."

Margaret leaned forward; her hands clasped one another tightly; her tragic apprehensive eyes were fixed on Lesbia Ravenna's face.

"Of course I didn't know about the marriage at the time— you mustn't think that. Esther told me about it the following

188

summer. It must have been the day you remember. It's funny your remembering what she said about marriage by declaration. That's just what she did say—she told me there had been a marriage by declaration, and then a frightful quarrel. I think he wanted her to come away and tell everyone, and she wouldn't—she wouldn't face old Archie. And it came to a really terrible quarrel between them. He was a hot-tempered young man, and he got it into his head she was ashamed of him—ashamed of his position, you know. And he went off in a rage, swearing she should never see him again until he could offer her a position that she wouldn't have any need to be ashamed of. He sailed for New York in a tramp steamer, and it went down. It was an awful shock of course; but after the first blow I think it was a bit of a relief too. He dominated her a good deal. She wasn't really what I would call in love with him, and after the first shock wore off, I do think it was a relief. And then—oh, my dear, you can guess what a terrible thing it was when she found she was going to have a child. *Of course* the marriage ought to have been given out at once—I've always said so—I said so to Esther the very first minute she told me about it, but then, of course, it was too late. They should have given it out at once—told the whole story from beginning to end. People would have been sorry for her then. But, as I say, by the time Esther told me it was too late to do anything. The baby was born, somewhere over in France, I believe, and put out to nurse. Don't ask me how people contrive these things—they do; and I'm sure I've often wondered how. The whole thing was a senseless piece of mismanagement. She was frightened to death of her uncle, and that was the beginning and the end of it. Well, about a year later she got married. I don't know how much she told him, or whether she told him anything. She married him, and two years later Edward Standing came back. Frightful—

189

wasn't it? Esther told me about it. It was just before I went out to the States to be married. I thought it all very shocking. But Edward Standing had his own violent temper to blame for it. He'd let her think him dead on purpose—wanted to come back with a flourish or never come back at all; and I suppose, like most men, he thought everything was going to stand still whilst he was away. Well, he came back, and he found her married to someone else. There must have been a very dreadful scene. It ended in his giving her up. He cared for her much more deeply and truly than anyone had given him credit for. He went away, and I believe he took the little girl. She didn't live very long."

Margaret spoke with dry lips:

"She's alive now."

"Oh no, my dear."

"She is."

Mrs. Ravenna stared.

"Alive? My dear, she died—oh, quite sixteen years ago. Poor Margaret!"

"Mrs. Ravenna, *please*—who are you speaking of?"

"Of Margaret."

"What Margaret?"

"My dear, who could I be speaking of? Your mother's sister, Margaret Brandon. She married Herbert Faring. I suppose you hardly remember her?"

Margaret put out her hand. It was a purely instinctive movement. Everything was slipping. Her hand went out into empty air and she slid forward in a dead faint.

Ten minutes later Mrs. Ravenna was still petting her, fussing over her, and accusing herself of stupidity.

"My dear, of course I never dreamt. It was too bad. But I had her so much in my mind, and of course to you she was only a name."

"Not even that," said Margaret. "I suppose I knew that my mother had a sister—yes, of course I did know that. But my mother never spoke of her—never at all."

"She didn't like Herbert Faring. She and Margaret never met except when he was away. And after Margaret died—no, I suppose Esther wouldn't speak of her—she was like that."

Margaret lay back amongst the soft cushions that had been piled behind her. It was true. Esther Pelham had lived very fully and sufficiently in the present; every day brought her so much that she had no time for the past. Margaret Brandon had slipped away into the past and been lost there.

After a silence she asked:

"Was the marriage legal?"

"The marriage with Edward Standing? Oh yes, my dear— that was the trouble. They had made a declaration in writing, and he had it. If he had chosen, he could have upset the marriage with Herbert Faring and made a most frightful scandal. In the end he gave her the paper and promised never to make any claim."

Margaret sat up.

"Nobody seems to have thought of the child," she said.

CHAPTER 35

Miss Silver called that evening at Mrs. Foster's.

She did not see Miss Greta Wilson, because Greta had gone out to dine and dance with Archie Millar. Mrs. Foster had, in fact, sent them out.

"It's no use, Archie. I've taken her in to please you, but I'm not going to put my table out. It holds eight, and it won't hold any more. So you've just got to take her away and dance with her. She won't mind."

Greta was frankly delighted.

"Does Charles dance as well as you do?"

"Haven't you danced with Charles?" said Archie.

"Not yet. Does he dance as well as you do?"

"Oh, he couldn't do that. I don't want to shatter any of your young illusions, you know; but after four years explorin' in desert wastes I shouldn't wonder if poor old Charles wasn't a bit of a back number."

Greta gave a little shriek.

"Oh! Archie! There's Ambrose!"

"Who's Ambrose?"

"There! He's Ambrose Kimberley. He came to the flat one day when Margaret was out. And I went for a walk with him, and Charles was in a most frightful temper about it. I do think Charles has got a temper. Don't you? He was in a frightful temper about Ambrose. Oh, Archie, he's seen me! He waved his hand! Did you see? Don't you call him frightfully good-looking?"

Archie eyed Mr. Kimberley coldly.

"He's the brand they grow for the movies—good old Hollywood vintage—full of bouquet—mellow on the palate—sweet as cream—flappers like it."

Greta giggled.

"He's got lovely eyelashes. Charles was frightfully cross because I told him they were yards longer than his."

"Men don't have eyelashes," said Archie sternly. "It's not done."

Charles, after dining alone, walked to Thornhill Square. He thought he would like to have a talk with Mrs. Lattery.

"I think I shall be coming to live in the house next week,"

he began, and had to endure Mrs. Lattery's very voluble plans for his accommodation.

"And I don't know whether you'll be wanting to entertain, sir."

"Probably," said Charles.

Mrs. Lattery embarked on the question of the staff that would be required.

"My brother, sir, will be looking for a place. I don't know whether you would consider him. He's been in very good places."

"As?"

"As butler, sir—he's been in very good places indeed, sir."

Charles found himself a good deal interested in Mrs. Lattery's brother. Pullen was the name—yes, Pullen.

"He was with Lady Perringham, sir, and before that with Mr. Mackay. He has always given every satisfaction."

"And where is he now?" said Charles.

"He was in the service of the late Mr. Standing, sir. But I hear the house is to be closed, and my brother—Pullen's the name, sir—he'll be looking for something else and I thought—"

"Quite so," said Charles. He wondered whether William Cole, alias Leonard Morrison, also wished to take service with him; and he wondered what would happen if he were to engage these two interesting persons.

He left the house and betook himself to call on Margaret. It was by now rather after half-past nine. He climbed the steep, narrow stair and stood for a moment on the dimly lighted landing. He had come to see Margaret, but having come, he was in two minds as to whether he would not turn round and go away. He came slowly to the door of the flat and stood hesitating. As he did so, he noticed that the door was not fastened. He pushed it gently, and heard a faint click. Someone had just put out the electric light.

Charles took one step across the passage and thrust open the sitting-room door. The room was in darkness. He called "Margaret!" and felt for the switch. Someone charged him with a headlong rush that carried him back through the door into the tiny passage. He fetched up against the wall with a bang.

In the half-minute's struggle that followed he had the man by the throat, was violently kicked on the shins, lost his grip, had an impression of a long, thin, twisting form, extraordinarily strong, extraordinarily supple, and gripped a bony wrist, only to have it wrenched away. The door of the flat slammed. Charles got it open and pursued. The intruder was away before he reached the entrance. After prospecting, Charles returned to the flat and put on the light.

The old green desk stood on the table. It had been turned inside out. The drawers of the bureau were standing out upon the floor.

Charles whistled. He went over to the bedroom, knocked, and then in sudden deadly fear, pushed in. The light showed him Margaret's black day dress lying across a chair. The room was empty. The little kitchen was empty too. Margaret was clearly out.

Charles returned to the sitting-room and sat down to await her return. He left the room in its disorder, and as he sat looking at this disorder he thought very deeply.

Margaret—what a mess she had got herself into! That little *ass* Freddy! If there *was* a comic opera conspiracy knocking around, it was just like Freddy to get mixed up in it—all very earnestly—very much *pour le bon motif*. He could imagine Freddy full of bright and boring enthusiasms, full to the brim of absurd zeal, and then suddenly discovering that he'd got let in by a lot of crooks and being scared to death. A well-meaning little fool if ever there was one. But Margaret—what could one do about Margaret? That she should have been dragged into the mess to save Freddy's skin! She must be got out again—that went without saying; and if Freddy had got her in, it was for Freddy to get her out. Those statements she had signed must be got back. By hook or crook Freddy must get them back. He couldn't have been mixed up with the Grey Mask lot for twenty-five years or so without getting to know a bit. He probably knew where the papers were likely to be; it was even barely possible that he had kept them himself. An early interview with Freddy Pelham was certainly indicated.

Margaret came in at eleven.

"Charles! What on earth?"

"You're not as surprised as I was when I got here and found a burglar in possession."

"A burglar!"

"Did you think I'd been going through your desk and bureau?"

Margaret gazed at the turned out drawers, the ransacked desk.

"What did he come for?" said Charles quickly. "What did he come for, and what did he get away with?"

"Oh!" said Margaret. "Oh, I left it locked."

"The bureau?"

"This drawer." She turned over the papers that lay in confusion. "Charles, it's gone!"

"What's gone?"

"The certificate. No, it wasn't the certificate—it was only the envelope. I forgot—you don't know that Greta found it. Charles, do you know who Greta's mother was? She was my mother's sister. She was Margaret Brandon. The certificate was in my mother's desk. Greta is my cousin."

"You found the certificate?"

"No—only the envelope, endorsed by Edward Standing.

The marriage was secret—a Scotch marriage by declaration. I've just been hearing the whole story from my mother's oldest friend." She told him what Lesbia Ravenna had told her. "I don't know how the envelope came to be in my mother's desk."

"You say Standing gave the declaration back to Mrs. Faring. She probably wouldn't keep it herself—I think she would have been afraid to keep it herself. But perhaps she wouldn't destroy it, for the child's sake and perhaps for her own sake too, in case the story ever came out. I expect she gave it to her sister to keep."

"But the envelope was empty."

"Well," said Charles, "Mrs. Faring had committed bigamy. They may have been frightened about that. It was certainly safer not to keep the declaration."

"They kept the envelope."

"Aren't women like that? They like to keep something. They don't go the whole hog and make a clean sweep of the past like a man does. You say the envelope's gone."

"Yes. It was in here. Look! The lock's been forced."

"What was on it?"

"Mr. Standing's endorsement—Greta recognized his writing at once: 'Our declaration of marriage. E. S.' I think she had signed it too, because something had been rubbed out—initials, I think, like his. I thought the second one was a B. You could only just see the marks."

"There was nothing inside the envelope?"

"Nothing at all."

The drawer that had been locked was full of tumbled papers. Margaret began to straighten them. As she lifted one, a snapshot of Charles looked up at her. She covered it quickly. That old boyish smile was gone.

"Here, let's put these things away."

Charles spoke from just behind her. She did not know whether he had seen the photograph or not. He helped her to put the drawers away. It was strange to be doing these things with Charles; strange and yet extraordinarily natural to be talking to him in her flat at midnight. It was the first time since their parting that they had talked without bitterness. The hour comforted Margaret. He would go away, and he would marry Greta; but at least there would have been this moment when he didn't hate her. Perhaps when he was married to Greta he would stop hating her altogether. The thought touched something that lay dead, and the old vehement, passionate Margaret woke.

All at once she was so intensely aware of Charles and of herself that they might have been new creatures in a new world. The colour came into her cheeks.

Charles looked at her in astonishment. The sad pale ghost of Margaret was gone. This was Margaret herself.

They looked at one another in silence. The little green clock which he had given her ticked from the mantelpiece. Charles pushed the last drawer home and rose to his feet. She was only a yard away, but there were four years between them still.

"Why did you do it?" he said. It was the third time that he had asked the question; he had not meant to ask it now.

"I told you," said Margaret with her head up.

"It wasn't an answer."

"It's the only answer I've got."

"Why didn't you tell me the truth four years ago?"

"What was the good? There was no way out."

"There's always a way out. We could have made one together." He spoke with extreme vehemence; the flood of it carried him beyond his own control. "You never loved me. That's the truth."

Margaret looked at him. The tide of passion rose and ebbed

197

again. She would not protest that old dead love to the Charles of today. She looked at him, and the strange sense of newness passed away. This was the flat, unprofitable everyday to which all romance came in the end. You had to go on and do your best without it—you had to go on. The colour and the fire went from her. She looked very tired.

Charles became intensely aware of having made a fool of himself. He gave a short angry laugh.

"It's a bit late in the day for scenes—isn't it? I don't know why I dug that up—it's rather a poor thing in ghosts. I meant to talk business with you. I'd like to still, if you don't mind."

"It's very late." The words came slowly. Charles was quite right—it was very late—it was four years too late.

"I won't keep you long. I wanted to ask you about those statements you signed. Have you any idea who's got them?"

"I suppose Grey Mask has got them."

"You don't think it possible that Freddy has them?"

"Oh no—I'm sure he hasn't. He told me he had to satisfy the others."

Charles frowned.

"Those statements must be got back. I can't move whilst you're compromised—and I've got to move for Greta's sake."

Margaret leaned against the mantelpiece.

"I'm afraid there's no way of getting them back. You had better leave me out of it."

"How can I?"

"Very easily."

Charles looked at her coldly.

"I call that unintelligent. Do you really expect me to do anything that would land you in a police court?"

A bright flame burned her cheeks.

"I don't ask to be considered. Do you suppose I care what happens to me? Do you suppose I want you to risk Greta?"

Charles's frown darkened.

"I haven't any choice. Please be practical. Freddy got you into the mess, and Freddy ought to get you out of it. When is he off?"

"He moved out of the house today. You heard what he said—he may be off any day. He hates to be tied."

"I see. All right, I'll be going."

He went as far as the door, then turned, strode back, and jerked a sudden question at her:

"Who's Grey Mask?"

"I don't know," said Margaret.

"You've no idea? None?"

She shook her head. She was frightfully pale.

"Does Freddy know?"

"I don't believe any of them know," said Margaret in a whisper.

CHAPTER 36

At eleven o'clock that night the Standing house in Grange Street was in darkness. On the three upper floors blinds were down, curtains drawn, and lights switched off; in the hall a faint glimmer from the small shaded bulb which burned all night over the telephone.

A man entered Grange Square by Caton Walk and proceeded at a slow and leisured pace round two sides of it until he came to the dark square house at the corner. Here he stood quite still. The railings which enclosed the plane trees, empty flower beds, and grass plots of Grange Gardens were at his back.

It was a black night, and he stood where the shadows were blackest. He watched the house for ten minutes or so, then walked across the road and up the steps. Here again he stood and waited.

The house was as quiet as a house might be. The basement windows showed no glimmer. The man opened the door with a latch-key and passed into the hall. It was quite pleasantly warm after the cold in the square. The tiny bulb over the telephone made the darkness here seem less dense than the dark outside.

The man crossed the hall and stood a moment by the study door listening. Then he opened the door very softly and went in. It was about ten minutes before he came out again. This time he went up the stairs, which crossed the back of the hall in a double flight. He had reached the landing, when the front door opened and closed again softly. The man on the stair put his right hand in his pocket, and then moved without haste into the angle made by the stair as it continued its upward way. He listened for the sound of another foot on the marble steps. The only sound that came was the click of an electric switch.

Instantly the hall below was lighted from end to end, and against this light the outline of the balustrade, showed black. The man on the stairs came forward, leaned on the balustrade and looked over into the hall. He saw the black and white tesselated floor all empty, and on the left the open dining-room door. As he looked, the light went on in the dining-room, and at the same time he heard a faint shuffling sound. It was the sound of someone moving, of someone coming down-stairs; but not down these stairs—the sound was too faint for that. If the man had not possessed phenomenally acute hearing, the sound would not have reached him at all.

Someone was coming down the back stairs. He had only to stand where he was to be unobserved. It appeared, however, that he not only desired to remain unseen; he wished, nay, he intended, to see. He moved quickly along a passage to the right until he reached a door that opened upon the back stairs. Here he waited, listening. The soft shuffling footsteps were below him. He opened the door. The stairs were dark. He followed the footsteps down into the darkness.

At the foot of the stairs there was a baize door. He opened it cautiously. The long passage was black, but even as he looked, light showed at the far end. A second door swung open, a man's figure showed against the light, and then the door swung to again.

After a moment the man followed. At the second door he listened. There was no sound, but the room beyond was lighted. He peeped cautiously. The lighted room was empty. He had come to the butler's pantry. A door led out of it through a short length of passage to the dining-room. He took this way with some assurance, and at the dining-room door the sound of voices gave him pause.

Very slowly and gently, he moved the handle round until the latch slipped and the door came a bare half-inch towards him. Through the chink he looked into the lighted dining-room. There were two men there, both fully dressed. He was able to recognize them both without difficulty. Facing him was the footman William Cole. He held a tumbler half-full of whisky and soda. His coat was torn at the neck, the right cuff was ripped, his hair a good deal disordered. The other man was the butler, Pullen. They were talking.

"Who was it?" This was Pullen, a little more hurried than when he was on duty.

"How should I know? I didn't wait to ask his name, I can tell you. It took me all I knew to get away—and all for nothing."

"You didn't find it?"

William took a drink.

"Found the envelope. What they've done with the paper beats me."

He pulled out a long envelope and flung it down on the table. Pullen picked it up and held it at arm's length to read the endorsement:

" 'Our declaration of marriage.' Yes, that's it."

"But it's empty. I'd hardly put my hand on it before I had to cut and run. When I looked inside I could have done murder."

"Where's the declaration? That's what I want to know."

"The girl's got it, of course. The question is—where's the girl?"

"Kimberley's found her already. I went on to the Foster's. There's nothing there, unless she had it on her. She was out with Millar."

"That girl's been here too long. She's got to go. Once she's gone, it don't matter if a hundred certificates turn up. She's got to go, and that's an end of it."

William finished his whisky.

"Well, do her in yourself," he said.

"It's not my line."

"Why should it be mine?"

"Well, it's yours—isn't it—Lenny Morrison?"

William's face underwent a horrible change. The stout Pullen recoiled.

"Less of that! D'you hear? Call me that again, and you'll be sorry for it. As to the girl, she's Egbert's job, isn't she?"

"He won't. I said so all along. Grey Mask's giving you the job. It wants neat doing, and Egbert's a bungler if I ever saw one. Now, look here! There are to be no more delays."

The man at the door went on listening for another ten min-

utes. Then he retraced his steps and vanished into the darkness of the house.

Outside in the square Miss Silver waited patiently for
another hour. When the man came out, she followed him.

CHAPTER 37

Mrs. Foster came down to breakfast on Thursday morning in
a state of nervous exasperation.

"Really, Archie's the limit! Yes, I know he's my cousin.
Now, George, it's no use your looking like that—I never said
he was your cousin or anybody else's cousin—I know he's
mine. But you needn't try and make out that all your relations
are angel beings who never do tiresome things, or land you
in holes, or shove strange girls on to you in the middle of a
dinner-party."

The broad face of George Foster emerged from behind *The
Times.*

"Got a bit off the rails, haven't you? Take a good deep breath
and start fresh."

"George!"

"My dear child, what is it?"

"I'm feeling simply too temperamental, and I could *kill*
Archie! First he dumps this girl on me in the very middle
of a dinner party—"

"My *good* Ernestine!"

"It was the next thing to it, and my table would have been
utterly spoilt if I hadn't been *firm* and *insisted* on his removing
her for the evening."

George grinned.

"I didn't notice your having to insist very much. Archie appeared only too anxious to oblige."

"Oh, of course he's in love with her. It's the only excuse he's got. George, if you go on rustling the paper like that, I shall scream."

"What *is* the matter?"

"*Really*, George, you might have a little consideration, after the shock of having burglars and a dinner party and Archie's stray flapper all happening together. And I want to know what brought Maud Silver here. She asked for that girl."

"Who's Maud Silver?"

Ernestine flushed scarlet and bit her lip.

"You know perfectly well. She got back those odious diamonds your mother gave me. And I must say I *didn't* think you'd refer to it now when I'm feeling as if I simply couldn't bear to hear myself *think*."

George said nothing; he returned to the golfing news.

"I do really think you might *say* something, George! You're simply immersed in that wretched paper. I believe you'd just go on reading it with a burglar in the very room."

"What d'you want me to say? Hullo! Sandy Herd did a jolly hot round yesterday."

"*Really*, George!"

"What's the matter?"

"If you talk to me about golf, I shall burst into tears."

"What d'you want me to talk about?"

"The burglar, of course. What on earth did he come for?"

"Anything he could collect, I suppose."

"Then why did he pull out everything in the spare room and not so much as *look* for my diamonds? Can you tell me that?"

George could not. He lacked interest in the burglar. Since

nothing had been taken, why make a song and dance about it? He reverted to golf.

Miss Greta Wilson was late for breakfast. When she had finished, she accompanied a slightly calmer but still fractious hostess on what George rudely described as a "nose-flattening tour."

"Men never seem to think you want any clothes," said Mrs. Foster. "George is perfectly hopeless. If I say I want a new evening dress, he boasts, positively boasts, of the fact that his evening clothes are pre-Ararat."

Greta giggled.

"I *love* looking at clothes," she said. "It's the next best thing to buying them—isn't it?"

They looked at a great many. Ernestine bought a hat, a jumper, and some silk stockings, which soothed her a good deal. At twelve o'clock she remembered with a shriek of dismay that she had promised, absolutely promised, to ring up Renee Latouche and give her Jim Maxwell's address.

"I looked it up on purpose. And then George interrupted me and it went right out of my head. Come along to Harridge's and I'll ring up from there."

As they turned into the big stores, a car came out of a narrow side street and drew up by the farther kerb.

Mrs. Foster left Greta to wander about on the ground floor whilst she rushed upstairs to telephone.

"But I shall be at least twenty minutes, because it always takes simply ages to get Renee to the telephone. I know I shall have to talk to everyone in the house before I get her. Maddening, I call it."

Greta was quite pleased to be left. She looked at bewilderingly lovely materials shining with all the colours of the rainbow, and planned a dozen dresses. She then wandered into a duller department which displayed travelling rugs. She was not really interested in travelling rugs, but she pinched a fold of one of them to see how soft it was. As she did so, a curious thing happened. A man's hand and arm came into view for a moment. She did not see the man, who was standing behind her; she only saw his hand and arm. The hand was broad and hairy, the sleeve of dark blue serge. The hand laid a note on the fleecy brown travelling rug and withdrew as suddenly as it had come.

Greta looked at the note with eyes as round as saucers. The colour drained slowly away from her rosy cheeks. She stared at the note and grew paler and paler. The envelope was grey— not the common Silurian grey, but a curious rough grey paper which was very uncommon. The envelope was addressed in a bold clear hand to Miss Margot Standing.

After a minute of terrified hesitation Margot took up the envelope and tore it open.

When Ernestine Foster had finished her conversation with Mrs. Latouche, she remembered that she had promised to bring home fruit for lunch. She bought a pineapple; then decided that it would certainly be sour and that George would inquire how much she had paid for it. After hesitating for ten minutes between grapes and Cape peaches she decided on bananas and apples, and then set out in a hurry to look for Greta.

Greta was not in the silk department, where she had left her, nor in the Bank, where they had agreed to meet. She was not in Jewellery, Furs, Gloves, Lingerie, Haberdashery, Glass, China or Gramophones.

Ernestine's temper mounted rapidly. During the morning Greta's sympathetic attitude towards clothes in general and Ernestine's purchases in particular had softened her a good deal towards her guest; but after Mrs. Foster had searched fifteen departments Greta had a very serious relapse into being "that odious flapper of Archie's." After half a dozen more departments, Ernestine was not only angry, but just a little alarmed. Of course the creature had got tired of waiting and gone home—girls of that age never have any manners. But—

She questioned the commissionaire at every door. The man at the door by which she and Greta had entered the stores remembered the young lady very well. He knew Mrs. Foster by sight, and he remembered her coming in with a young lady. He remembered more than that; he remembered the young lady coming out about ten minutes later. Oh yes, he was quite sure it was the same young lady—she came out, and she got into a car that was waiting at the other side of the street.

"Was she alone?"

"Oh yes, madam, quite alone. There was a gentleman in the car."

"What sort of gentleman?"

"I couldn't say, madam. It was a closed car with a chauffeur. The chauffeur went into the stores and came out again a minute or two before the young lady."

"What kind of a car was it?"

"It was a Daimler, madam."

Ernestine went home very angry indeed. She rang up her cousin, Archie Millar, and was told he had gone out for lunch. She left an urgent message, and upbraided George all through lunch for the total lack of courtesy and consideration displayed by his sex.

"If Archie wanted to take the girl out to lunch, why didn't he say so? Heaven knows where he raised the car from. Archie with a Daimler and a chauffeur, if you please! And isn't it just like a man to dump a girl on me one minute, and then positively abduct her about five minutes before lunch and without saying a single word? I don't suppose he'll go near his office again till three o'clock. Then he'll shoot the girl back here and expect me to look after her. Would anyone but a man be so exasperating?"

At half-past two Archie rang up.

"Hello, Ernestine!"

"*Really*, Archie, you're the limit!"

"My dear girl, why so peeved? If you're not careful, you'll be gettin' wrinkles in the voice. What price voice massage?"

"I must say I think you might have let me know you were going to carry the girl off like that. I might have imagined something had happened to her."

"I say—what's all this?"

"I think you might just have told me."

"Told you what?"

"Of course George takes your part. He would—men always do."

"What have I done?"

"If you were going to take her out to lunch—and I suppose you arranged it last night—why on earth couldn't she have said so instead of leaving me stranded at Harridge's?"

"Ernestine, what are you talkin' about? Where's Greta?"

"I'm sure I don't know. Hasn't she been lunching with you?"

"No, she hasn't. I say, suppose you tell me what's been happenin'?"

"You *didn't* fetch her from Harridge's?"

"No, of course I didn't."

"Then who did?"

"Look here, tell me what happened."

"I went upstairs to telephone to Renee Latouche, because I'd promised her Jim Maxwell's address, and George was so exasperating that I forgot all about it till Greta and I were passing Harridge's."

"Well?"

208

"It took me ages to get Renee—it always does. And when I'd finished, I couldn't find Greta anywhere. I went into every department. D'you know, they've got departments for things I've never even heard of. I went everywhere, and she simply wasn't there. And then I asked the commissionaires. And one of them had seen us go in, and he said he'd seen Greta come out only about ten minutes afterwards. He said she got into a Daimler that was waiting and went off. And of course I thought it was you."

"A Daimler!"

"With a chauffeur. The commissionaire said there was a man inside. Wasn't it you?"

"No, it wasn't. I haven't seen her since last night."

Ernestine hardly knew Archie's voice.

"Then who was it?"

"What time did all this happen?"

"Well, it was about twelve when I remembered about telephoning to Renee, and the commissionaire said Greta came out about ten minutes after we went in, so—"

"Ernestine! I told you not to let her go about alone!"

Ernestine became sharply offended.

"Well, if you call that letting her go about alone!"

Archie rang off.

CHAPTER 38

Charles spent the afternoon going through a stack of papers at Thornhill Square. It was about five o'clock when he finished with them and went out by the garden way. It was dusk but not yet dark. The alley-way was much darker than the garden.

When he had shut and locked the door in the wall, he stood for a moment, and then turned to the right instead of to the left. The impulse which made him do this was so slight and undefined that it took no definite shape in his mind. He turned to the right instead of to the left and walked slowly along the alley-way.

On his right were the other gardens of Thornhill Square, on his left the smaller, narrower gardens of George Street. On both sides, brick walls broken at intervals by wooden doors. The slope of the ground hid all but the top storeys of the houses on the right; but the George Street houses showed back windows lighted and curtained.

Charles had walked a dozen yards or so before it occurred to him that it was a sentimental desire to look at the Pelhams' house which had brought him out of his way. That he might have looked at it any day since his return was true; and it was equally true that he had never felt impelled to do so. He discovered the reason now. It was the empty house that drew him, because, empty, it held a thousand memories.

He walked past the bend in the alley and stood where he had often stood waiting for Margaret to slip through the garden door. The house was larger than the others in the street—

larger, and older by a hundred years; a square Georgian house with modern additions. The study was an addition, and a hideous one. It jutted out, breaking the square lines, and from it a frightful iron stair descended to the garden. From the alley you could see the French window and the looped spirals of the stair.

Charles had stood a hundred times where he was standing now and watched for the window to open. He watched now with a definite feeling of what a fool he was to stare at an empty house and people it with memories. The dusk was darkening into night; the house was just a black square. He could no longer discern either window or stair, when suddenly the window sprang into view, a brilliant oblong crossed with black lines. It showed for a moment, and then a man pulled down the blind.

The man was Freddy Pelham; and the sight of Freddy sent all those romantic memories back into the past to which they belonged; their place was taken by the practical consideration that here was a most excellent opportunity of tackling Freddy about the whole stupid Grey Mask imbroglio.

Charles tried the garden door, found it open, and walked briskly up the garden path. The iron stair was wet and slippery under foot, the hand-rail coldly insecure—a beastly contraption like seaside lodgings. He rapped on the window, and could have laughed at Freddy Pelham's scared face when he raised the blind and peered into the darkness—"Probably thinks it's one of Grey Mask's little lot."

Freddy's relief at recognizing Charles Moray was touching.

"I'm all alone in the house, you see. And I shouldn't be much use if it came to a rough-and-tumble with a burglar—what? Now there was Hugo Byrne—you remember Hugo—no, he was before your time—his mother was Edith Peace, and his sister married one of the Dunlop Murrays—no relation of yours of course. Let me see, what was I going to tell you? Oh yes—burglars. Well, poor old Hugo got up in the middle of the night and thought he heard a burglar and—let me see, did I tell you?—he'd got his wife's uncle down from Scotland staying with them—he married Josephine Campbell, you know. No, no, not Josephine—she was the dark one—Elizabeth Campbell. Yes, I'm sure it was Elizabeth, because she had red hair, and we used to call her Red Liz—behind her back, you know, behind her back. And—where was I? Oh yes—poor old Hugo and the burglar. Of course it turned out to be old Robert Campbell. And he never left them a penny. Rather too bad—what?"

The study was in its usual condition of disorder. How Freddy ever found anything in it was a mystery. He appeared to have been making some slight attempt to clear things up.

"Frightful mess—what? Sit down—sit down. Here, put those photograph albums on the floor. No—perhaps better leave those. This chair now—we can shift these papers. Nothing of importance there—what? Only bills—nothing to break one's heart over, if some of them did get lost—what?"

He tilted a confused mass of papers on to the floor.

"Thanks, I won't sit," said Charles. "I'm afraid I'm interrupting you. Fact is I wanted to ask you about something, and when I saw the light I thought I'd come up and get it over."

"Well, what can I do for you? I don't suppose I shall do much more here anyway. I thought I'd try and clear up some of this mess; but I'm off tomorrow, and there's too much of it—I can't tackle it. Margaret's coming up to say goodbye. I telephoned to her place to let her know I'd be here, and she'll come along as soon as she gets off. That's why the garden

212

door's open—she'll come along that way. Well, well, I shall be glad when I'm off. I don't like saying goodbye—that's a fact. Stupid of me—isn't it?"

He was fidgeting with the litter on the table. There was something pathetic about the aimless movements and the deprecating glances which accompanied them.

Charles felt very sorry for him. He said,

"Oh, I don't know," and then, "It was about Margaret I wanted to speak to you."

Freddy brightened into curiosity.

"About Margaret—what? You don't mean to say—no, no, of course not—much better let bygones be bygones. I remember Tommy Hadow now—he got engaged to the second Jenkins girl—I can't for the life of me remember her name—something short. Dot? No. May? No, it wasn't May."

"It's nothing of that sort," said Charles firmly.

"Well, well, I'm sorry—in a way, I'm sorry. But all the same I don't know that it does to bring these things on again. It didn't answer in Tommy's case. Separated in a year—and that's worse than a broken engagement. Gwendoline! That was the girl's name—Gwendoline Jenkins! And her sister married Sam Fortescue."

"No, it's nothing of that sort," said Charles. He thought Freddy vaguer than ever, and did not feel the slightest interest in the Jenkins family. "Look here, Freddy, I really do want to talk to you. Naturally you've got Margaret's interests very much at heart, and I thought perhaps if we put our heads together, we could do something to help her out of her present false position."

It was incredibly difficult. The words he was using seemed to him of a stilted ineptitude, a sort of cross between the Meanderings of Monty and the platitudes of the Reverend Mr. Barlow.

Freddy looked across the table at him with a curious fluttered expression.

"Charles—you distress me. I don't think I understand. What's all this about a false position?" He did not say, "And what has this got to do with you?" but there was just a hint of it in his manner.

Charles plunged on:

"Margaret is certainly in a false position. And look here, Freddy, you're going abroad—your plans are apparently very uncertain—you may be away for years—anything may happen. I think you'll agree that Margaret ought not to be left—" He hesitated for a word, and finally produced "involved."

Freddy rumpled his mouse-coloured hair.

"My dear boy, you distress me very much. Has Margaret been getting into debt? I've offered her an allowance, and she won't take it. I really don't know why."

"I wasn't talking about debts."

"But you said 'involved.'"

"I didn't mean debt. I think you must know what I mean—" he looked away for a minute—"in fact you do know. I want you to understand that I know too." He paused, and added, "Margaret has told me why she broke off her engagement."

He looked back at Freddy and saw a blank, white face, small eyes peering, hands shaking. "Good Lord, what a blue funk he's in!" Rather horrible to see poor little Freddy like that—horrible to see anyone in such a ghastly funk. Why, the forehead under the mouse-coloured hair was streaming wet.

Freddy put up one of those shaking hands and pushed the damp hair back.

"What did she tell you?"

Charles repeated what Margaret had told him.

"She said you'd slipped into it when you were a boy. She said the affair was political—but of course you won't expect me to believe that. I don't say you didn't believe it when you were seventeen. I don't know anything about that, and it doesn't matter. But you know as well as I do now that this Grey Mask business is just a big criminal organization run for gain."

Freddy put his head in his hands. The white wet face was hidden, but Charles felt that the terrified eyes still peered at him through the shaking fingers. A little contempt flavoured his pity. No wonder Margaret had had to bear the brunt if this was a sample of how Freddy went to bits in an emergency.

"Look here, Freddy," he said. Then, with sudden impatience, "For heaven's sake, man, pull yourself together! Don't slump like that."

An inarticulate sound, half-sob, half-protest, came from behind Freddy's hands.

Charles walked up and down.

"I don't want to reproach you—I'm not going to reproach you; but you must see that it's up to you to try and get Margaret out of the mess you got her into. You can't just go off abroad and leave her to it."

Another sound. Charles made nothing of it.

"Of course she was an absolute fool to sign anything. She told me she put her name to two statements, both highly damaging. Those statements must be got back. That's really what I've come to talk to you about. When people are on the wrong side of the law like this Grey Mask crowd, there must be ways of doing a deal with them. That's where you come in. You know them—you're in touch with them—you're in a position to—"

Freddy dropped his hands.

"You don't understand. I can't do anything."

"Something's *got* to be done."

Freddy leaned back, his hands on his knees, his whole figure limp.

"You don't know them. You must forgive me—Charles, it was such a shock—to find that you had any knowledge of—" He spoke in a series of jerks, and at the end of each short sentence his voice was almost gone.

"I suppose it was. I want you to understand my position. I'm concerned for two people. Margaret's one of them, and Greta Wilson is the other. I'm very deeply concerned for Greta, because I believe she is in a very dangerous position; and I'm so placed that I can't do what I ought to do to protect Greta without running the risk of finding that Margaret is involved."

"What do you mean?" said Freddy Pelham.

"It's obvious, isn't it? Unless we can get back those two statements which you got Margaret to sign, I can't put Greta under police protection. You heard her story about being followed by a strange car. I believe she was within an ace of being carried off then, just as I believe she was within an ace of slipping to her death under the bus last night. You know she was pushed. Do you know who pushed her?"

Freddy stiffened; everything about him seemed to go rigid. The effect was one of extreme terror, of a creature in a trap with every muscle tense—waiting.

Charles looked at him with something like horror.

"Freddy! For heaven's sake, don't say you knew!"

Freddy shook his head. The tension relaxed. He said faintly,

"It was a shock"; and then, "she slipped."

"She slipped because she was pushed. I mean to know who pushed her. I mean to bring the whole damned crowd to justice. And I want you to help me. For Margaret's sake—for your own sake—I want you to help me. I don't ask you to

216

appear in the matter at all. You can go off abroad tomorrow and be out of it all. If you're wise, you'll keep out of it. I want to know who's got those statements of Margaret's."

"Grey Mask," said Freddy with a shudder.

"Who is Grey Mask?"

Freddy shuddered again.

"No—one—knows."

"Don't you know?"

Again that curious rigidity, that fixed stare of fear.

"Freddy, pull yourself together! I'm not asking for anything that will compromise you—I only want your help for Margaret. I can't work in the dark. Give me a hint of whom to approach."

"I can't tell you anything."

"Look here, Freddy, you're forcing my hand. If you don't help—if you *won't* help me, I shall have to take my own way. I shall have to take it more or less in the dark. Margaret may suffer—you yourself may suffer. Don't you see that the minute I move I may pull the whole thing down? If you'll help me, I believe we can get Margaret out, and I swear I'll do my best for you. But if I have to go on without knowing where I am, it may very easily mean the worst kind of smash."

Freddy sat silent.

"You see you force my hand. I can't delay any longer. I can go to the police and tell them what I know or—" he spoke very slowly and deliberately—"I can go to Pullen and try to do a deal with him."

Freddy Pelham started forward. His left hand gripped the table edge; his right fell fumbling on the handle of a drawer.

"Who's—Pullen?"

Charles laughed angrily.

"Don't you know? I think you do. Well? Are you going to help me? Or am I to try Pullen or—Lenny Morrison?"

Freddy's mouth opened, but for a moment no sound came. Then in a whisper, he began to say "Go"; and having brought the word out once, it seemed as if he could not stop saying it:

"Go—go—go—"

Charles walked to the door. The scene had become as useless as it was painful. He walked to the door, and with his hand already on the knob, he turned.

He saw the untidy littered room. He saw the untidy littered table. And he saw Freddy Pelham with an automatic in his hand. He saw Freddy's face, different, quite hard, quite cool. He saw Freddy's eyes, the eyes of a stranger. And he saw all these things in a flashing moment that could not be counted as time. It had the instantaneous character of thought. And before the next second followed, two things happened simultaneously—Freddy Pelham fired, and Charles ducked. He heard the shot as a muffled sound that passed into the ringing of a thousand bells. He plunged down into darkness.

CHAPTER 39

Archie Millar had been spending the most horrible afternoon of his life. He went first to Harridge's, where he questioned the commissionaire without adding anything to what Mrs. Foster had already told him. He then rang up The Luxe, only to discover that Charles Moray was not in the hotel.

He found Miss Silver's office closed, and again rang up The Luxe. Still no Charles.

After this he rushed into Sauterelle's and demanded

Margaret Langton. Miss Langton had taken a selection of hats to a customer on the other side of London. On the plea of very urgent family affairs Archie extracted the customer's address and proceeded there. Margaret had left ten minutes before.

He rang up The Luxe again from a public call-office and returned to Sauterelle's. Margaret had just come in. He had to wait whilst she was fetched. She found a very distracted young man.

"Margaret, she's gone!"

Margaret did not need to ask who. A most sickening feeling of fear drove the faint colour from her cheeks.

"What has happened?"

"She's disappeared. Ernestine had no business to leave her." He poured out the commissionaire's story. "I'm nearly off my head. Charles told me about the bus. They've carried her off. Heaven knows why she went with him, but she's such a darlin' little innocent, she'd never think—Margaret, what *are* we to do?"

"You must go to the police." Her voice was quite steady.

"Charles said—Look here, I'll have another shot at Miss Silver first."

"I've heard of her. But I don't see—"

"Charles was seein' her. She knows all about everythin'. He told me last night. I wish to heaven I could get hold of Charles. It's past five—he may have come in. I'll go and have another shot."

"Wait," said Margaret. "Wait a minute. I—there's something I can do. I get off at six. There's someone I can go and see. I don't know that it's much good, but—it might be. Where shall I find you?"

"Better telephone to Ernestine. I'll ring up at intervals and find out if there's any message. I can't tell where I shall be."

He went off once again, tried to get Charles, and, failing, asked without hope for Maud Silver's number. To his overwhelming relief he got it, heard a most welcome click, and then Miss Silver's voice saying "Hullo!"

"Miss Silver, is that you?"

"Speaking."

"It's Archie Millar. I've met you at my cousin's. Charles Moray told me—"

"Quite so, Mr. Millar. I may say I've been expecting you."

"I came round, and your office was shut up."

"Quite so—I had to go out. You wish for news of Miss Wilson?"

"Miss Silver, d'you know where she is?"

"I know where I think you may have news of her. Will you take down the address? Number ten, Grange Square."

"But I say, Miss Silver, that's where—I say, you know what I mean—isn't that—"

Miss Silver rang off.

Quarter of an hour later he was ringing the doorbell of No. 10. The door was opened by a plain, neat young woman in cap and apron. Of butler or footman there was no sign. Up to this very moment it had not occurred to Archie that he had no idea for whom he was going to ask; his idea had been to get to the house, to get news of Greta, to—well, to get to the house.

He looked at the plain young woman, and felt like a fool.

"Mr. Millar?" said the maid.

Archie walked into the hall and followed dumbly up a marble stair. On the first floor, a long corridor with Persian runners; a dim, soft light; an air of hushed expectancy.

Archie stopped being harassed and torn by doubts and fears. An overpowering sensation of having walked straight into a story from the Arabian Nights removed all other feelings. He breathed the air of hushed expectancy and found it pleasant.

The maid opened a door.

"Mr. Millar," she said.

Archie passed into the room and heard the door close behind him.

The room was large and solemn; it had the ordered richness of a shrine. The Persian rugs upon the floor were dim and soft and old. The light came from crystal sconces set on the panelled walls.

Archie looked down the room and beheld Miss Margot Standing curled up on a purple couch. She wore a white frock and a pleased expression. She was eating chocolates.

He had no very clear idea of how he got across the room. He found himself with his arm around Margot's waist; he had an impression that he had just kissed her, and that she did not seem to mind; he was saying things like "My blessed little darlin' "; and she was staring at him with round, surprised blue eyes.

"Archie! How f-funny you are!"

Archie kissed a sticky little hand and held it to his cheek.

"My blessed child! Darlin', where *have* you been? I've been nearly off my head about you."

Margot took her hand away and sucked the stickiest finger. She looked through her black lashes at Archie and giggled.

"Did you think I was lost?"

Archie nodded.

"I said you would—I said you and Charles would both think I was lost. Were you in a frightful state? Is Charles nearly off his head too? I do *hope* he is! It's frightfully exciting to have people in a frightful state about you."

Archie began to pull himself together.

"You leave Charles alone—he's not in on this scene. You fix your mind on me. What d'you mean by runnin' away like that? I haven't had time to look in the glass, but I shouldn't be a bit surprised if my hair hadn't been doin' the turnin' white in a single night stunt."

Margot giggled.

"It hasn't." She pushed the chocolates towards him. "Have a choc. That's a most frightfully good sort, only it comes off creamy on your fingers. I'm sticky all over from mine. *Do* have one."

Archie shook his head.

"I only eat that sort in my bath."

"Tell me about Charles. Is he looking for me?"

"I don't know."

"Doesn't he know I'm *lost*?"

"I don't suppose he does."

"Oh, but I want him to—I want him to be frightfully upset, and then frightfully pleased to find me, just like you were. You *were* pleased to find me—weren't you?"

She put her face up to his.

Archie kissed her again, this time quite deliberately. Margot returned his kiss with engaging frankness. Then she sat back. Neither of them heard a door open and close again.

"Are you proposing to me? Because you haven't done it at all properly if you are. You ought to have *said* things first, and not kissed me till I said 'Yes'." Her mouth quivered a little. "It's my first proposal, and I did want it to be a proper one. I don't count Egbert." Archie took both her hands—they were still rather sticky. He kissed them gently.

"My darlin' child, I'd propose to you from here till the end of next week if it was the slightest good. I love you quite a lot, you know."

"That's better," said Margot. Then her mouth quivered a little more. "Why isn't it any good? Aren't you going to? Why aren't you?"

"Because you're not old enough," said Archie. "You're just a blessed baby, and I should be a perfect brute if I asked you to marry me."

Margot's bright round eyes filled with angry tears. She pulled her hands away with a jerk.

"Why, I'm eighteen! Lots of people are *married* by the time they're eighteen. One of the girls at school had a sister who was engaged six times before she was eighteen." She began to cry. "I think it's *frightfully* horrid of you. And you've spoilt my first proposal. And—and—you needn't think I wanted you to propose to me. And you needn't think I'd have said 'yes.' And you needn't think I like you the least little bit, because I *don't!*"

"Look here, darlin'—"

"I think you're *frightfully* horrid!" said Margot with a sob. Then suddenly she caught him by the hand. "You *did* say you loved me, didn't you?"

"I oughtn't to have said it."

Margot pinched him very hard.

"I *hate* you when you talk like that. You kissed me, and you *did* say you loved me—you *know* you did. And then you go and spoil everything by saying I'm not old enough." She made a snuggling movement towards him. "Archie—*darling*—*do* propose to me properly. I might say 'yes' if you ask me frightfully nicely." Then she looked up and gave a little scream.

Archie turned round.

A man with thick grey hair and rather hard features was leaning on the end of the sofa. His expression was one of amusement.

Archie sprang up. He stared at the man, and his jaw dropped. A dozen different photographs of this man had frowned or smiled in just this sarcastic manner from the pages of every illustrated paper in London. The shock of recognition was so great that he forgot everything else.

The man spoke. There was a suspicion of a northern burr in his voice.

"How do you do, Mr. Millar? I must introduce myself. My name is Edward Standing."

CHAPTER 40

Archie felt a tug at his sleeve. Margot had jumped up, scattering her chocolates. She hung on his arm, laughing and excited.

"Archie, you didn't guess, did you? Papa, I didn't tell him. I wanted to frightfully, but I didn't. So you see I *can* keep a promise. I didn't tell him a single word—did I, Archie? Archie, isn't it *frightfully* exciting about Papa not being drowned? Papa, may I tell him *all* about it now? Because we're very nearly engaged—aren't we, Archie? Papa, he won't propose to me because he says I'm not old enough. Archie, if *Papa* says I'm old enough, will you do it properly? Papa—"

Mr. Standing put a hand on her shoulder.

"I want to talk to Mr. Millar. Run away and play."

Margot pouted, then brightened.

"My hands are a bit sticky. If I go and wash them, will that be long enough?"

Mr. Standing gave her a push towards the door.

"I'll call you when I'm ready."

When she had gone, he turned a cool, hard gaze upon Archie.

"So you think Margot's too young to be engaged?"

The back of Archie's neck burned.

"I don't quite know when you came in, sir."

"Well, I heard you tell her she was too young. I agree with you. We'll leave it at that. You didn't, I take it, expect to find me here."

"I didn't expect to find Margot. I came because Miss Silver told me to come."

"Yes, I know all about that. I have met Miss Silver. She tells me I am very considerably indebted both to you and to Mr. Charles Moray. I am very glad to have the opportunity of thanking you and of explaining some of the rather extraordinary things that have been happening. Sit down, Mr. Millar."

Archie sat down. He was irresistibly reminded of interviews, now happily remote, with his headmaster; there was the same feeling of unpreparedness.

Mr. Standing laughed suddenly. The atmosphere changed.

"We're being a bit solemn, aren't we? That's my fault, I'm afraid. I must have been a bit of a shock to you. Now Margot took me with perfect calm—she merely remarked, 'Oh, Papa, you're *not* drowned! How frightfully nice!' and at once proceeded to pour out a full account of some very curious adventures. Well, I'm beginning at the end of the story. I must go back a bit."

Mr. Standing sat forward in his chair.

"I want to begin by saying something about all this rubbish that has appeared in the papers on the subject of my daughter's legitimacy. I am sending a statement to the Press tomorrow. I married as a young man, and I am now a widower. My marriage did not take place in England. Margot is my legitimate daughter. I had *not* failed to provide for her future. I made my will fifteen years ago. The document was in the hands of my solicitor, Mr. Hale senior. It was destroyed after his father's death, and after my supposed death, by Mr. James Hale."

"He *was* in it then! Do you know, sir, it was Margot who wouldn't let us go to him—and a jolly good thing we didn't.

225

Charles Moray was tellin' me all about it last night."

"Yes, James Hale was in it. And so, I regret to say, was my nephew Egbert. Well, that disposes of the will. About a year ago I became aware of the existence of a criminal conspiracy directed by a singularly cunning and able rascal. Certain things came to my knowledge; but I hadn't a shred of evidence against anybody. Then, about two months ago, my man Jaffray came to me with a most extraordinary story. He was a good fellow whom I used as a sort of steward-cum-valet on my yacht. He'd been left stone deaf after shell-shock. Well, a queer thing happened—he got his hearing back. He said it came quite suddenly one day when he was crossing Hammersmith Broadway. He said one minute everything was quiet, and the next the roar of the traffic nearly knocked him down. Well, he didn't tell anyone except me. He said he wasn't sure it would last. And then he had another reason. He went down to the yacht to get ready for my cruise, and he overheard a conversation between the understeward and my butler, Pullen. It was an appalling conversation. He came off and told me about it. Pullen and this man Ward were discussing the best way of murdering me— that's what it amounted to. Well, I thought things out, and I made up my mind to give them a helping hand. D'you see?"

"Well, I don't exactly."

"I might have called in the police, and I suppose I could have got Pullen and Ward. But I wanted the others. Most particularly, I wanted the man who was running the show, Grey Mask. I thought I'd let them think their plan had succeeded, and see if they didn't come out into the open a bit. So I told Jaffray to see if he couldn't get taken on as second murderer. He did it very well—started by grumbling to Ward about his wages and one thing and another, got up some good red-hot Communist stuff, and let it off at discreet intervals. In the end Ward told him the whole thing. But Ward only knew Pullen—and he didn't know him as Pullen or as my butler. He didn't know any of the others. Well, Jaffray and I fixed up a very nice high-class assassination. We lay off Majorca, and I hired a boat to hang round and pick me up after Jaffray had pushed me overboard on a dark, windy night. I'm a first-class swimmer, and I had a life-belt in case of accidents. It came off nicely enough. I went over to Paris and waited for news. Jaffray went back to London. And then the fun began. They came out into the open just as I hoped they would. James Hale gave himself away by saying there was no will—he had handled it in my presence only a week before I sailed. My nephew Egbert also knew that there was a will—I had acquainted him with the terms of it no farther back than last August. He and Hale trumped up a forged letter from me alluding to Margot being illegitimate. They staged the affair so that one of Hale's clerks, a perfectly innocent young fellow, found the letter. It would all have been very clever if I had really been dead. What I want to say to you is this, I never dreamt of any risk for Margot—it didn't occur to me that Hale would get her back from Switzerland. As soon as Jaffray wrote and told me she was here alone, I came across. By the time I arrived she had disappeared. It was Jaffray who discovered her whereabouts. I decided that she was safe with Miss Langton. I was extremely anxious not to be recognized, as I had not yet got the evidence that I needed against Pullen and another man, the footman called William Cole. I was also extremely anxious to find out who was really running the show. On Tuesday, however, I made up my mind to fetch Margot away. I went with Jaffray and the car to fetch her. But she took fright. I had told Jaffray to tell her I was there. He said 'Mr. Standing', and she jumped to the conclusion that it was her cousin Egbert who was trying to carry her off. Not unnaturally, she ran away."

"Yes, she told me. So that was it?"

Mr. Standing nodded.

"As you know, you upset my plans by taking her to a new address next day. It took me all day to find her. This morning Jaffray and I followed her in the car, and I sent Jaffray into Harridge's with a note for her. She came at once, and I brought her here. A conversation which I myself overheard last night between Pullen and William Cole convinced me that I could not risk waiting any longer. The two men were arrested this morning. James Hale, I am sorry to say, got out of the country. My nephew has thrown himself upon my mercy. I believe him to be a mere tool. The man I want—the man who's at the back of everything, the cold-blooded ruffian who gave orders to have my daughter 'removed,' in other words murdered—Millar, I'm no nearer knowing who he really is than I was when I began."

"He isn't Hale?"

"No, he's not Hale—though I believe that Hale knows who he is. I don't believe any of the others do, and—Hale's out of the country."

The door opened and Margot came in with a doubtful air.

"You didn't call—but you've been simply *ages*."

CHAPTER 41

Charles came back to feelings of extreme discomfort. He opened his eyes and saw light coming down from above. There was something dark on either side of him; the light came down between two dark walls. The right side of his head felt just as it had felt when he was nine years old and had run into the corner of the dining-room cupboard. He blinked at the light and tried to move. He couldn't.

He had an instant of intense fear, and then realized with relief that the reason he couldn't move was that his hands and feet were tied. At the same moment a horrible choking feeling was explained by the presence of a gag.

He was lying on his back with his knees drawn up. A thick wad of something filled his mouth. He stared up at the light, and his head began to clear. The dark wall on the right was the study wall; the dark wall on the left was the back of Freddy Pelham's sofa. He was lying on the ground between the sofa and the wall with his hands tied in front of him and his ankles strapped together. There was a most abominable gag in his mouth.

These things, which belonged to the immediate moment, presented themselves with increasing definiteness. What on earth had happened? His unconsciousness hung like a black curtain between him and the events which had preceded it. He could hear Freddy Pelham moving in the room. He crossed the floor and threw back the lid of a box. Then he crossed the floor again. Now he moved a chair, and there was a rustling of papers.

Charles knew that it was Freddy who was moving to and fro in the room. He could remember coming up the iron stair from the garden and seeing Freddy pull the blind aside and open the door to let him in. What on earth had happened after that? Something about Margaret. Something about Grey Mask. Quite suddenly he had a swift, unnaturally brilliant picture of the study as it looked from the door—not the door into the garden, but the other door that led out on to the staircase. He saw the room, and he saw Freddy Pelham with an automatic in his hand and cool, cold murder in his eyes. He saw Freddy's finger move. That was the picture, everything in it very hard and bright and clear. It kept coming and going; and as it came and went, he began to remember.

He had got as far as the door; he had turned; he had seen Freddy; he had ducked, and Freddy had fired. The shot must have grazed the right side of his head and knocked him out. Freddy had trussed him up and shoved him away behind the sofa. He had done this because Margaret was coming. At this point his mind became quite clear. He heard Freddy Pelham get up and come towards him. The sofa was moved some inches. Freddy leaned over the back of it and looked down at him.

Freddy? Freddy Pelham? Charles stared at a stranger with Freddy Pelham's features and Freddy Pelham's clothes. This was not the Freddy whom he or anyone else had known—the foolish, amiable Freddy whom one laughed at and was fond of, and who bored one so terribly with his reminiscences. Hard merciless eyes looked coldly down at Charles; a cruel mouth relaxed into a smile; a clearer, harder voice than Freddy's spoke:

"So you're not dead? It's a pity—for you."

Charles glared. At the sight of Freddy's smile such a hot rage boiled up in him that he felt as if he would burst.

Freddy nodded.

"You're beginning to realize what a damn fool you've made of yourself. Amusing—isn't it? Just think of all the times you've laughed at me behind my back and been nice to me in a pleasant condescending way for Margaret's sake. And just think what a howling fool you were making of yourself all the time. It's really rather a pity that I can't take the gag out and hear what you've got to say about it. Perhaps later on, in a more secluded spot— I'm afraid it won't do here, but I really should like to hear what you've got to say. I'm afraid you're not very comfortable; but that can't be helped."

He held the back of the sofa and began to laugh, rocking gently to and fro. "My dear Charles, you've no idea what a fool you look! I'm really delighted that you're not seriously hurt.

230

In case you're worrying about it, do let me beg you not to be fussed about your wound. It's really a mere nothing—a graze. You can't think how pleased I am, because there are things that I'm really going to enjoy saying to you. I've always disliked you a good deal. You had the impudence to admire Esther, for one thing, and to combine it with a scarcely veiled contempt for myself. When I broke off your engagement to Margaret, I was really combining business with pleasure. I hope you realize how entirely you owe the pleasure of being publicly jilted on the eve of your wedding day to me."

Charles had mastered the blind rage which betrayed itself. He kept his eyes on Freddy in a stare of contempt.

"Margaret told you that she saw part of a letter of mine. Naturally I couldn't risk her marrying you and telling you what she had seen. As a matter of fact, I don't know how much she did see—but none of it was really fit for publication. I don't think I've ever been so careless before or since—I shouldn't have lasted so long if I had. I've had twenty years of it, and you're the very first person who has ever guessed that I was Grey Mask."

The name fell like a spark into the vague gaseous imaginings that had been coming and going in Charles's mind. There was a flare which illumined all the dark places. By its light Charles read his death warrant. The only person who had ever guessed the identity of Grey Mask would not be given the chance of passing the secret on. Something of this knowledge must have shown in his eyes, for Freddy laughed.

"You've got it, have you? Think it over for a bit."

He disappeared, crossed to the window, and almost immediately returned.

"Margaret is coming up the garden. Now please realize this—if you make the slightest sound, if you attract her attention in any way, I shall shoot—not you, but her. Don't imagine

231

for a moment that this is bluff. If it comes in the way of business, I don't care who I remove. But as a matter of fact, I dislike Margaret almost as much as I dislike you, and if you provide me with the excuse, I shall be charmed. Make as much noise as you please. You can kick the leg of the sofa, I expect, if you try." He leant over and flicked Charles on the cheek.

The next instant there came a tapping on the window. The sofa was pushed back into its place, and Freddy Pelham's footsteps receded.

Charles lay quite still. Freddy meant what he said. He had not the slightest doubt of that—not the very slightest. He lay perfectly still, and heard the French window open; Margaret's voice; Freddy's voice—the old half-hesitating voice;

"Now this is very nice of you, my dear—very nice indeed. I meant to come round, but time's getting short, getting terribly short—first thing tomorrow morning, you know, and I don't feel as if I should ever be packed in time—I'm not good at it, you know, not at all good at it—never was, never will be—what?"

"Can I help?"

The sound of Margaret's voice, tired, soft, kind, hurt Charles so much that he could hardly bear it. He could only see those two dark walls and the light coming down between them; but he knew in his heart how Margaret looked when she said that— she was pale, she had dark shadows under her eyes; she looked beautifully and kindly at the little mocking devil who would be charmed to have an excuse for removing her.

Margaret spoke again:

"Freddy, you look bothered, and I'm afraid I've come to bother you more. But I must."

"Anything I can do, my dear."

"Freddy, I'm in dreadful trouble about Greta."

"About Greta? There, my dear, don't distress yourself. What's she been doing?"

232

"Freddy—she's disappeared!"

"Oh, come! Disappeared! You mean she's gone out with some young fellow and not come back yet. Give her time—what?"

"No, no, it's not that. She disappeared in broad daylight from Harridge's. The commissionaire saw her get into a strange car and go off. Archie's wild with anxiety."

Freddy laughed, the old rather foolish laugh which was so familiar.

"Master Archie's in love. He's jealous because Miss Greta has gone off for the day with someone else."

"Freddy, it isn't that. Look here, Freddy, you may have guessed—I don't know whether you have or not. Greta is Margot Standing."

Freddy's exclamation of astonishment sounded so natural that Charles started.

"No! Not really!"

"Freddy—" Margaret's voice sank low and troubled—"*Freddy!* Margot Standing—Grey Mask—did you know there was anything?"

Freddy said "Hush!" in a shocked breath.

"Did you? Freddy, did you know that they wanted her *removed*? Freddy, I'm so dreadfully frightened."

Margaret had sunk into the chair beside the writing-table. She leaned across the corner of the table now and caught at Freddy's hand.

"You told me it was political. I believed you until the other day."

"My dear."

"Freddy—I believed you." She looked up at him through a mist of tears. "Freddy, Charles was in his house the day you were ill and sent me to the meeting there. He—heard things. He heard things about Margot. He heard them say she must be *removed* if her mother's marriage certificate were found—they talked about a street accident. He heard them. If he hadn't seen me, he would have called in the police then and there. I wish— I *wish* he had, for I'm desperately afraid about Margot."

"Now my dear." Freddy was patting her hand. She pulled it away with a jerk.

"I think they've got hold of her. You'll help—won't you?" Charles could hear how her voice shook. "Freddy, she's only a child really—just a pretty baby. You liked her. You *can* help if you will, because you know where to find *him*." The last word came with a gasp.

Freddy Pelham had turned away. He put his hands over his eyes and did not speak.

"Freddy, you did like her. You'll help."

"What can I do?"

"You can go to them."

"No, no."

"You must go to them, or else—" her voice fell and steadied— "I must go to the police."

Charles heard a sudden sharp exclamation—protest, terror; then Margaret, very steady:

"If there's no other way, I must."

Freddy spoke, terror rushing into panic.

"Don't be a fool! Charles likes her—do you want him to like her? Aren't you—fond of him yourself? Let her go. What does it matter to you? Do you want him to fall in love with her? Are you going to ruin yourself and me—and me, to give Charles an heiress? Is that what you're going to do?"

"Don't!"

"If it's ruin for me, you're in it too. Don't forget that!"

Charles knew the mockery of that shaking craven voice.

"Yes—I know. But I can't let that child be hurt." A strange passion came into her voice. "I ought to have done it before—

I see that now. But I didn't know the risk she was running—I didn't—not till the other night. Freddy, that bus—it wasn't an accident. She was pushed. Freddy, who pushed her?"

With every word she spoke Charles Moray's agony of apprehension was heightened. He was helpless, voiceless, dead already; and he had to see Margaret draw nearer step by step to the pit into which he himself had fallen. That she was lost from the moment she mentioned the police, he was persuaded; and to listen whilst Freddy played with her, used her to torture him, was the last indignity of pain.

"Who pushed her?"

He heard Margaret say that, and then silence fell—a long, cold silence. He did not see Freddy Pelham's hand drop down upon his knee. He did not see the mockery that looked out of Freddy Pelham's eyes.

Margaret saw these things. Only a yard away from her there sat someone whom she had never known, someone whose eyes gave her an unbelievable answer to the question she had asked. The silence went on. Margaret's very heart was cold with it. She began slowly to believe that unbelievable answer; she began to believe the other things which the silence and those horrible eyes were telling her. She would have been very glad to faint, but her mind was clear and steady; it was her heart that was numb with pain.

After a very long time Charles heard her say "Oh!" The sound broke something, for immediately Freddy Pelham laughed.

"So you've answered your very naïve question for yourself. As your friend Archie would say, you've got it in one. I was aware that Miss Greta Wilson was Margot Standing. And when she so obligingly prattled at my dinner table about a certificate she had found, I thought myself justified in taking a slight personal risk when an exceptionally favourable opportunity presented itself. I reached behind you and at the critical

235

moment I pushed her. If you hadn't interfered, she would have been very neatly disposed of."

Margaret sprang to her feet.

"You're mad! You don't know what you're saying!"

"People are always mad when they run counter to the established order. I've been very successfully mad for twenty years. I have had very few failures, and not one disaster. I am, in fact, a successful madman." His tone was coldly amused.

"Who are you?" said Margaret. Even her voice shrank.

Charles could guess at the horror in her eyes. He could guess at Freddy's smile.

"Don't you know?"

"No." It was just a breath.

Freddy Pelham put his hand in his pocket and drew out a small automatic pistol.

"I'm afraid you will have to pay the penalty for knowing that I am Grey Mask," he said.

CHAPTER 42

The room was silent. Charles could hear nothing, see nothing. He strained, and heard only the horrid beat of his own pulses.

Margaret's hands had fallen on the back of the chair by which she stood. It was a heavy mahogany chair with an old-fashioned horse-hair seat. Her hands closed on the smooth mahogany in the hard grip that felt nothing. The pillars of her house had fallen. She stood in the disaster and held blindly to the nearest thing that offered support. The shock was too great for crying out; it struck her dumb. She saw the pistol and the cruelty in

Freddy's eyes. She hoped he would shoot quickly. It was too horrible. She hoped he would shoot quickly.

He did not shoot. He balanced the pistol in his hand and laughed.

"I'm glad you didn't scream. Marvellous self-control! If you had screamed, I should have had to shoot you at once—and that would have been a pity. I should like—" his voice slipped back into the hesitating voice that she had always known—"I should really like now to have a little talk with you first, my dear—a comfortable talk—what?"

Margaret drew a long, deep, shuddering breath, and he laughed again.

"Not any louder than that please." It was Grey Mask speaking. "I don't want to have to put an end to our little party just as we're all really beginning to enjoy ourselves—but I'm forgetting you're not aware that it is a party. They say three isn't company; but it does so depend on the three. Doesn't it? Now you and I and Charles—"

Margaret said "Oh!" It was a quick involuntary cry.

Freddy Pelham took her by the shoulder. She had not known that there could be so much strength in his fingers.

"You haven't said how d'you do to Charles," he said. "Come along and have a look at him. He's been having a most entertaining time, and so have I. It's time you had a share in the fun. Let go of that chair!" This last was a sharp command with a sort of snarling fury behind it that was quite sudden and very daunting.

Then in an instant, as Margaret's rigid fingers still held on to the mahogany rail, he struck her across the knuckles with the little pistol. The blow cut the skin.

Charles heard her gasp and catch her breath. The next moment the sofa was pulled aside. Freddy was grinning at him, and Margaret looking, looking with her bruised hands at her breast and sheer heartbreak in her eyes. She said "Charles" and again "Charles" very faintly; and then "Is he—" and long, long pause before her failing voice said, "dead?"

"Not yet," said Freddy.

Margaret cried out and wrenched away from him.

"Steady now—steady! If you make a noise, I shall have to shoot him here—and now. You can look, but you mustn't touch. He's a lovely sight—isn't he? You needn't be alarmed by the blood on the side of his head—it's a mere scratch and won't interfere in the least with his enjoyment of the next few days. I'm not going to hurt either of you, you know, unless you positively oblige me to—I'm only going to leave you in a comfortable dry cellar where you may, or may not, be found when the ninety-nine-year lease of this house has fallen in, in— let me see, it is seventy or seventy-one years' time from now— I'm really not quite sure."

Margaret turned on him with a courage which stirred Charles Moray's pride.

"Freddy, you're not well. You—what are you saying? Freddy—*think!*"

Freddy Pelham let his amused gaze touch first one and then the other of them.

"My dear Margaret, it will save trouble if you will realize that you are not dealing with an amiable stepfather who has suddenly gone mad, but with a man of intelligence who has built up a most successful business and is prepared to remove anyone who endangers it. Though I dislike you both acutely, I should never have lifted a finger against either of you if you had not foolishly threatened me with the police. I never mix business and pleasure. It will save time if you realize this. As an illustration, I may tell you that the cellar of which I spoke just now was the reason for my buying this house, and for my continuing to stay here all these years. It has often been—exceedingly useful. It was constructed by the eccentric Sir Joseph Tunney in 1795. I came across a reference in an old book of memoirs which caused me to buy this house when it came into the market. When I say that not even your mother has ever suspected the existence of this extra cellar, you will admit that Sir Joseph Tunney was a highly ingenious person. Why, Mark Dupre was there for a fortnight, with the police scouring the country for him, and not a soul ever suspected where he had been. He was wise enough to pay up, and when we had collected the money, he was found—as perhaps you remember—on the top of Hindhead in his pyjamas without the slightest idea of how he got there."

Margaret had been falling slowly back step by step with her hands out before her as if to keep something away. As Freddy finished speaking, she sank down in the chair by the writing-table, flung out her arms across the scattered papers, and bowed her head upon them.

"Well now, we'll go down and look at the cellar—what?"

The reappearance of the old Freddy was the last touch of horror. Margaret cried out and lifted her head.

"Freddy—there's one thing—Freddy—mother—will you tell me the truth? What happened? Is she—dead?"

He stiffened.

"That's a very extraordinary thing to say. What makes you ask a thing like that?"

"An old friend—I met an old friend of hers. She said—she said—she'd seen her a fortnight ago in Vienna. I thought—" Her voice died as he looked at her.

"Who is this—friend?"

"I shan't tell you. She only saw her for an instant. She didn't speak to her. Freddy, *tell* me!" Her fingers clasped and unclasped themselves, tearing a piece of paper to shreds. "Freddy, *tell* me!"

"Who is this friend?"

She shook her head.

"You don't know her. She doesn't know anything. She thinks it was a likeness. Please, *please* tell me."

"What does it matter to you now? On the other hand, it doesn't really matter to me; so, as it happens, I don't mind telling you. Esther is alive—or was three days ago when her last letter to me was posted."

"*Alive!*" The word came with a rush.

"I've already told you that it makes no difference to you. It's very irrational of you to feel any pleasure in a matter which won't concern you in the least."

Margaret said "*Alive!*" again. This time the word was only a whisper.

Freddy Pelham began to walk up and down the room.

"Yes, she's alive. If even the strongest of us hadn't got his weakness, she wouldn't be alive. She's been my danger always—*always*." He repeated the word with a certain fierce energy. "A man in my line of business should never allow himself a serious affair with a woman—it's dangerous. You needn't think of me as a fool who gave way to a weakness. No, I always knew that she was my danger point, and I ran the risk deliberately, because she was the only woman I have ever met who was worth it, and because I felt myself strong enough to surmount the danger."

Margaret's eyes rested on him with a horrified surprise. Was this Freddy?

He went on talking all the time in a low, hard tone:

"I risked it, and I risked it successfully until six months ago. Then she discovered something. If she had been an ordinary woman, I could have put her off—you know how quick she is. Besides I was not altogether sorry. One gets a little tired of acting the poor fool whose only merit is his capacity for

240

humble adoration. I welcomed the chance of showing myself to Esther as I really was." He paused, stood in the middle of the room looking down at the pistol in his hand. "I ought to have ended it at once when I found how unreasonable she was. Instead, I went back to my acting—I played the penitent—and ye gods, how women do revel in forgiveness! She produced a plan she considered a stroke of genius—we would go abroad, making her health the excuse. I was to renounce my profession and any profits derived from it. A deliciously feminine piece of impracticability. Well, we went abroad. I allowed Esther to think that she was choosing our route. As a matter of fact, I had a plan of my own. I have for some years possessed a charming estate in eastern Europe. I took Esther there by car. She had no idea of where she was when we got there. Fortune played into my hands; she fell ill after a scene in which I explained my plan to her. Then, I must confess, I displayed weakness. I did not accept what chance offered me. I found myself unable to do so—I found that I could not contemplate life without her. It was a weakness. I temporized. I sent telegrams announcing her death. At one moment I hoped that she would die; at the next I drove three hundred miles to fetch a doctor. In the end she lived. I left her in trustworthy hands and came back. If I found that I could live without her, she could still be removed. If I was unable to conquer this foolish weakness of mine, she could remain in seclusion, and I could so arrange my affairs as to be able to go backwards and forwards. This morning—" He stopped, looked down at the pistol with a cold, furious stare, and then went on quickly: "This morning I heard from her— from Vienna. She had made her way there—how, I shall make it my business to find out. She could not have got away except by treachery—it was impossible. She writes that she is well—that there are things she does not understand—that she is waiting in Vienna for a personal explanation. I propose to give her one

241

that will remove all further danger from my path."

Margaret turned her eyes from his face. Another moment, and she would have screamed aloud. She caught at the arm of her chair and stood up. She was trembling very much. As Freddy came towards her, she went back step by step, her hands behind her, until she reached the window. She touched the edge of the blind.

Freddy levelled his pistol.

"If you lift that blind or call out, I'll shoot."

She shook her head, leaning there with half-closed eyes as if she were about to faint.

"Come away from that window at once! Do you hear? One—" he wheeled suddenly and aimed at Charles—"two—"

Margaret ran forward sobbing and catching her breath.

"No—no—*no!*"

He caught her roughly by the arm.

"We've had enough of this. Come along! Walk in front of me to the door and open it! Remember if you make one sound, it'll be your last."

He turned and took an electric torch from a shelf.

Charles saw the door opened. As Margaret passed through it he thought, with a frightful stab of pain, that he had seen her face for the last time. She looked over her shoulder just before the door swung in and hid her from his sight. He strained with all his might against his bonds, only to realize that he was exhausting himself uselessly. He lay still, and suffered for Margaret. The sudden break in her self-control, the pitiful sobbing—if only she had not broken down—if only her fine pride had held to the last. Charles Moray remembered that he had wished to see it broken.

He remembered all the times she had looked pale, and he had been angry, and all the times she had been sad and he had been cruel. And he remembered that he might have comforted her,

242

and he had not. And now it was too late. He could not tell her now that he had loved her all the time—he could never tell her now. He had meant to tell her. He had meant to kiss the sorrow from her eyes and the sadness from her lips. He had meant to hold her close and hear her say, "Forgive—forgive the years I stole" . . . It was too late.

Half-way down the stairs Margaret sank down. The hand on her shoulder closed in a bruising grip and jerked her to her feet. They passed out of the hall and through the door leading to the basement. Margaret's steps faltered; she had to lean against the wall. The hand on her shoulder forced her on and down.

In the basement, the empty kitchen and other offices; and at the back, a small flight of steps that led to the cellars, three in number—one for coal, one full of packing-cases, and the third a locked wine-cellar.

Freddy Pelham unlocked the door. There was a good deal of wine in the bins and, at the far end, a cask or two and some more packing-cases. He shut and locked the door on the inside, and then proceeded to shift one of the casks and to move the packing-cases.

A low, stout wooden door barred with iron came into view behind them. It was barely three feet high, and was secured by three strong bolts.

Freddy shot them back.

"When I bought the house, all this was very cleverly hidden—match-boarding and whitewash—very clever indeed. Without the information which I had extracted from an otherwise extraordinarily dry book of memoirs I should never have found it, and you wouldn't be here. Let us praise the pious memory of Sir Joseph Tunney."

He pushed the door, which opened inwards. A horrible darkness showed beyond. He stood back with the mockery of a bow.

"It's perfectly dry, and on the warm side. Your last hours should be quite comfortable."

Margaret leaned against the packing-cases.

"And if I won't?"

"I shoot you here and push you into that most convenient vault. In with you!"

"Freddy—" The word died on her lips. There was nothing to appeal to. There wasn't any Freddy. There was only Grey Mask.

She had to bend almost double to pass that horrible low door. Freddy's torch threw a dancing ray beyond her into the darkness. Her head swam as she watched it flicker. The rough floor seemed to tilt and tremble. Her foot slipped and she fell forward. Behind her the door slammed and she heard the bolts go home. The flickering ray was gone. It was dark.

CHAPTER 43

Margaret lay where she had fallen. The strength had gone out of her. She lay quite still and strained for any sound from beyond the bolted door. There wasn't any sound. She could not hear Freddy's retreating footsteps or the opening and closing of the wine-cellar door. She could not hear anything at all. The place was soundless, lightless, utterly cut off. The warm, heavy air weighed on her with a deadening pressure. She kept her eyes shut so that she could not see how dark it was. Minutes passed.

It was a very little thing that roused her. Her left hand lay on a sharp point in the uneven floor, and a good part of her weight rested on this hand. The pressure became unbearable. She moved, shuddered, and sat up.

Instantly she wished that she had not moved, that she had let the sharp point prick her to the bone. The darkness of the place was dreadful. In every direction there was a gloom so dense that it seemed to forbid movement and breath as well as sight. Only thought remained—Charles. Was she to die alone in the dark? What had happened to Charles? Would she ever know? What was happening? The door and the darkness were between her and the answer to all the terrified throng of thoughts that clamoured to know.

She covered her face with her hands and bent her head upon her knees. She mustn't let herself lose grip. Grey Mask couldn't touch them really. Nothing could touch you as long as you held on—not darkness, nor silence, nor anything that anyone could do. She stopped minding the dark.

It seemed to be a very long time before a sound reached her. It came suddenly, harshly, as the bolts ran back and the door swung in.

She sat up, her heart beating violently, and saw the beam from Freddy's torch cutting across the corner of the nearest packing-case. The wood was rough and splintered. The beam gave each splinter its own black shadow, then, shifting, touched Charles Moray's foot. His ankles had been untied. He seemed to be leaning against the case. Behind him, Freddy spoke:

"Pride goes before a fall. Get down and get in! I haven't any more time to spare for either of you. Get inside!"

Margaret was filled with a curious trembling joy. Charles was here. Whatever happened, they were going to be together. She drew back and saw him come through the low doorway bent double. Suddenly he pitched forward as Freddy thrust at him from behind.

Margaret gave a sharp cry of pain, and had the light flashed full upon her face.

"Well, well," said Freddy Pelham, "you can now make the most of your time together. You can break your fingernails trying to undo my knots, and when you've got them undone, you'll be just as far from getting out of this as you were before. It may save you a good deal of trouble if I tell you that this place is absolutely sound-proof. You won't even hear me lock the wine-cellar door as I go out, and from the other side of that door. I shouldn't hear a sound if you were shouting through a megaphone. There are eight feet of earth between you and the garden, and six men couldn't break down the door. I don't know what old Joe Tunney used this cellar for; but I know what we've used it for, and it has stood the test every time. The ventilation is quite adequate and rather ingenious."

He shifted the torch and allowed it to light up his wrist watch for an instant.

"I must be going. I have still a few things to do, and I have to be up early. Perhaps it may solace you tomorrow to think of my flying to Vienna. With any luck we shall get above the fog. You can think of me bathed in sunshine. There was an old-fashioned song which I remember an aunt of mine used to sing very charmingly:

'For I am content to abide in the shadow
So long as the sunshine falls brightly on thee.'

In Vienna—I have an account to square." His voice had changed; the words came slowly; there were strange undertones of reluctance, effort, fear. Grey Mask's one weakness was a weakness still. It was not the least of Esther Brandon's many triumphs.

With a quick jerk Freddy Pelham slammed the door on them. The bolts were shot with violence.

Margaret listened as she had done before, and heard no further sound. She put out her hand and groped for Charles. And then a dreadful thought struck her rigid. Suppose Freddy hadn't really gone. Suppose he were just waiting there on the other side of the door to see what they would do—listening, waiting, ready to break in on them and snatch away their little lingering hope.

She crept to the door, laid her ear against the crack, and listened with such an intensity that it seemed to her as if she must hear every sound in the world.

She could hear nothing.

Then in the dark beside her Charles Moray moved, struggling into a sitting position. Instantly she forgot Freddy. Still on her knees, she turned; her arm flung out, struck against his shoulder and came about him in a movement astonishingly full of protecting strength. She began to whisper to him:

"Charles—are you all right? I'll get this dreadful thing out of your mouth—if I were only sure he'd gone—do you think it's safe? Wait—wait—just a minute—whilst I listen again. Are you all right? Move your head if you are."

She felt it move, and turned back to the door. Not a sound—not one smallest sound. After all, why should he wait? He wouldn't wait—he would want to get away.

She turned round again.

"I think it's all right. He'd want to get away. I want you to lean against me—yes, like that—so that I can feel just where you are. I came straight from the shop, so I've got my scissors. I've been thinking of them all the time. I can cut that horrible bandage, only you must keep awfully still."

The fingers of her right hand went to her coat, unbuttoning it. The scissors hung at her side, a good strong pair, really made for use. She cut through the ribbon that held them, and then, shielding the point with a very careful finger, guided them to where the bandage crossed his left ear. The gag had been tied on with a silk handkerchief. Once the point was under the tight fold, it was easily cut.

Charles had never experienced a more blessed relief. He coughed, spluttered, and spat out the gag—another handkerchief by the feel of it. Margaret was fingering the rope at his wrists. This was silk too—one of those heavy cords that are used to loop back the old-fashioned type of curtain. The knots might have defied her, but the strands were soon cut through.

"That's great!"

He stretched his arms, then felt his head gingerly.

"Are you all right? Charles—"

"Right as rain."

"Ssh! Perhaps he's still there. He mustn't hear you speak. Do you think he's gone?"

"My dear, what does it matter?"

"He—why did you say that?"

Charles put his arm round her.

"We'd better face it, old girl. We're through. If he came back and shot us, it would be quicker."

She did not speak for a minute. She did not speak, because for a long minute she was too happy to speak. She leaned against Charles in the darkness and felt his arm about her, very strong, very steady. Nothing seemed to matter.

The arm about her tightened.

"Margaret!"

She turned her face to him.

"Margaret—we're together!"

"Yes—" The word was a sighing breath.

"I've been an utter beast to you. I—I loved you all the time."

He felt her draw away.

"I thought—you loved Greta."

"Good Lord! I'm not a nursemaid! The creature's about five years old! You didn't really think so!"

"I did."

"My darling idiot!"

He kissed her.

"Do you think so now—now—*now*? Why are you crying—Meg?"

Margaret hid her face against him.

"Because I'm so—happy."

There was a blessed silence. The cellar, the darkness, the desperate, hopeless state in which they stood, were just the outer shadow which could not touch them. Margaret, at least, was in some joyful place of heart's desire, the haven which she had longed for and never hoped to see.

To Charles the shadow was a visible menace. He spoke first:

"They'll look for us—they're bound to look for us."

But even at the sound of his own words his heart sank. They might look; but how would they ever find them here?

"If we'd a light. Do you know how big this place is?"

"No. I don't think there's any way out, or he wouldn't have left us. But, Charles, they *will* look for us."

"Did anyone know you were coming here?"

"One of the girls at the shop did. I told her I was going to say goodbye to my stepfather. And—and Archie knew—" She stopped, trying to remember exactly what she had said to Archie.

"What?"

"I'm trying to think. I said—yes, I'm sure I only said—I didn't mention Freddy's name—I told Archie to go to the police. And he didn't want to. Did he know about me?"

"I told him last night. It seems about a hundred years ago. What did you say to him?"

"I said there was someone who might know where Greta was. Oh, Charles, I wonder where she is?"

"Is that all you said?"

"I think so. But if he was to ask at the shop, they might think—"

"This place is so damnably well hidden."

"Charles, I want to tell you—does it make it worse for you to hope? I *do* think there's *some* hope."

"Where?"

To Charles there seemed to be no hope at all.

"Because—I'll tell you—you know when I was sitting at the table up there in the study—I was desperate—I felt I must do something after he said that about the cellars. I don't know if you could see me. I had my arms on the table, and I put my head down and pretended I was crying. I wasn't crying. I'd seen a pencil, and I got it in my fingers and wrote on a bit of paper. I wrote 'Cellars—C and M.' I kept the paper in the palm of my hand. I'd thought what I would do—it was just a chance, but it was the only thing I could think of. All the time he was talking and walking up and down, I was trying to think. And I tore up some little bits of paper quite small and kept them in my other hand. When I went back to the window as if I was frightened—oh, I *was* frightened—I didn't have to pretend—I was horribly frightened—because I thought he'd shoot you if he found out—I—"

"What did you do?" said Charles quickly.

"I stuck the paper on the glass—on the windowpane. I'd sucked my finger and made it wet, and stuck the paper on the glass—the bit I'd written on. I wasn't sure if it would stick, but it did. It's only a chance, but if he doesn't find it, they will."

Charles held her tight.

"It's behind the blind?"

"Yes."

250

"He won't pull up the blind. Why should he? I don't believe he'll find it. Archie's bound to come here. Margaret—darling—darling—darling—I believe you've saved us!"

"I couldn't think of anything else except—except—I dropped a little bit of paper on the stairs, and here and there on the way down to the basement, and one at the wine-cellar door, and two or three where the packing-cases are hiding this little door. I had to chance his seeing them. But he only had a torch. I thought I was bound to risk it. Do you think—do you really think they'll find us?"

A cold revulsion sobered Charles. The hope which had carried him away offered so much. It gave him happiness, love—and Margaret. He was afraid to look at what it offered him.

"I—don't—know," he said.

CHAPTER 44

Long hours of the night—very long—very dark.

Charles explored the cellar and found it about twelve feet square. There was no sign of any other opening. He lifted Margaret as high as he could hold her. She could just touch the roof.

Later he broke her scissors in a vain attempt to dig through the wall into the wine-cellar; the points slid and broke on very hard cement. The door itself would have withstood a battering ram. There was nothing for it but to wait.

They talked. There was so much to talk about. And then, quite suddenly, Margaret fell asleep with his arm about her and her head against his shoulder. The air was heavy and rather warm; it had the curious smell of underground places where no light ever comes. Presently Charles slept too.

He awoke with a consuming thirst; and as he moved, Margaret stirred and woke too. Her little cry of surprise cut him to the heart. She had forgotten. Now she must remember and face a black day of dwindling hope. In those night hours Charles had come to think their chance of being discovered a very slender one indeed.

Margaret said, "I'd forgotten—I was dreaming." A little shuddering laughter shook her. "It felt so real—a great deal more real than this. I suppose—Charles, I suppose *this* isn't the dream?"

If it were. If they could wake up and be together in the light. Charles put his face against hers.

"What did you dream, Meg?"

"I don't know—it's gone. It was something—happy. You were there. We were frightfully happy."

If they could wake up. He held her hard for a minute. Then his clasp relaxed, and he said with sudden violence.

"That little devil must be starting."

"Is it morning?"

"Yes—seven o'clock—quite light outside."

A most terrible longing for the light swept over Margaret. She had a picture of the grey morning, and an aeroplane rising higher and higher until the sunlight struck the wings and made them shine. She cried out:

"I can't bear it! Charles, if they don't come today—if they don't come soon, he'll get there—he'll get to Vienna! And she doesn't know—she'll be waiting for him, and she doesn't know!"

"We're all in the same boat, my dear."

"I can't bear it!" There were tears in her voice. "It's so awful not to be able to do anything. When I think that she's alive, I want to sing for joy; and when I think of him—getting nearer and nearer, and no one to warn her, I—I—*Charles*!"

She clung to him in a passion of bitter weeping.

"She's got more chance than we have, darling." The blunt fact came out bluntly. "In a sort of a way he cares for her, and—they may find us, you know."

Margaret's passion sank strangely into calm.

"You don't think they will."

Charles Moray was silent.

CHAPTER 45

"Miss Silver! Thank Heaven!"

Miss Maud Silver looked mildly at an agitated young man. She took a latch-key from a neat capacious bag and opened her office door.

"Come in, Mr. Millar."

Archie came in, flung his hat on a chair, and rumpled his hair violently.

"I've been walkin' up and down waitin' for you till I thought I should go mad."

"*Dear me*, Mr. Millar—and why?"

"Where's Charles Moray?"

Miss Silver paused in the act of taking off a long drab rain-coat.

"I really have no idea."

"Where's Margaret Langton?"

"Mr. Millar—what do you mean?"

"I mean they've disappeared—that's what I mean. I've been trying to get on to Charles since two o'clock yesterday. He's never been back to his hotel. I went to Miss Langton's flat last night, and she wasn't there. And she hasn't been to work. What's happened?"

A faint, fleeting smile just touched Miss Silver's face.

"They might have gone away together."

"Don't you believe it! Somethin' has happened. Now look here! Charles went down to his house yesterday afternoon and stayed there till it was dusk sortin' papers—I've seen the housekeeper. He let himself out by the garden way, and nobody's seen him since."

"And Miss Langton?"

"I'd just been seein' her when I rang you up yesterday. I was all worked up about Miss Standing. Miss Langton told me to go to the police. I didn't want to do that." Archie hesitated; he wasn't sure how much Miss Silver knew. "There were reasons for not bringing the police into it."

Miss Silver gave her little cough.

"I am aware of that. It was, if I may say so, exceedingly courageous of Miss Langton to suggest your going to the police. But—" she coughed again—"have you considered the probability that she has disappeared as a consequence of that suggestion?"

Archie nodded.

"I thought about it."

"Mr. Moray may have taken her away."

"I don't think so, because, you see, I said I wouldn't go to the police."

"You said you wouldn't go to the police?"

"Not till we'd tried everythin' else. And Margaret said there was someone who might know where Greta—where Miss Standing was. She said she'd go and see this person as soon as ever she got off, and she promised to ring me up at my cousin's. Well, she never rang me up at my cousin's. And she never went back to her flat. And it seems to me she might have seen this fellow, whoever he was, and he might have cut up rough."

"On the other hand, he might have known that Miss Standing was safe. And Miss Langton may, as I suggested before, have thought it wiser to disappear—there have been several arrests."

"She'd have rung me up," said Archie doggedly. "She said she'd ring me up, and she'd have done it. Don't you believe she's disappeared of her own free will—she *hasn't*. I'm very worried about her, and I'm goin' on worryin' other people till I find her."

Miss Silver took the brown exercise book, turned to a blank page, and wrote. In a moment she looked up.

"Yes?"

"I went down to Sauterelle's this mornin'—that's Miss Langton's hat-shop. I asked to speak to the other girls—bit of a V.C. job that—and one of them says Margaret told her she was goin' off to say goodbye to her stepfather. Look here, Miss Silver—it's damned ridiculous, but I can't get it out of my head—Margaret's stepfather is Freddy Pelham. He lives in a house in George Street. The gardens run down to the gardens of Thornhill Square, with just an alley-way between them. Margaret went to say goodbye to Freddy Pelham at six o'clock. Charles came out of his house in Thornhill Square at somewhere about five. He came out by the garden way. That's to say he was within fifty yards or so of Freddy Pelham's back gate. Supposin' he went up to say goodbye to Freddy Pelham too? Margaret went, and she hasn't come back. Charles hasn't come back either. It's *damned* ridiculous, but I can't get it out of my head that old Charles may have gone there too."

"There are other explanations," said Miss Silver. Then she coughed and asked abruptly:

"Where is Mr. Pelham?"

"Gone abroad. I told you Margaret was sayin' goodbye to him. Left this mornin' by aeroplane. Address *poste restante*, Paris—and a fat lot of good that is!"

Miss Silver tapped with her pencil.

"Are you suggesting that we should apply for a search warrant?"

"No, I'm not. I'm suggestin' doin' a little job of breakin' and enterin'. Look here, Miss Silver, are you game? I'm suggestin' you and me goin' boldly in by the garden door and openin' a window with a skeleton key, or chisel, or what not. Unless Freddy's done somethin' drastic since I used to play in and out of the garden with Charles and Margaret, there'll be some odd window I can get through. The question is, are you game?"

"I've my reputation to consider," said Miss Silver. She coughed. "If I were walking along George Street and were to ring Mr. Pelham's bell—" she paused and gazed at him mildly. "If you opened the door to me, it really would not be any business of mine how you got in."

"Right! I do the breakin' and you do the enterin'. Come along!"

Three-quarters of an hour later Mr. Millar crawled through a scullery window. It was a tight fit, and there was broken glass about; his clothes sustained some damage. He dusted himself, wondered why a scullery always smelt of cabbage, and proceeded upstairs, where he reconnoitred George Street through a hole in the drawing-room shutters. Miss Silver, in her drab raincoat and old-fashioned turban toque, was walking slowly along the opposite pavement. She held a newspaper in her hand.

Archie proceeded to the front door and oscillated the brass flap of the letter-box.

Miss Silver crossed the road and rang the bell.

The door was secured by bolts at top and bottom. They creaked a good deal. Archie opened the door with a flourish, and Miss Silver came in. As soon as the door was shut, she turned to Archie as if she were about to speak; then suddenly changed her mind. Instead she folded the newspaper and put it into her bag.

They went together into the drawing-room. The closed shutters made a gloom there. Miss Silver took a torch from the pocket of her raincoat.

After ten minutes they went to the dining-room, and then up the stairs. About halfway to the study Miss Silver stopped and picked up a little piece of torn paper. It was just such a piece as might be torn from the corner of a letter. She flashed the light to and fro, but found nothing more.

The study was not so dark as the drawing-room; there were no shutters here, and the maroon curtains had not been drawn. A light blind reaching to within an inch of the floor screened the long French window.

Archie went over to the window and released the blind. As it left his hand, Miss Silver called to him:

"Mr. Millar—come here."

He came quickly. He had not thought that placid voice could be shaken. Most undeniably it shook now.

"Mr. Millar—look!"

She pointed, and Archie looked. At about the level of his shoulder the woodwork at the side of the door was cracked. The edge of the jamb showed a small semi-circular furrow, the wall behind a neat round hole.

Archie gave a faint whistle of dismay.

"A bullet hole, by gum!"

"I think so. I think the bullet's in the wall. I trust he missed whatever he was aiming at."

She walked over to the table, stooping on her way to pick up another torn scrap of paper. This one lay near the chair which was drawn close up to the side of the table. She stood for a moment, small grey eyes intent, hands clasped on the old-fashioned reticule she always carried. Then she leaned over the table.

Half a dozen little bits of paper lay amongst Freddy Pelham's letters, just as they had slipped from Margaret's hand.

Miss Silver nodded, straightened up, and looked about her. The table stood a couple of yards from the window. She looked across it and saw the garden sloping to the alley-way. The trees had a mournful, drooping look, half their leaves gone, and those that were left to them poor, torn, draggled survivals. She saw the ugly spirals of the iron balustrade guarding the garden stairs. She saw the long window between heavy, maroon curtains, one looped back, the other hanging straight. And she saw a piece of white paper lying at the foot of the straight curtain.

She went over, picked it up, and held it out at Archie.

"Well, Mr. Millar, you were right. They're here."

Margaret had stuck her piece of paper on the glass, but as it dried, it had fallen.

Archie read the scrawled pencil message:

"Cellars—C. and M."

He read it, turned to stare at the hole Freddy Pelham's bullet had made, and once more whistled softly.

"What's it mean?"

"We shall doubtless find out. Perhaps you know the way to the cellars. I think we had better go there at once."

She was through the door before she finished speaking. Archie followed.

At the door leading to the basement Miss Silver found another piece of paper. She coughed approvingly.

"It's a pleasure to work with anyone so intelligent."

"I say, that's awfully nice of you!"

"I was not referring to you, Mr. Millar. Miss Langton must be a highly intelligent person, even for a woman."

They went down into the basement, and farther down to where three cellar doors opened upon a dark flagged passage.

"These two always were open," said Archie. "Freddy liked messin' about and doin' a bit of carpentering in this one, and the other's for coal. The third's the wine-cellar." He tried the door. "It's locked all right."

He rattled the latch and shouted:

"Hello—ello—*ello*! Charles! Are you there? Is anyone there?"

A booming echo came rolling back along the low roof. It said "There," and "Charles," and died. Something fell with a clang.

Miss Silver turned her torch down, picked up a metal bar, and put it into Archie's hand.

"What is it?"

"Well," said Miss Silver—she gave a slight cough—"I believe it is called a jemmy—an instrument in use amongst burglars. I, of course, have my reputation to consider. But if you—" she coughed again. "It really seems quite providential—doesn't it?"

"Heaven helps those who help themselves, in fact," responded Archie.

Miss Silver proceeded to give him expert advice as to lockbreaking.

The silence of the inner cell had not been stirred. It settled heavily and more heavily still. It was half an hour since Charles had spoken and Margaret answered him. Their torment of thirst had begun. It was long past midday, and hope waned as the light wanes after sunset. Their sun had set. The little light of hope that had remained failed and was forgotten. They were forgotten in a dark, hidden place out of mind.

The first sound was faint. It jarred that settling silence—but so faintly that it might have been some ghostly mirage of sound, causeless and unreal.

Margaret stirred, moved her hand to meet Charles Moray's hand, and turned her head to say on a whispering breath,

"Charles—"

His hand pressed hers.

"Did you hear it?"

"Yes."

"Charles—what was it?"

The silence settled again. That faint sound had reached them when the wine-cellar door gave way with a crash and set all the underground echoes calling.

Miss Silver flashed her torch round the well-stocked bins, up to the low roof, down again to the flagged floor. At the far end a cask or two, packing-cases, a shred of white torn paper. She picked it up.

"They've been here, Mr. Millar. I think we'll move those casks."

On the other side of the casks and of that thick, deadening wall Margaret was listening as she had not listened since Freddy Pelham had left her in the dark alone. She could hear nothing.

But she had heard something. Suppose they came and went away again. The thought pierced to the quick. She tried to call out, but the terror of the thought took away her voice; it failed in a dry throat. She tried to tell Charles to shout. Her hand clung to his.

And suddenly the door swung in. The silence broke into harsh sound. The bolts went loudly back, and the door swung in. The noise was overwhelming. Archie's shout shook the cellar, and a dancing, flashing ray struck her eyes like a blow. Darkness closed over her.

When she opened her eyes again, someone was giving her water to drink, and it was light. She looked at the light and wondered at it. Grey London light, but how beautiful! She drank again. Water—how lovely! Light—air—water! She drew a long, long breath, and came back from the half-way place between dream and waking. She was lying on the sofa in the study. A little woman in a drab raincoat was holding water to her lips in a cracked breakfast-cup.

Margaret took another lovely sip and sat up. She saw Charles, dusty, bloodstained, unshaven, his face smeared and dirtier than anything she could have imagined. He put down the cup from which he had been drinking, and came to her and kissed her. It didn't matter how dirty his face was. How lovely! How lovely to be alive—to be together! The most exquisite happiness filled her. She began to cry.

Then all of a sudden she remembered Freddy Pelham, and her mother waiting in Vienna. She said,

"Freddy—someone must stop him!"

She sprang up.

"Charles—it isn't too late! It isn't, it *isn't* too late—*Archie!*"

She turned to him with outstretched hands, and Archie Millar turned away.

Charles Moray put his arm about her.

"Better tell her," he said in a low voice—he spoke to Miss Silver. Then, "Margaret—"

Miss Silver spoke in her colourless tones:

"Miss Langton, your mother is quite safe. Mr. Pelham has been—arrested."

Margaret leaned against Charles. She felt weak and cold. Miss Silver took her hand and patted it. Her touch was kind.

"I bought a paper on my way here. Mr. Pelham was arrested in his flight. His aeroplane crashed in the fog. The pilot was picked up by a Channel boat. Mr. Pelham was drowned. Your mother, my dear, is quite safe."

Margaret tried to say "Thank you." She knew Miss Silver was kind. She knew that there had been deliverance. But she had come to the end of her strength.

She turned and hid her face on Charles Moray's dusty coat.

Part of a letter from Miss Margot Standing to her friend Stephanie:

. . . I'll tell you all about it at Christmas. We'll have a lovely time. And you shall see Archie. We're not engaged, because Papa says I'm not old enough to be engaged, and Archie says so too. Archie's *frightfully* in love with me—at least he won't say he *is*, but I'm sure he is. And Papa likes him most frightfully. I think I shall have a sapphire ring. But I don't want to be married for simply ages.

Margaret and Charles are going to be married next week. I would love to be Margaret's bridesmaid, but she isn't going to have any because of her stepfather. He was a nice little man, and I expect she's frightfully sorry about it. He was drowned in an aeroplane, so she and Charles aren't really going to have a wedding—they're just going to be married. I call it *frightfully dull* . . .